THE NEIGHBOR

SOPHIA KARLSON

This is a work of fiction. Names, characters, places, and incidents are either the product of the author's imagination or are used fictitiously, and any resemblance to actual persons, living or dead, business establishments, events, or locales, is entirely coincidental.

The Neighbor © 2022 by Sophia Karlson

All rights reserved. No part of this book may be used or reproduced in any manner whatsoever without written permission from the author, except in the case of brief quotations embodied in critical articles or reviews.

Cover art: Najla Qamber

Editing and proofreading: Leanne Rabesa

Proofreading: Meg Chronis

April 2022 edition

To the readers who need this book.
You'll know who you are.

1

MARLÈNE

Marlène swore that every article ever written about getting clean was penned by someone who hadn't tried to get clean themselves—ever. The next two weeks should be easy in theory, but in practice it was going to be hell.

These articles always had nice, simple bullet-pointed lists that described the things you'd experience, step by step, without the honest details of how excruciating and exhausting withdrawal would be. A sterile scientific approach labeling a messy, warm-bodied, and visceral human experience.

She had no clue how she was going to do it, because she'd tried twice already and relapsed both times. But she had to get clean because this time, her job was in the balance. Her editor-in-chief had never said anything in so many words, but when Olivia had signed her leave request, the message had been clear: get clean or find a new job. She only had two weeks to pull herself together. Being booted off the editorial team of the biggest fashion magazine in the States wouldn't only be a blow to her career, but it would also mean she'd have no work permit. She'd need to move back to France, and that was the last thing she wanted or needed.

This job had been a saving grace in so many ways, and to spend her two weeks' annual leave in withdrawal to keep it was the least she could do.

It was now or never.

She hitched her arm and shoved her hip upwards to resettle her groceries and the paper bag crinkled as she tightened her grip. The elevator pinged, the doors swooped open at her floor, and she stepped out. A water drop gathered on her hairline from the dusting of snow that she hadn't managed to wipe away. It lost the battle against gravity and slipped down her temple in a slow and annoying tickle. At least it hadn't been a cloudburst, but snow this early in November in New York? What was up with that?

Her purse strap was slipping from her shoulder and with the polystyrene container of her hot pho soup clutched tight in her other hand, she was falling to pieces. She should have taken the offered plastic bag instead of doing her bit for the environment.

Marlène widened her steps as far as her pencil skirt would allow. Only around the corner and then three yards to her apartment's door. If she could make it there without dropping any or all of it, surely that would be a good sign. A sign that she'd manage and not cave in this time. A sign that the universe would allow her to be the master of her own life, that she was in charge and that yes, she could choose her destiny and how this ended—at last.

She slowed down as she rounded the corner, but her foot blindly connected with a pair of legs that stretched out into the corridor. Her body lurched forward. Her ankle wobbled on her high heel, and she lost her balance midstride. Fright pulsed through her as she stumbled, sending her heartbeat into a sprint. She gripped the container of pho tighter on instinct; the lid popped off as she swayed, and her knees buckled.

A hissed *fuck* and a sharp inhale followed in quick succession as she collapsed on top of the legs and her groceries crashed down hard on a pair of large, booted feet. The contents scattered over the floor in a chain of clangs as the pho's star anise and cardamon scents filled the air. Scorching hot soup splattered over her hand, which had found purchase on a taut stomach.

"Oh my God," she whispered as she tried to collect herself, watching in horror as the hot noodles slid from the cup in her hand onto a masculine chest. Two strong male hands shot forward to firmly stabilize her, and she glanced at the face that came with them.

The neighbor. The guy she knew only from the few times they'd navigated the short space between their respective doors and once or twice around the lobby. She hadn't seen him in months; in fact, it could almost be a year. They had never spoken a word to each other, just given each other a courteous nod.

"I'm so sorry." She managed to get to her knees, away from his body and strong hold.

"No-no, it's my fault. You okay?" His voice was deep and reassuring but from the sweat that beaded on his forehead the soup was still burning where it had spilled.

She nodded as she stared at her handiwork. The pho had wetted the whole of his chest and rounds of scallion and meat slivers clung to his checked blue business shirt as if it were a tablecloth. Red oily spots were spreading where the sriracha had made its mark.

"It still burns? It was simmering when they served it up." She picked up the empty container from where it had landed in his crotch. With quick scoops, she tried to gather as many of the noodles into the cup as she could, shaking them off her hands as she went along.

She navigated the noodles around his pecs and belt bordering his trousers. God, this couldn't get more awkward, could it? At least the soup didn't go *there*.

With the patchy cleaning job done she leaned back, and he shot up and pulled at his shirt, breaking the vacuum between liquid and fabric with a sucking pop. "It smells great, if nothing else," he said with a small smile, the relief palpable in his voice. "It's from Go Go Pho on the corner, isn't it?" He was holding out his hand to help her up.

Her fingers trembled as she placed her hand in his. It was too early for any withdrawal symptoms. It must be the sticky heat of the pho and the shock of tripping.

He pulled her up and her purse's strap scraped down her arm. It fell to the floor as they let go of each other's hands.

"Yes, I'm so sorry." Her fingers tingled from his touch, so she stared down at her cream cashmere coat to ignore his gaze. Flawless, warm, beautiful. *Ruined*.

She glanced to the side and noticed a suitcase and laptop bag lined up against the corridor wall, a jacket and black coat flung over the luggage. He'd been away for so long that dust and cobwebs had gathered in the corners of his apartment's door jamb.

"Sorry, I must have fallen asleep—"

"I think we can stop with the sorries now." She shot him a smile. "Why are you sleeping outside your apartment? It's normally done inside, you know."

He gave her a wry smile. "I'm locked out. Got mugged in Paris nine months ago and as I didn't need my key, I forgot it had been inside that wallet."

"Ugh. Mugged in Paris? That sucks." Her fingers itched to pick at the green scallions still glued to his chest. "You're waiting for a locksmith?"

"No, my brother. He has a spare."

"He's still going to be a while?" This brother of his was taking his sweet time if he'd managed to fall asleep in the corridor.

"I'm not sure. The last time we spoke he had to cut the call short for some emergency."

"Well, since you're locked out, come inside and clean up. You need to get something cool on your skin." She reached for her purse to dig out her apartment keys.

As she took the few steps toward her door, she sensed him hesitating. She pushed the key into the keyhole and glanced at him.

"You're just going to let me walk into your apartment?" he said.

Why would he even ask that? "It's not like you're a stranger."

"You don't know my name, and this is New York."

Right.

"Marlène Desrosiers." She held out her sticky hand to him. "Originally from Paris but I've been working in New York for more than two years. I like travel and Vietnamese food. Obviously." She pulled a face and made a wink at the last three words. "Nice to meet you, neighbor."

He smirked as he took her hand in his. Smooth, warm fingers. A sure, steady grip. A calculated look as he inspected her face. "Ruben Scott. Currently jet-lagged. Back in New York for now but lately working in Paris. I love pho, too, once it's cooled off a bit." He smiled at her. "*Enchanté.*"

Marlène grinned at his French, heavy with an American accent. "*Enchantée.* See? We have two things in common." They both liked pho and she got splattered, but he was drenched in it. She opened her apartment door. "Come inside."

She walked in, put her purse on the foyer table and switched on the small lamp. As she stripped off her cashmere coat, she stared at the mirror above the foyer table. Maybe a good dry-clean could get out the sriracha stains. His footsteps faltered and stopped short just outside her door, so she turned to him.

What was eating this guy? "You good?"

"Yeah, it's just that I don't usually walk into my neighbor's apartment to deal with spilt pho. But I really need to take off this shirt."

Marlène took in his face. She couldn't gauge his age. Dark hair with some grey strands by his temples. The grey had a different texture; it was hardier, willful. He wasn't hiding or getting rid of it, that was for sure, but he seemed to be too young to sport any grey hair. His brow sloped to a Roman nose, to eyes that hardly had any wrinkles around them. The lines that bracketed his mouth spoke more of cynicism than laughter, especially with the way he pressed his lips together now.

He was handsome in a way that ticked all her boxes. She shrugged off the thought and tore her gaze away from his mouth because those lips, the scratch of stubble on his jaw, his firm touch when he'd held on to her earlier, all reminded her of how long it had been since she'd touched a man's skin, since she'd slipped her fingers into hair, since…since so many things.

A tingle of need spread over her, and her breath caught in her throat. To have the sensation run through her body was fresh, belated, and a total relief.

She walked deeper into the apartment, switching the lights on. "That's all it is. Dealing with spilt pho. You can use my bathroom."

Unless he was a serial killer. The thought had crossed her mind. She'd brushed it aside and moved on. If he offed her in some gruesome way, at least she wouldn't be dealing with her little addiction over the weekend. The thought was somewhat sobering and hovered weirdly on the precipice of delightful.

She didn't wait for him to follow. The anticipation of withdrawal messed with her head.

Men were men and she'd known all the types. To be honest, it would be refreshing if Ruben Scott did something to her that hadn't been done before.

2

RUBEN

Ruben watched Marlène as she switched on the lights. He'd always sensed something was different about her. Now he knew. After spending nine months in France, he could spot a Parisienne from a mile away. Not only did they dress with style, but they also carried themselves with an air no foreigner could replicate, try as they might.

Someone had told him it was their underlying sexual satisfaction. Had it been Marc? Probably. French women took pleasure in pleasing and being pleased. Something like that. Marc would know. He'd been in France for two years longer than him and had worked his way through every arrondissement. Every one of them had a way to deal with the job, and that was Marc's release.

He wasn't cut from the same cloth as Marc. For Ruben, French women had confidence in their femininity, and it affected men more than anything else. The way she stared at him, her silhouette cut out against the foyer's soft light, spoke of all of this without a single word. That he could see her like this, a beautiful woman unaware of her allure, came to him as a surprise. He'd lost all sense of reality and needed this break more than he knew or maybe understood.

The distance also helped. Having a whole ocean between him and Paris helped him breathe. Sometimes, when the problem was with people, they managed to tarnish a place too.

Honestly, he was all Frenched out and now here he was, about to enter her space. Marlène Desrosiers. There was more here. She was familiar beyond being his new neighbor whom he'd seen maybe twice in the month before he'd left for Paris. He couldn't put his finger on it, and it bothered him.

Instead of dealing with his shirt or entering the apartment, he scanned the corridor. Five cans of tomato soup. Three bags of salad. Brie, Roquefort, and a hard goat's cheese. The trifecta of the balanced French cheese board. Two baguettes. Butter. And three freaking bottles of champagne. No wonder it had hurt like hell when her groceries hit his legs.

Ruben gathered the lot in the torn paper bag and went inside. Her place wasn't bigger than his, but it was a corner unit and had more windows in the living room. The layout was similar: one bedroom with a separate bathroom and kitchen, but the small foyer was extra. Her furniture was a mismatch of antique and modern that somehow worked.

He watched as she closed the blinds to the city view and wanted to stop her, because the familiar cityscape was comforting, but he said nothing. He walked into the kitchen and placed her groceries on the counter.

"You might want to wait a moment before you open your champagne," he called out. For all he knew, the three bottles were ruined by their tumble. At least nothing had broken.

"It's going to pop perfectly, if you ask me!" Her heels thudded on the wooden floor, but Marlène didn't walk into the kitchen; instead, he watched her head towards the front door.

She strolled back seconds later with his suitcase and laptop bag in tow and parked them in the small foyer.

"Thanks for picking up the food."

"No problem."

She came to a standstill in the kitchen doorway and there it was. That French poise. The hint of a chemise peeking from her white shirt which had a wide collar, upright and stiff even after an entire day at work. A pencil skirt accentuated her small waist, and her heels elongated her legs so that she appeared much taller than she was. She was dainty and probably a head shorter than him once she ditched her shoes. Bottom line, she looked striking and sexy without exposing a bit of skin. It was a look that kept men intrigued and let the imagination loose.

"Do you have a clean set of clothes in your suitcase?" Marlène asked. "I'll get you a towel and I can put your shirt in the wash if you'd like?"

He needed more than a clean shirt. He needed a shower not only to wash off the soup, but also to wash off Paris and the whole horrid year, followed by a long walk in the streets of Manhattan. He needed to breathe in this city's foul air and let the fumes from its subway's ventilation grates perfume his clothes.

He needed to feel himself again. Find himself again. Somehow, being here with her already made him feel calmer. It could be her apartment and the simple fact that it was next door to his.

She didn't extend the invitation to a shower, and with Bryce arriving at some point, he didn't want to invade her privacy if it wasn't necessary.

"It's okay, thanks. I'll deal with it."

"The bathroom is this way."

He followed her and started to unbutton his shirt. She continued to her bedroom and as he entered the bathroom, he had to stop short. It wasn't dirty, but it *was* a mess. There were two laundry baskets full of beauty products against the wall, and more stuff on the counter. The shower floor had a domino row of scented soaps, scrubs, and shampoo lining the walls. Glancing over them, he could see they were all the expensive type, though most of them seemed to be discarded into the baskets. Women took this shit seriously, but this was extreme. He'd never seen so many beauty products tossed together in one bathroom in his life.

Ruben shook his head as he stripped, exhaling a relieved sigh as the warm fabric peeled off his skin. His torso was flame red and still hot to the touch. He dropped his shirt in the basin, wanting to dunk his whole body into a pool of cold water.

"I—" Marlène stopped in her tracks in the door, which he hadn't bothered to close as he waited for her to bring the towel.

In the mirror, he watched as her gaze travelled over the expanse of his pecs and abdomen, taking in every bit of him. She tried to school her face, but her eyes widened as her gaze roamed and snagged over his upper body.

He had scars, and they weren't all obtained in the line of duty. The stabbing scars were the marks of a misspent youth.

"God, I'm sorry. It's so red, it looks like it hurt. It looks like it *all* hurt."

She met his gaze in the mirror and he cut her a smile. "I'll be okay, don't you think?"

"Yes. Obviously. You didn't blister?"

"Doesn't look like it."

"Great." She placed a fluffy white towel on the counter. "If you want to take a shower, please. Feel free to use any of the products. There's so much of it, I'll never work my way through it all."

Marlène closed the door, but not before he spotted the warm blush that spread to her cheeks like the burn that fanned over his chest.

Sharing was caring, and she had so much to share. He wouldn't know where to start with her ridiculous amount of beauty products. He was a soap, shampoo, and shave kind of guy. He dragged his hand over his stubble and with relief recalled that he had his own toiletries in his suitcase and didn't need to wade through her collection.

As much as he'd like to take a shower, he didn't want to be in it when Bryce arrived with his apartment key. He missed his brother. With a sigh, he pulled his phone from his pants pocket and scanned it for messages, but there was nothing new from Bryce. He could be on his way, but chances were that he'd never gotten on the road.

Ruben pressed dial and cursed when the call went straight to voicemail. What was up with Bryce? A one-liner would do to let him know if he couldn't make it. He'd have to sit it out a bit longer before he made the call to go to a hotel for the night or fork out the after-hours pay for a locksmith, but at least he could clean himself up.

Ruben killed the call and went to pocket his phone, but his gaze homed in on his work portal icon. His thumb hovered. He shouldn't do it. He should step away as he'd been told a hundred times in the past few weeks. There was a reason he was in New York and no longer in Paris and his fucking head was going to have to play along for once.

He'd do whatever it took to get back to Paris, and he had a few weeks to steer his mind into the right lane. Failing to finish what he'd started didn't even bear contemplating.

3

MARLÈNE

Ruben Scott had been through the wringer, and not just once. A few times.

She'd spotted two stab-wound scars on his rib cage and one where his trousers hung low on his muscled abdomen. He had a bullet wound scar on his shoulder. And on one pec, peeking through the dusting of hair on his chest that narrowed until it disappeared into his trousers, was the faint scar of a cut. Beyond that, he was all six pack, shoulders and biceps with muscles that flexed as he'd watched her in the mirror.

He was no metro male, for he wasn't showing off. He was just a shirtless man with scars he wore with indifference. Ruben had rough edges below his checked business shirt. Rougher than anyone that she'd ever been with, probably tougher too. She'd never been with someone who had stab-wound scars. Her usual consisted of rich men who liked to dominate, be it at work or in the bedroom. If any of them had a dirty job to be done that involved bullets and knives, they'd have henchmen to do it for them. The Paris upper crust was a deceptively clean clan.

Maybe she hadn't known all the types of men after all.

Not that she wanted to get to know Ruben in any way. All she needed was to get through tonight, then through tomorrow, then through the weekend and then—

It didn't pay to think ahead in this game. This game was won second by second, minute by minute, hour by hour.

She took off her work clothes and inspected them for soup splatter before she hung up the designer skirt and blouse. She wanted to put on pajamas, but with him in the apartment, it would be inappropriate. Instead, she reached for the quintessential unexpected-guest attire—grey yoga pants and a black tank top, comfortable and sensible—and got dressed again.

Imagine inviting a criminal or a member of the mafia into her apartment and that he could actually do more than simply use her shower. As if. He might be rough and far from innocent, but something deep down in her gut told her he was good.

Long ago she'd learned to trust her instincts when it came to men. With Ruben, there had been no slow clamping inside her, like fingers slowly circling a wrist and tightening their grip.

Marlène closed her eyes and shook her head. A dull fog clouded her brain. At least he was a distraction from what her body and mind were going through, and she could do with a distraction. She wasn't sure she wanted to deal with the whole package of distraction a man like Ruben Scott presented her with. Her fingers yearned to touch his scars and ask him when and how he'd gotten each and every one of them. How it had felt as the blade had pierced his skin. And how had he buried the memory of that violence afterward and kept it six feet under?

For all she knew, his scars weren't something he talked about. She understood that mindset. Buried inside her was a cavern filled with things she never talked about or wanted to talk about. It was the moon to her inner earth, sometimes full and bright, sometimes obscured by clouds, sometimes dark and invisible. It was always there, even when she couldn't see it.

It was this type of thinking that kicked her behind the knees every time and made her stumble. She couldn't go there already, so she wrenched her thoughts back to the mess in the corridor she needed to clean up.

She tied her hair in a ponytail, then opened her bedroom door to listen for sounds in the rest of the apartment. The shower was running so she headed into the kitchen, fitted a bucket under the faucet, filled it halfway with warm water, and added floor cleaner. Mop in hand, she went out to the corridor to clean up her soup spill.

When she came back inside ten minutes later, Ruben stood in the bathroom door, dressed in a gray T-shirt and faded jeans, but barefoot and with the used towel in his hands. His hair spiked where he'd roughly towel-dried it.

"Where do I go with this? Laundry?" he asked as he raked his hair back with his fingers.

He was younger than she would have guessed. He was on the right side of thirty-five, max thirty-seven. No chance he had a year beyond forty on him, not with a body like that and only those few wrinkles.

"Sure, drop it in the basket. You hungry? I'm famished." She lifted the mop and bucket as explanation. "And my dinner's all mopped up."

Ugh. Why was she offering him dinner? It might be the combination of his comment on Go Go Pho's delicious food or the guilt for stumbling blindly around the corner in the corridor.

He didn't answer immediately.

"Unless your brother is going to be here soon?"

"His phone's switched off. I don't know if he's even on his way."

It was late already, almost ten o'clock on a Friday night. She didn't usually work so late, but with her two weeks' leave, she'd wrapped up a few things before heading home.

"Let's get delivery then, it won't take long and I'm sure you must be hungry too. My treat, for having ruined your shirt."

It would kill time for her too because the tender hold of the first withdrawal symptoms circled around her waist, python-like. She'd rather have him here to keep her company for as long as she could hide what was happening to her body from him.

He chuckled. "Add some shrimp rolls and rice with mango for dessert and I'm sold."

"Sounds like a deal." Marlène smiled and reached for her purse to get her cell phone. She put in the order on the restaurant's mobile app. "Right, looks like it will only take twenty minutes. Champagne?"

"If you dare."

"God, yes. It's been earned." She led the way into the kitchen and unpacked the food from the paper bag. The champagne was meant for later, for afterwards, but she needed some now.

"By the looks of it, you have something to celebrate this weekend," Ruben said as she pulled the last bottle from the bag. He came to lean against the counter and the small space shrank as he filled it with his presence.

"Hmm. You could say so." How much would anybody care to know? How much would *he* care to know? This didn't hurt anymore; it had been over two years now. It was more like the end of an era and here she was, still alone, afloat on open waters. It was never a good place to be. "My ex is getting married tomorrow. That's a champagne-worthy event, don't you think?"

"I—" He faltered.

She shrugged. "Don't worry about it. Our relationship was somewhat toxic."

"Okay." Ruben turned towards her, hip against the counter.

She glanced at him, and his frown deepened. "Did he hurt you?"

Funny that he'd think her ex had been the problem right off the bat. It implied the problem couldn't have been with her. It was kind of cute and sweet and somewhat enlightening as to how he saw her.

Marlène hated to disillusion him, but beyond tonight, they didn't owe each other anything. "No, nothing like that. James and I—" She hesitated. "I was the poison, and he kept on taking the antidote and we carried on like that for years. He's much better off without me, as I'm honestly much better off without him." Marlène turned to the fridge to pack away the groceries, but for a split second she had to pause as emotions swelled inside her. She wasn't going to cry. She swallowed them down deliberately. "But that doesn't make it easy, you know? I have some regrets."

"Don't we all." Ruben opened the fridge for her and held out his hand. "Let me help."

She shot him a woeful smile and said nothing as she passed him the salads and cheese.

There was nothing to say. Nobody goes through life without regrets. They came in threads of all colors, one layered upon the other, and only when you looked back could you see the tapestry you wove for yourself.

She, for one, should never have started using drugs with Damien. James had done all he could to stop her, but what he didn't understand was that in the cavern inside her, there lived a monster, and the monster needed to be fed. She'd merely swapped one addiction for another and here she was, a few years down the line, knowing a drug addiction was much worse than a sex addiction. In the bigger scheme of things, for her, personally, sex was the lesser of two evils.

What she regretted most was never telling James anything, not even giving him a hint of what had been going on in her head and heart when she was with him. For four years, James Sinclair had only known her on the surface, and it had been for the better.

"It's water under the bridge, and trust me, you don't want to hear about any of my regrets," she said. "Least of all when it comes to my ex. We will raise a glass to the happy couple, and now that you're here, you can stop me from making a stupid drunk-dial call where I don't get anything coherent out—least of all a sorry."

Ruben chuckled. "I thought we were done with the sorries for today."

For today, maybe, but she'd stood on the drunk-dial ledge several times. One day, maybe, when enough time had passed, when she'd finally cleansed her body and soul, she'd ring James up and tell him. Something. Anything. A snippet. And James, being the man he was, would probably forgive her everything without further ado.

"We sure are done with the sorries. That is, until I pop this bottle and manage to get champagne all over you." She handed Ruben the bottle of champagne with a sly smile. "I'd rather see what you'd make of it."

He laughed as he took the champagne from her and started twisting the muselet. "I'll just take another shower. No shortage of soap and shampoo here."

4

RUBEN

Ruben removed the champagne's muselet and pressed his hand to the cork. "Do you have champagne glasses? Best have them handy."

"Yes, in the cupboard. I just—" Marlène moved in the direction of the cupboard on his other side.

He took up a lot of space as her kitchen was small. As she scooted past him, he flattened himself against the kitchen cupboard so that they didn't touch. Her scent drifted from her hair, intensifying the intimacy of the small space. Something flowery with a touch of vanilla.

"Here." Marlène opened the cupboard and rose on her toes to reach the champagne flutes on the top shelf. "We're good to go." She held the two glasses ready over the sink and he helped the cork out with his thumb. It popped in his hand but there was no spray, only a ghostly swirl that escaped the bottle.

"No spill. I see that as a good sign," he said as he took a glass from her and slowly filled it to the top. "Don't want to waste any of the good stuff."

"I'll take it as a good sign too. As long as you don't play ten-pin bowling with it, or shake it like mad, champagne settles after a couple of minutes if it had some rough handling. Generally speaking."

"You know about wine then?"

"I'm French," Marlène said as if this explained everything. "It wouldn't be very patriotic if I didn't."

"No, it wouldn't." He filled the second glass and put the bottle on the counter.

Marlène raised her glass and took a deep breath. "To exes."

"To regrets." He should never have signed up for the job in Paris.

"And to neighbors." She smiled as their glasses kissed and a soft clink sounded through the kitchen.

"To neighbors," he echoed, and they both tilted their glasses and sipped.

Marlène closed her eyes as she savored her mouthful. For a moment, he could study her openly. She'd gathered her blonde tresses into a ponytail and had changed into a sleeveless top and long yoga pants. The feeling that he knew her from somewhere else struck him again and he found he couldn't take his searchlight gaze off her, wanting to pinpoint where he'd met her before.

Maybe he'd met her by chance in Paris during the past nine months and they'd both forgotten. But that was impossible. Nobody forgot a woman like Marlène.

"God, that's good." Marlène opened her eyes and caught him staring. "I haven't had any in ages and it used to be my go-to drink for years."

"Not something you saved for special occasions?"

"Every day is a gift, so every day is a special occasion, *non*?" She squeezed past him, not waiting for a response, and led the way towards the lounge.

It was a flippant remark, but he couldn't bury the notion that her truth was much darker than those words gave away. Trust him to put his foot knee-deep in it within ten minutes of getting to know her. On the comment about her ex and their toxic relationship, his gut reaction had been that the fucker had hurt her. At least he'd stopped short of asking whether the hurt was physical, emotional, or mental, because for the past year it was all he'd been dealing with. Over time he'd learned that abuse somehow encompassed all of the above, irrespective of the starting point.

What if she'd said yes? He'd go find the fucker and make sure he couldn't see his bride through his swollen, beat-up eyes on his wedding day.

The thought was impulsive, but that his head could even go there in two seconds flat rattled him. He had to get his anger under control, even if it only existed in his head, otherwise he'd never go back to Paris and months of relentless work would've been in vain.

Marlène settled on the short end of her L-shaped sectional and waved a hand towards the other side for him to sit down. They should change the topic of conversation. His heart rate was still elevated after the internal flare of anger. His neck felt flushed and that muscle in his jaw ticked away like a time bomb. What had Marc said? *You're a time bomb, Ruben, and that's the last fucking thing we need on the team right now.*

He sank into the sofa, defeated by the knowledge that he was going to have to deal with his anger issues in the next few weeks, or Marc wouldn't allow him back on the job. The line had been drawn in the sand.

"Still jet-lagged?" Marlène asked.

"Yeah." Sleep had become less of a priority, but ditching his insomnia wasn't going to be the cure-all some would think it to be. "So, what's with all the toiletries and make-up in the bathroom?"

"They're samples. I'm the beauty editor of a fashion magazine. We receive product samples all the time. Those are all the good ones. We share them at the office, but I've managed to fill those baskets since I moved in here."

"Sounds like a good perk."

"Mostly, until it becomes too much. There's no way I can work through it all, but I suppose suppliers feel the need to spread the love where it has the biggest reach."

He nodded. As he had no use for these things, he didn't know how to make a conversation about it. He should say something though, anything really to avoid the reciprocal job questions that were bound to come up.

"You've been working in Paris for how long, you said?"

"Nine months. Give or take."

She nodded, waiting for details. When he didn't volunteer more information, she shifted in her seat. "You're on leave now?"

"Yes." Something like that. His absence from work still needed a label. What do you call forced leave you have to take because you'd been fucked up beyond logic by the work you were doing? This wasn't annual leave, and yet, Marc gave him a month's break with a weekly check-in of sorts and something about overtime that he'd approve in lieu of something as long as Ruben got out of the fucking room.

"What do you do, back in Paris?"

He took another deep sip of bubbly and tried to recall whether his NDA included talking to sexy blondes on plush suede leather sofas who looked like they were born to relieve men of stress. Any stress. All stress. If he'd chosen a shrink, he sure as shit wouldn't choose this one. He sank deeper into the cushions, which were way too comfortable for his level of exhaustion. The drink didn't help. The alcohol hit his bloodstream quickly on his empty stomach.

"I work in IT." Keeping it vague and simple. Just the letters IT were enough to put off the average technophobe.

"You don't strike me as an IT guy."

She was on to him already. "There's a stereotype?"

Marlène harrumphed. "Never mind," she said with a smile. "Next you're going to tell me you're into programming, or systems, or something internet-y to make me feel out of my depth so you can divert the conversation to something—" She broke off laughing. "About soap and shampoo. *Merde.* I've been so bored with my job lately."

She was cute when she cursed with such passion in French and a smile twitched his lips. Imagine leaving France for home only to find a French woman next door who he could actually talk to.

"It involves some programming. The project has been going for some time. Debugging and so on." He raked a hand though his hair. "I won't bore you with the details."

"I want to be bored. Very much. By someone else's job."

This should make him smile, but all he could do was shake his head, wishing she'd stop probing.

She opened her mouth to tease some detail out of him, but the apartment doorbell buzzed, and she got up with a wink. "Saved by the bell."

Ruben suppressed a sigh of relief as she answered the door. It was the takeout delivery. At least now they would have the food to talk about, or their mouths would be full and chewing. He'd be able to avoid any further discussion of his work.

He followed her movements. She had the grace of a dancer, light-footed and sure. Her body was toned, from her tight butt to her shoulders and the bits of her back exposed by her racer-back top. Her ponytail swayed, revealing creamy skin as she fumbled for her wallet in her purse. Her fingers trembled and she dropped her wallet twice, then struggled with its zip.

Was she nervous? She seemed chirpy and full of flirty jokes. Maybe she wasn't a fan of the situation either and had hidden it well earlier, but now she regretted asking him to stay for dinner. He'd leave after the meal that she'd forced on him.

"I'll get the tip." He stood and went to his jacket where it was flung over his laptop bag in the foyer and pulled out his wallet.

"New wallet? Post Paris pickpocket?"

"Yep." He smiled. "They only got me once, and that was embarrassing enough." For someone who used to work the streets, first on the wrong side, and then on the right side, he couldn't believe those girls managed to trick him. He was new and in a foreign country; that could be excuse enough, but honestly? He blamed Paris. He blamed Paris for a lot of things.

Marlène opened the door, and he tipped the delivery guy.

"Grab the champagne in the kitchen, will you?" Marlène asked as she headed back to the living room with the bags, skipping the small two-seater dining table that stood against the wall.

He obliged and returned to fresh wafts of pho soup as she unpacked the takeout on the coffee table. Her ponytail slid over her shoulder, drawing his eye to that bit of naked skin her racerback top didn't cover. She flicked her hair over her shoulder to keep it from dangling over the food. As she repeated the movement again, his gaze homed in on the scatter of moles that graced her smooth skin over her shoulder blade.

He blinked and focused on the spots again as a slow shudder rippled, then clawed its way through his gut as the picture fell into place.

Almach. Mirach. Alpheratz. He must be hallucinating. He looked closer. The line was clearly there, each mole in perfect relation to the next. Smaller spots to the bigger ones. The conclusive spots were hidden by her top, though he couldn't be sure they were even there or if they were natural. If they were though, he knew the ones that were hidden had been tattooed to make the perfect representation of the constellation.

The moles were bigger than what he recalled from the images, but of course they would be. Still, he couldn't be sure. It wasn't possible. Not in a lifetime. Not in this universe. He'd need to see the whole of her back to make sure. It couldn't be. He'd been studying the constellation and searching for any connection for months now, on and off, borderline obsessively.

But it could be. What if she was?

She could be Andromeda. Their chained maiden.

5

MARLÈNE

"You feel like watching something on TV?" Marlène settled back with her soup and reached for the TV remote on the sofa's armrest. She scooted forward again, putting the soup down on the coffee table.

It was too soon, this restless feeling. TV and chill were a good excuse not to make conversation and would keep his eyes on something other than her growing unease.

She stared at Ruben where he sat holding his shrimp roll. He hadn't taken a bite yet and now that she looked at him, he'd gone deathly pale.

He wasn't well, that was clear, so that made two of them. For all she knew he was in shock after waking up with scorching hot liquid cascading down his chest.

"Are you okay? Do you need a painkiller?" She wasn't okay and the knowledge of what was coming strained her frail resolve. She'd managed to ditch the cocaine because she'd been upping on the opioids, but now, even though she'd managed to lower her doses progressively over the past few weeks, this was like going cold turkey.

"I just feel knocked. Hard." He glanced at her, searching her face before his gaze dropped to her hands. "Work had been stressful over the past few weeks. My flight here was delayed by two hours, and you know how it goes with the jet lag. You get home and all you want to do is collapse in your bed."

She reached for her soup again to hide the tremor in her hands, but she couldn't let go of the feeling that despite being exhausted and pale, he was taking everything in with a sharp eye. She sat with the remote in one hand, soup in the other, failing to stifle another yawn.

"Are *you* okay?" he asked after a stretch of silence.

Marlène swapped the soup for a napkin and blew her nose. This was how it started, like a common cold. Hopefully it was all he'd perceive it to be. The previous two times she'd tried to get clean, the withdrawal's physiological effects had started the same, but they'd felt worse. His presence muffled her physical awareness, so instead of homing in on every twitch and dull ache begging in her body, she'd been breathing through them. "Just tired, too."

"I should go to a hotel," he said. "I don't feel like waiting for a locksmith. I'll eat and then go."

She wanted to apologize, and she wasn't sure for what. That he was locked out because he got mugged in her hometown, that she was withdrawing, that his brother was missing in action?

"You can stay if you'd like. Sleep on the sofa." The words were out before she registered that she was even thinking them.

Ruben stared at her but didn't answer. His phone vibrated where he'd placed it on the coffee table, and he reached for it with a sigh of relief on scanning the screen. "It's Bryce."

He stood as he took the call, and his feet made no noise on the plush carpet that anchored the living room in the open space. In the quiet of the apartment, she heard every word.

"Ruben, I'm sorry. We had a fatality at one site, and I've been busy the whole afternoon."

"Jesus," Ruben said. "What happened?"

"I'm not a hundred percent sure, but a contractor fell from the scaffolding. I've been with the police and investigators and the paperwork..." The voice trailed off as Ruben walked toward the kitchen, his hand at his temple, rubbing. He made a turn and walked back in her direction. "...I'll fly in tomorrow, first thing."

"It's all good, I'll sort it out," Ruben said. "Don't worry about me, you just deal with what you have to deal with."

"But I do worry. I want to see you. It's been too long."

Ruben dragged a hand through his hair and met her gaze across the room. "I want to see you too. Let me know when you board, and I'll meet you at the airport."

"Skip the airport. Get some sleep. You haven't slept for weeks."

She averted her gaze, no longer keen to follow the conversation. Where the hell was his brother if he was going to fly in to bring Ruben the extra key for his apartment? She dug into the paper bag for the cutlery that came with the takeout, making enough noise to block out their voices. Ruben had turned his back on her again, but she still caught the final see-you-tomorrows before he hung up.

He pushed his phone into his back pocket before rubbing at his temples with both hands. "Bryce had a fatality at work. No wonder he switched off his phone. He had to deal with the police, the paramedics, and everything else once he got called to the site. Judging by the background noise it sounded as if he was still there."

"That's horrible. And super stressful." She couldn't imagine having to deal with that type of trauma at work. "The person who died, does he have family, a wife and kids?"

"I'm not sure. Probably." He took two steps to the sofa and dropped down with a groan. "It's the worst."

They both went quiet and after a moment he murmured,

The Neighbor

"I'm sorry. This isn't how you wanted to spend your Friday night."

"No worries." It was going way better than anticipated, she could have told him if she'd dared to be honest with him and be unsympathetic to his distress for his brother. "Where's your brother? Don't you want to go to him?"

"He's in Boston."

"He's in Boston?" she echoed, her jaw going slack. "You were waiting for him to drive here from Boston?"

"Yeah. It would've been a few hours and I wasn't in the mood to go sit in the lobby or go to a bar and wait."

She could understand that. He wanted to be home and not in a hotel. He wanted to be alone. He didn't want to deal with a locksmith. Close family was about all he had energy for.

Now he got to deal with her. Lately, she didn't want to have anybody around her at all. Especially at times like these. The thought of anybody seeing her like this, as things tensed, how she knotted up with need until she wanted to explode, would drive her nuts with shame. But having him here, in this distress, split her focus and subdued her physical withdrawal. Worrying about someone else shrank her anxiety. It was a novel approach and one she would cling to for as long as it lasted. By tomorrow morning, the novelty would have worn itself thin.

Ruben would be long gone by then.

"What does he do? That there was a fatality?"

At this he shifted in his seat and her body begged to do the same. She couldn't for the life of her sit still anymore, and this was only the beginning. Once the restless leg syndrome kicked in good and proper, things were going to get real. Sleep deprivation was torture, and no one slept with restless legs.

"He's an architect and has his own construction company. Works his butt off."

"Seems to run in the family," she said, hoping to ease the tension a bit.

"We're not blood relations," Ruben said as he reached for his shrimp roll. "We lived in the same foster home for a few years. We're the family we choose to have."

He said it in the same way he'd stood in the bathroom earlier, chest bare in front of the mirror: indifferent to her scrutiny or opinion. These were his facts, his life, and even if those words held an undercurrent of tragedy, like those stab wounds, they had formed him and he wasn't ashamed of where he'd been, or what he'd become.

She'd like to say she was sorry, but they were done with those. She would've liked to know how he ended up in the foster care system, but they weren't on that level of intimacy—yet. And maybe they never would be.

He was staring at her again, searching. His gaze kept flowing over her features, as if he were drawing a contour map of her cheekbones, the hollows of her eyes, and the rise of her lips in his mind.

"You two are close," she murmured, the swell of emotion at the thought of her sisters almost too much to be borne.

"Blood brothers, in our own way." He dipped his shrimp roll in the sweet chili sauce, and she drew in a shaky breath as a tremor ran through her on cue. "You have brothers and sisters?" he asked as he looked up again and bit into his shrimp roll.

"Two sisters. They're both younger than me," Marlène managed, her voice level. "By four and six years." She missed them so much, the longing had become a physical ache that often rose in her like it did just now, a sharp squeeze to her heart as if it had tightened into a fist.

"They're in France?"

"Yes, the one is married, the other engaged." The way the words came out, she sounded a bit desperate, what with her ex getting married this weekend and her obvious single status. Home alone on a Friday night, with three bottles of champagne in the fridge she'd planned to drink alone.

He must think she was an alcoholic.

She reached for her champagne and finished the glass in an attempt to keep her composure. "Sounds like your brother will do anything for you," she said, eager to steer the conversation away from her own desperate existence.

"As I would for him," Ruben said. "And I bet you'd do anything for your sisters too."

"I would," she murmured.

And I did.

6

RUBEN

Ruben hardly tasted the shrimp roll. His head was too busy with the traffic jam of thoughts that had been trying to disentangle themselves since his tentative discovery. He couldn't jump to conclusions here, and there was no way he could ask her to kindly strip and show him her naked back.

And yet, it would only take him a second to be certain.

The food was turning cold on the coffee table. She hadn't touched anything; instead, like a magician trying to fool someone about which cup she'd hidden the sponge ball under, she'd been shifting between her soup, the TV remote, and now the napkins.

Except that he couldn't be fooled. She'd lost her appetite. She'd been stifling yawns, blowing her nose every two minutes, and with the tremor that ran through her it was obvious that she was withdrawing from something, and it clearly wasn't alcohol.

Maybe this was another conclusion he shouldn't jump to, and apart from asking her outright, he could wait it out and see what she did when her withdrawal intensified. He could, no, he *would* take her up on her offer now, without thinking twice about spending the night on her sofa. That was, if her invitation still stood.

With Bryce's call coming through, he hadn't responded when she asked and now all he wanted was to stay and open up this unexpected find. Carefully, like an archeologist who, after months of methodical excavation, finally stumbled upon hidden treasure. With a soft brush and delicate strokes, he needed to unearth her secrets, one by one, making sure nothing could hurt her or his own discovery in the process.

His knowledge could startle her, but even worse, it could break her. He bet she was brittle underneath all those layers that covered her secrets. If his suspicions were true, she might take flight when she realized he knew...*everything*.

He'd bet a million dollars that she'd never told a soul.

Marlène shifted in her seat again, her restlessness another indication of her anxiety. Her body was begging for that overdue hit.

"Do you want to stay?" she asked, perched on the edge of the sofa. "I have blankets and pillows. You already know my sofa is very comfortable."

Why would she ask him to stay if she was going to go through the excruciating process of withdrawal? Unless she was stretching the time between taking drugs, trying to wean herself off them.

Anything was possible and knowing where she possibly came from and what she'd gone through, nothing about it surprised him.

She stood, her hands clenching and unclenching by her sides, and for a moment he could take in her body full frontal where she waited for his response. His gaze traveled the length of her, trying to match her body to that of the girl in the photos, but of course it was a fools-gold method. Marlène was a woman, and the photos he'd worked with were those of a child, a girl on the cusp of womanhood. This beautiful woman in front of him had hips and deep concave curves made for a man's hands to spread up, in tender worship, toward full breasts.

He swallowed. He hadn't noticed before—he wouldn't lie and say he didn't look—but now...she must have changed her bra because a thinner fabric layer covered her breasts. Her nipples were pierced, two tiny barbells pebbling against her tank top and clearly visible in the soft light in the room.

Fuck. Inside him, arousal, long ago killed by his job, stirred awake.

This was the last thing he needed. And yet. The feeling was so longed for and missed that for a few sweet seconds, it was hard to suppress and contain.

"I—"

"Don't make a fuss, please," she said. "It's the obvious thing to do. Your brother's coming tomorrow, you're tired and really don't need to drag yourself and your suitcase to the nearest hotel that's going to charge you six hundred dollars for a shoebox. And that for a few hours. Stay here and relax." Marlène shrugged, then shot him a small smile. "I figure if you had an ulterior motive for coming inside my apartment, you would have acted on it by now."

Her short speech made him chuckle. If only she knew half of what was going on in his head. His physical reaction to her made him pause. When it came to this, the last thing he wanted her to be was Andromeda. If she were, he wouldn't be able to touch her. He shouldn't want to touch her. And he wouldn't be allowed to touch her—ever.

He'd had no ulterior motive when he first came into her apartment, but now his reasons rose up dark and sharp and selfish. He needed time to consider whether staying would be about her or about him, and whose needs he'd be putting first.

One thing Ruben already knew: he wouldn't rest until he

The Neighbor

had ruled out that she was the girl in those images. He suppressed a groan. He came home for a break and now this.

If she was indeed going through withdrawal, she wouldn't sleep either. Only in short snatches that made everything worse. If she was going through withdrawal, why on earth was she doing this alone? One thing he *was* certain of: she didn't plan to have anybody over tonight.

She could have an ulterior motive in asking him to stay. He stood, unsure of his decision and the iceberg of ethical issues that surrounded him in staying, going, asking her questions, getting closer to her, anything and everything. It was too complex to unravel in a minute and this was just the tip.

"Do you need me to stay?" he asked. A few simple words to open the conversation about was really going on with her.

Marlène blinked and crossed her arms over her chest, covering herself up as her mouth opened and closed in search of a response. He cursed under his breath because that came out wrong. She'd been aware of his slow inspection of her body, and now she thought he wanted to stay and have sex.

"That's not what I meant—"

She laughed. "You know, funny that. If you'd asked me three years ago, this wouldn't have been half as awkward and the answer would have been a simple, resounding yes. That is, if my ex was game too."

Her answer covered so much ground, he felt as if he had motion sickness. No, it was the churn in his stomach at digesting her words and what they actually meant. She'd had an open relationship with James. She'd been into some kinky stuff. And three years ago, she would have said *yes*.

Was she attracted to him and echoed his own suppressed desire? The thought made him inhale slowly, not knowing where to file it in the onslaught her few words unleashed.

"That's not what I meant," he restarted. He had to keep this simple and keep his work out of it. "My mom was a heroin addict, Marlène. Let's just say I've made it my business to know the first symptoms—all the symptoms—as if they've been hammered into my head like the two-times table."

She bit her lip, but that didn't stop the tears from welling up and spilling down her cheeks. "God," she whispered on a shaky breath and turned away from him.

Ruben shoved his hands into his jeans pockets to prevent himself from reaching out to her. As much as he wanted to give her a comforting, innocent squeeze on the shoulder, now wasn't the time. She didn't want to look at him now. He'd stumbled upon her truth, and she hadn't expected it at all. Probably didn't want him to know this of her either. The turn of her back, with the corner of the Andromeda constellation teasing him, was her hiding from him, possibly in shame.

He closed his eyes, not wanting to stare but begging for the rest of the stars to glow through the top's fabric and show themselves. "It's okay, you know, to admit the truth, to yourself, to anybody really. It's often the first step to acceptance and healing," he murmured. When had he become so wise? And yet, it had taken him years to be open about growing up in foster homes when it came up in the conversation naturally, like it had earlier. "And you shouldn't be doing this alone. No one should be doing this alone."

And no woman in her state should be alone on the eve of her ex's wedding day—not if she wanted to mark the event with three bottles of champagne and an attempt to stop using.

It would seem Paris hadn't left him empty-handed. At least it had taught him how isolated you were in a foreign place if you weren't passing through as a tourist. If you didn't speak the local language and the only people you could hang out with were your work colleagues—the last batch of people you'd want to see over a weekend. Life became monotone. This isolation had been one reason why he'd spent more hours at work, getting in deeper than he should have.

The Neighbor

She had no family here to support her as they were all in France. It could be she hadn't made the type of friends in New York she could casually ask to hold her hand while she vomited and then shat her guts out for days on end. No surprises there. That type of friend surfaced once in a lifetime if you were lucky.

He had Bryce. The one friend from his fucked-up childhood, who'd told him simply: we have one of two options. Be good or turn bad.

Being good took daily effort, walking the straight and narrow, every decision always made in the direction of goodness. Turning bad was just that. A slow slip into the wrong company, a few petty thefts, a few uppers, a few downers, and soon your decisions only led in one direction with no space for a U-turn. Bottom line, people weren't born bad, they turned bad because of the company they were forced to keep and then chose to stay in, and the things they chose to do and believed in.

Yep, Bryce Sutherland had had a shitload of wisdom at the tender age of twelve. He wasn't shy about sharing and for five years made it his business to keep Ruben Scott, primed from conception to end up in one system or another, on the fucking straight and narrow.

"Marlène?"

She turned back to him and wiped at her eyes, and for the first time, he noticed how green they were, rimmed red by her tears. "I've tried twice now, and I couldn't do it," she said. "And I'm not going to some rehab for the two weeks I have to do this. I don't want to be surrounded by addicts. I don't want to know their stories, and I don't want to tell anybody anything about mine."

Their gazes locked as she quietly challenged him. "There's no need," he said. "You don't have to tell me anything. I understand."

"You're so perceptive," she said, her tone edged with accusation.

"You have no idea." A lifetime in training how to read people and situations would do this to you.

She chewed her lip and slid her hands up and down her arms as if she were cold. "Have you ever done this before? Helped someone go through withdrawal?"

"I wish I had. I wasn't any help as a kid with my mom, but here's my chance to make up for it."

She groaned a guttural *God* and buried her face in her hands. "I don't know why, but you being here—"

Helped. He understood. "I've got a month with nothing better to do, and honestly, I dread all those empty hours. Let me support you. I'll stay and we'll manage it second by second, minute by minute."

"Why must you be so *in tune*?"

"For now." He gave her a wry smile. "You're going to hate me so much in about six hours, I would say. When was your last hit?"

"This morning, before work."

"Where's your stash?"

She groaned but nodded with her head in the direction of her bedroom. He followed her and she stopped in front of her nightstand. "Here." She opened the drawer and stepped aside. His stomach dropped as he saw the neat rows of pill containers that filled the whole drawer. A clean set up for a deadly game.

He pulled one of the containers out and scanned the label. The prescription was in French, but it didn't take much to decipher the gist of it. Opioid painkillers. Strong little fuckers too. Prescribed by a Dr. Phillipe Toussaint. "Do you need this for physical pain?"

"You know the answer to that," Marlène whispered. "Look at me."

He wanted to look at her, so much. He wanted to examine

every inch of her skin for his missing stars and track marks and scars that told secrets. She could be injecting too.

For the rest, she was in good shape and sexy as fuck. Too young to be this broken and desperate. The perfect high-end user who lacked nothing, except the next hit, which she'd have no issue procuring. "I'll take that as a no. Do you have a bag we can store them in?" He didn't want to up her anxiety with threats of getting rid of it, at least not yet.

"Sure." She left the bedroom, and he tossed the containers one after the other onto her bed, feeling them for weight and listening as the pills rattled inside, whether the bottles were full or empty.

Marlène returned and held out a shopping bag.

"Thanks. Now show me all your hidden stashes."

7

MARLÈNE

She was either insane or desperate beyond anything she'd ever experienced before.

A perfect stranger.

In her apartment.

On her sofa.

Listening. To. Her. Every. Move.

Her legs twitched at the thought, and she stared out into the dark, trying to breathe through it.

So it started.

And she just knew he was awake and waiting, staring into the same darkness. Maybe Ruben stared at a slice of sky between the blinds. One without stars, invisible above New York's smog and blinding lights.

Ruben had been thorough. He'd taken her pills and all the over-the-counter stuff she had, tossed his clothes out of his suitcase, and locked every last container up, turning the built-in numerical lock so that she couldn't see the code. Baskets of beauty products now stood in the corridor outside her apartment. He'd scanned the bathroom cupboard's contents with an expert eye and proceeded to peek into every tampon and band-aid box to make sure she wasn't hiding pills in there. He was fast and sure of every step he had to take to clean the apartment of her stashes.

She had one left. In the kitchen. Fat chance she could get all the way there without him intervening.

He hadn't asked questions. He hadn't poked and prodded. He'd merely done what needed to get done by distancing her from her drug supply.

There had been a short interrogation, but her refusal to go to rehab had given him enough insight as he kept his questions brief and to the point.

"Do you have a local doctor you see for anything?" he'd asked.

"No. I haven't needed to see a doctor since moving here. Anything I need I sort out in France when I'm home for business."

"Right. Do you have a local dealer for when you run out?"

She'd almost choked up at his question. She didn't run out. She made sure she had a business trip booked to France a good three weeks before she'd even think she might run out.

The script would be ordered, prepared, delivered, ready for her arrival. She somehow managed to separate her two worlds. Paris on the one side, New York on the other, and this addiction of hers was the last bridge between the two. She'd never sourced a local dealer, because from the beginning she'd planned to come to New York and get clean. She would never have been able to do so in Paris. She'd thought it would be easier on this side of the Atlantic, alone, away from her usual triggers. But this last hurdle had become a mountain. "No local dealers. I don't get out much."

His eyes softened at her response, and she had to look away from his penetrating gaze. "How many days did you manage the first few times?"

"Those times I didn't last two days." She hadn't explained more, and he'd only asked one last question.

"Here, in this apartment? Alone?"

"Yes."

It was pathetic. Her fear of rehab was partly rooted in her fear of being caught smuggling opioids. Having a script for the drugs was irrelevant as the quantities spoke for themselves. Ending up in jail for trafficking wasn't how she wanted this to end.

Her bigger fear was that she'd actually crack. Literally crack open like a rotten egg and the world would see what hid under her smooth, pure façade.

She'd never been to rehab, and she wouldn't be going either. Rehab could involve a lot of talking. Talking. Talking. Talking.

The last thing she had the right to do was talk.

With Ruben, she didn't need to talk. He just concluded. He took in everything with those dark brown eyes, sinking his gaze into her, deeper and deeper. He'd stared straight into her with such frankness, his gaze knocking on the trapdoor to her soul.

Marlène turned on her side but couldn't get comfortable and rolled onto her stomach. Her limbs ached. She turned to her other side and hugged her legs close. Given the current going rate, by morning it was going to feel like the dentist drilling into a tooth without local anesthesia, except that the pain would pound in every single bone in her body.

Twenty years was a long time not to talk.

Weird how time washed away and stood still too, stagnant in some memories. When she closed her eyes, she could go back in time to seconds, minutes, hours of her life in such vivid color, as if the earth hadn't circled the sun for twenty years and no rays had discolored her memories or burnt them to dust.

She shouldn't let her mind wander. Ruben wouldn't understand that opioids helped her avoid that cavern inside her, filled with full-color flashbacks that only led to nightmares. Tonight, there had been no nightly ritual of taking her pills, with their calm permeating her cells and soothing her before going to bed.

Thinking of her morning and evening drug routine intensified her craving, making her mouth go dry with the need to swallow something.

If she wasn't going to fall asleep, she needed to keep her mind busy with other things.

She sat up and glanced through the open door to the living room. The no-closed-doors situation happened without them discussing it. She hadn't bothered to change into pajamas, another part of her ritual missed. They'd brushed their teeth together, staring at each other in the bathroom mirror as if they were a couple going to bed.

If it wasn't so weird, it would be hysterical.

Ruben didn't trust her. Good for him. How much experience with withdrawal did he honestly have? With his revelation that his mother had been an addict, she couldn't begin to imagine what his childhood must have been like. Her first impression of him was that he was clean-cut, but those scars told a different story. Nobody got through life unscathed, but everybody could pretend. She chuckled at the thought. Maybe he was just another human who had perfected the art of the smooth façade.

"What's so funny?" Ruben called from the other room.

She couldn't see him from her bed as he was lying on the longer part of her sofa, but she'd heard him being restless, mirroring her every move.

"You," she called back. Nobody had ever invaded her life with such precision. He'd obliterated her privacy and yet she trusted him. If anybody was going to see her through the next few days, it was this guy who had nothing better to do but dread his empty hours.

No way did he work in IT. And everybody worked on or with a computer nowadays. It wasn't lying by omission. He'd chosen not to tell her. She should be petrified, but she'd indirectly trusted him with her body when she opened her apartment to him. He hadn't overstepped one single boundary, until it came to her secret stashes and raiding her cupboards.

She slipped out of bed and dragged the comforter with her. "I thought you'd be asleep with your jet lag and all."

He stared at her from the sofa, his hands cradling his head, still in the same jeans and T-shirt he dressed in after his shower. The blanket she'd given him hung over his legs and to the carpet. "I'm waiting."

"For what?"

"For you to go into the kitchen. That's the one room I didn't deep-clean."

Merde. Hate sprouted in her chest. Her legs caved in, and she slumped into the short end of the sofa. "Fuck off already."

"It's sweeter when you curse in French. It suits you better." He sat up and shot her a smile in the dark.

"But you won't understand me perfectly," she said with a smirk.

"It's the only French I picked up. Trust me, I'll understand it all." He reached for an extra pillow he'd discarded on the floor and tossed it in her direction.

She caught the pillow and watched as he shifted so that his head was on her side of the sofa. He settled back with a sigh and stared at her, his head almost touching her thigh. "Get comfy. It would be better for you to sleep here in any case. Break with all routine."

This was starting to feel a lot like rehab. "You know, if I were religious in any capacity, I would have thought you were a gift from the devil himself."

"And here I thought I was being absolutely saintly."

She curled up next to him, trying to ignore the tremors and

nausea that sat shallow in her throat. His head was mere inches from her own, and she stared at his hair, dark against the white pillow. "I'm going to be sick," she whispered.

"I know."

"I'm going to have diarrhea. You're going to be here and not getting any sleep." *As he listens to every sound coming from the bathroom.* The apartment was tiny—almost claustrophobic, with him here experiencing her withdrawal secondhand. But her anxiety trampled any embarrassment dead in its tracks.

"I know. It's okay. I have insomnia in any case."

She wanted to know why, where he went in his head, but she closed her eyes and bit her lip to focus on the pain she inflicted for a few brief seconds on herself, and not the aches tightening in her body, the slow, painful squeeze of a python.

Ruben turned on his side and reached his hand over to her. "Hold on, right here." She placed her hand in his and he wrapped his strong, warm fingers around hers in a reassuring grip. "I've got you."

8

RUBEN

Ruben woke to the soft vibrations of his phone on the carpet. He glanced at Marlène where she lay twisted in her comforter, forehead beaded with sweat and her hair clinging to her temples. She was drenched but actually asleep.

That had taken forever. During the night, Marlène's anguish had become too much to bear but he'd forced himself not to step away. Instead, he'd held her closer. The calm in the living room seemed unnatural now.

Faint sunlight striped the floor through the gaps in the blinds. He unfurled his fingers from her delicate wrist where she'd trapped her arm under his pillow. That had been one desperate move. She'd literally shoved her arms under his head in an attempt to stop them from quivering and begged him to hold on to her wrists.

He reached for his phone and killed Bryce's call, sending him a message that he couldn't talk right now. He sat up straight, trying to make zero noise, and typed a message:

I'm in my neighbor's apartment. The one on the corner, one door up. Where are you?

A reply came directly: *On my way from the airport. Be there in twenty.*

It was nine o'clock on a Saturday morning and traffic should be manageable.

Don't call when you arrive, just send me a message.

All good? Bryce asked.

Fucking fantastic.

All good.

He'd hardly slept, but neither had she. Once the diarrhea and vomiting had started, things had gotten real. He'd tried to keep her hydrated, but she'd kept bringing it all up again. If it continued like this, he would have to call a doctor to help manage the situation. She didn't need to suffer like this. Had she lied about her dose? At some point, she'd yelled at him that she'd been trying to taper off. Maybe she hadn't realized how high a dose she'd been taking. Addicts tended to lose perspective of these things. Between the time spent by the toilet, her chills, sweats, and heart rate in overdrive, there hadn't been an opportunity to bundle her up and take her to the nearest emergency room.

Bryce would provide a brief interlude and he had to make the most of it. He got up, pocketed his phone, and went to her bedroom to pack some essentials. He had to get her out of her apartment. It might be the shortest move in history, but they'd both get more rest in his place. She had a stash or two he hadn't managed to sniff out yet, probably in the bottom of a cereal box or with the cleaning products under the sink. They could deal with those once this was over, once she was ready to tell him where they were.

A cash-strapped addict lived from high to high, working the streets in any and all ways to get money for the next hit. Marlène wasn't cash-strapped, and by the look of the clothes in her closet, never had been. But the way she was flying shit between Paris and New York, she could end up in serious, life-changing trouble.

By the time his phone buzzed, he had everything ready at the door and had dragged her laundry baskets of beauty products back into her bathroom. He bet there could be some pills stashed in there too and wanted to make sure he'd wake up if she sneaked out to go find them. He shot one last glance at the sofa where Marlène still slept, then unlocked and opened the door wide, holding his finger to his lips to silence Bryce.

Bryce's eyebrows hitched up, but he said nothing as he glanced over his shoulder into the apartment. "You look like shit," he whispered.

"You look like shit too," Ruben whispered back. The dark circles under his brother's eyes and gray tinge to his skin spoke volumes.

"Fuck," Bryce muttered as he dragged him close and Ruben hugged his brother back, his fingers digging into Bryce's back muscles. "Sorry about yesterday."

For a long moment, they held each other, and Ruben felt how the tension in his body eased. It was so good to be home. "You good?"

"Yeah, it'll be okay." They let go of each other and Bryce nodded in the direction of the sofa as he pulled his keys from his jacket pocket. "What's up?"

Ruben took the keys and found the one for his apartment. "Long story. Keep an eye on her and don't freak her out if she wakes up. If she stirs, call me. I'm going to air out my place and then move my things."

"Right. No dodgy shit I need to shut my eyes and duck for?"

"Nah. You're good."

They both knew the dodgy shit Bryce referred to wasn't the usual one-night stand scatter of clothes and condoms. He didn't even want to think about the dodgy shit Bryce referred to. He unlocked his apartment door and snapped the cobwebs as he opened it wide. The wall of stale air didn't move, and he strode to the far windows, which opened a few inches at the top. He lifted the shutters, opened the windows, and continued to his bedroom to open the window the few inches it allowed there too.

A ribbon of cold air sliced through the apartment, and he inhaled a deep breath. His place was more a man cave than Marlène's designer abode. Functional, with his wide desk against the one living room wall, monitors and a keyboard covered in a layer of dust. He'd do a cleanup later, wouldn't take more than half an hour with his minimalistic furnishings. In the kitchen, he checked the fridge. Mustard, ketchup, mayonnaise, pickles. He smirked. A hearty meal in itself.

Ruben left everything open and went back to Marlène's apartment, where Bryce leaned against the wall, hands in his jacket pockets, his mouth pulled into a grim line.

"What's up with her?" he mouthed as Ruben padded up to him.

"Opioid withdrawal."

"What the fuck?" Bryce muttered. "Don't tell me you're involved with her?"

"Would be a helluva welcome home, wouldn't it?"

"Jesus Christ, Ruben. Don't joke. I'm worried about you as it is. You know you can't dip into that shit."

"I'm fine. Only trying to do some good, helping out a neighbor."

Bryce pinned him with his gaze and Ruben shook his head. That scowl told him his brother didn't approve one inch. "What happened in Paris?"

"Now's not the time."

"Are you going to tell me?"

Marlène stirred and for a blissful second Bryce's intense stare broke away to look at her. Bryce wouldn't allow him to sidestep that interrogation. As soon as he'd let him know that he was flying home for a month, Bryce had smelled a rat. It hadn't helped that a day before that message, he'd let Bryce know they were on the brink of a breakthrough.

He chose to ignore Bryce's question as he scooted past him to where Marlène now struggled to get up, pale and teary. "*C'est qui, ça?*" she muttered, pulling her comforter tighter.

During the night she'd strung several unfamiliar French swear words together, shooting them at him like bullets. Her voice didn't hold that desperate aggression now. She looked bewildered and fragile.

"It's my brother, Bryce. He came to open my apartment, remember? From Boston."

Marlène stared at him, goosebumps sprouting over her arms. "How much was that, you think?"

"Of sleep? Two hours, at least."

"Consecutively or in total?" she groaned, and he couldn't help but smile. She was teasing him and though the worst wasn't over by a long shot, he loved that she showed some spirit.

"Come on, we're moving to my place. You'll be better off there."

"Less temptation?" She eyed his suitcase where it stood by the wall and swallowed convulsively.

"Yep." He reached for the glass of water on the coffee table. "Only two sips. Please."

Marlène rolled her eyes at him and muttered something sinister which only made him smile. She drank and handed him back the glass. "I love meeting your brother like this, you know. All sweat-drenched and hideous."

"Ignore him. He's easy to ignore." What a lie. His brother walked into a place as if he owned it, and anybody seeing him walk in believed it. *Fake it till you make it.* More Bryce Sutherland wisdom to live by. "I have a bath in my place. You can soak it all off and warm up." He held out his hand, hoping she'd have the energy to walk there herself.

"*Non*," she muttered as she shook her head. "*Non-non-non*."

"Only until you see the sense of it, I promise. You know by now you're safe with me."

"I know. I see the sense of it, it's just—" She sat straighter and let her legs hang from the sofa, but she was weak. "I'm drained. Top to bottom. You were there. You heard it all." Color bloomed on her cheeks, and she dropped her gaze.

During the night, her embarrassment was black and white; now in daytime, it was in full color and shone from her face.

"Allow me," he said softly as he took her hand in his and bent over her, guiding her to circle her arms around his neck. "I'll get you there." He burrowed his hands underneath her body and ignoring the soft protests that he thankfully couldn't understand, lifted her up, making sure that her comforter came along.

"The things I have to endure," she whispered in his ear as she turned her face into his shoulder, away from Bryce.

"It'll all be worth it in the end." He ignored the devil whispering in his head that he was doing this for himself, and not for her.

9

MARLÈNE

As Ruben carried her out and into the corridor, Bryce's eyes pierced her with a thousand swords. If looks could kill... It severed the last bit of self-respect she had left hanging from a thread.

Ruben had told her to ignore his brother, but Bryce's cold blue gaze told her everything. Bottom line: she shouldn't even think of *messing with his brother*.

The last thing she wanted to do was to *mess with his brother*. Literally, physically, figuratively. Ruben Scott had misplaced his wings. She'd never been around a person who was more guardian angel incarnate than human. The way he'd helped her, supported her, carried her through the night had been selfless given that they were strangers. He'd done everything right, nothing being too much. At times he'd spoken to her softly, encouragingly. At times he'd wiped the sweat of dry heaving from her forehead. At times, with only a closed bathroom door between them, he'd told her snarky tales of things that happened to him in Paris which he didn't find funny at the time. He'd made her laugh.

When she'd slumped out of the bathroom, thinking that

maybe that was the end of the diarrhea, he'd merely taken her hand and led her back to the sofa, where they'd settled again until the next wave of something struck.

And now he was carrying her into his apartment because he wanted to keep her safe. Widening the distance between her and that suitcase of his. She hated him for it. Everything had been drained from her, everything except the will to get a hit by any means. At some point during the night, she'd wanted to die and had told him so many times. He'd waited, sometimes holding her until some other withdrawal symptom forced her out of his supportive embrace. She'd wanted to claw his suitcase open and bury her face in pills, but she had no energy to fight his gentle resolve. He wouldn't allow it and kept her from caving in with soft words.

Ruben padded over to his sofa and lowered her onto it. He was so consistently gentle, and she couldn't find the anger in her to lash out at him anymore.

"It's cold," she whispered as he loosened his arms around her.

"Just some fresh air. I'll close the windows." Ruben wrapped the comforter around her. "You can warm up in the bath and then you need to eat something, okay?"

She nodded and hugged the comforter tighter around her body. Ruben disappeared into the bathroom and her gaze locked with Bryce's as he strode into the apartment with Ruben's clothes in his arms. Water started to run into the tub and Bryce looked away as if he couldn't stand looking at her.

"It's okay, you know, I really hate him right now," Marlène whispered.

"Good. Keep it that way—if you can," Bryce muttered before he disappeared into Ruben's bedroom. When he reappeared and continued to the front door again, he didn't even look at her.

A minute later, Ruben came out of the bathroom and

followed Bryce out of the apartment. Bryce returned with a second batch of Ruben's clothes and his laptop bag, but when Ruben walked back in, he had a bundle of her clothes in his arms.

"I helped myself to your closet," Ruben smiled, somewhat apologetically. "Hope you don't mind."

"Nothing to hide from you after last night. Nothing you haven't seen." Marlène's body temperature was all over the map, but now a blush flushed her face. Her sexy French bras and panties cascaded from the pile, with what appeared to be her whole silk pajama collection. If she'd known she was going to hang out with her neighbor, she would have stocked up on plainer clothes.

Bryce rolled his eyes with an *ugh* as he dumped her clothes next to her on the sofa. "Anything else you need?" he asked, looking towards Ruben.

"Groceries. Some calcium and magnesium supplements, electrolytes. And ibuprofen for the pain."

"Hmm. I was hoping to go for breakfast?" Bryce said.

"I won't leave Marlène here alone," Ruben said as he pulled Bryce toward the front door.

Now he was missing out on breakfast with his brother, whom he hadn't seen for nine months. Plus, Bryce had flown from Boston to be here. Not only was she indebted to him now, but the guilt was going to eat her alive.

"Please go, I'll be fine," she lied.

"No, you won't," the brothers chimed in unison. They looked at each other and grinned.

"It's okay," Bryce said. "I'll sort out the shopping."

She watched as the brothers walked out of the apartment. Ruben pulled at the door to close it. She was trapped and yet she hadn't felt this free in a long time. Ruben had taken the weight of her ordeal on his shoulders, allowing her to be where she needed to be in the moment, surviving from one second to the next and through the night.

In the bathroom, the faucet still ran, and since Ruben had gone into the corridor with Bryce, he might have forgotten about the bath. She shivered as she unwrapped her comforter from around her shoulders. Her top was glued to her body with sweat, and she groaned in disgust. At least her legs no longer felt like they would cave in if she so much as attempted to put weight on them. She straightened slowly. The hardwood floor was cold under her bare feet, and with her body exposed to the cooler air filtering in from the windows, painful chills rippled over her skin and into her bones.

By the time she walked into the bathroom, she was trembling. The bath was half full and she closed the faucet. She glanced at the empty space. If her bathroom was yin, his was the yang. The space was empty, except for toilet paper and some towels hanging from a railing. Everything else was stored in the mirrored cupboard and underneath the sink.

Surely Ruben wouldn't mind her getting her toiletries if she had the energy to go fetch them. She stroked her arms with her hands, longing to get into the warm water, but she couldn't get naked without having everything she needed to get out of the bathroom again, fully dressed.

She walked to the door and the men's voices came through the small crack. Ruben hadn't closed the door completely. They spoke softly, but she could hear every word.

"I'm not going back to Boston until you tell me what happened in Paris," Bryce said. "You're my family, Ruben, and if you're in trouble, I want to know."

A short silence followed, feet shuffling on the floor, a soft groan from Ruben. "You know I can't talk about my work."

"In detail, no, but you can tell me why you seem to have been put on furlough." Another silence. "And yes, I'm going to push you until you tell me. If you need me, I want to be here.

We can be a very cozy threesome in your one-bedroom apartment."

"Okay. Jeez." Ruben sighed. "I lost my shit and broke a chair from the break room against the wall."

"Your freaking temper. Break rooms aren't for breaking shit," Bryce muttered drily. "I thought you had it under control. Ever since that day I had to drag you off the asshole who groped that other kid at school—"

"He so had me coming his way, long before I caught him cornering someone half his size." Ruben paused. "We both know he wasn't after that kid's lunch."

"Yeah, okay. It's a miracle you weren't suspended," Bryce said. "You're thirty-five, Ruben. You need to contain that fucker."

"Whatever. We'll see how your temper fares with the shit I have to deal with. And it was just one chair. And one table. And some drywall. And a chipped mug." He paused. "That last one had to go."

Ruben's tone changed towards the end, trying to make light of something that wasn't. She closed her eyes, but it was impossible to imagine Ruben breaking walls with a cafeteria chair. He'd been so gentle with her, that he could have a violent streak was incongruous with everything she'd experienced since last night. The only hint of a violent past were those scars on his body, but now, her inner being contracting with dread. There were two sides to every story, the one in the light, the other in the shadow.

"So, what now? You'll get back on the job or what?"

"I need to talk to a psych. Marc will only let me get back on the job after a month's break and if I've spoken with one. We need an ocean between us for a while."

"You've talked to a shrink before so—"

"That was different."

It was quiet for a drawn-out minute, and she envisioned

them measuring each other up, neither wanting to look away first.

"Okay," Bryce sighed. "You phone me when you need to talk. I know, not about your work, about…shit. Or come up to Boston and stay a week or so, or even just for a few days."

"Yeah, sure. Let me just catch up on sleep first."

"And ditch the addict."

"Don't go there. You have no idea—" Ruben broke off and inhaled sharply.

"I have no idea, no. But whatever you do, don't get involved and for fuck's sake, *don't* fall for her."

Ruben muttered something inaudible.

"There's a first for everything," Bryce said, his tone somewhat dry.

More shuffling followed and footsteps fell on the floor. The door opened and her breath caught as Ruben's gaze met her own.

"You're up."

She wrung her hands together, caught out and now cautious with knowledge she hadn't planned on gaining. "I was hoping to get some of my toiletries in my apartment."

"How much of our conversation did you hear?" Ruben walked through the door and stepped away so as not to crowd her against the wall.

"Most of it?"

"Right." He stared at her, searching her face, and she couldn't look away. "I've never hurt a woman or a child, and I never will." He sighed and the exhaustion was etched in hard lines around his mouth and his brow, where frown lines slashed over his forehead.

But he had anger issues and the scars on his body spoke volumes. Somehow she believed him and just nodded. "I know."

"How can you just know?"

"I've been around a lot of men." And nothing showed someone's true colors more than how he reacted to her worst withdrawal to date.

"Yeah. Okay. Whatever." Ruben rubbed a hand down his face and closed his eyes in what looked like a moment of prayer. "Still want to do this?"

"Do what?"

"This detox. With me here. And you here."

She'd lashed out at him so many times last night and at one point she'd punched him on the chest. He'd been nothing but caring, a gentleman in every sense of the word. Some of her actions had become hazy between everything else and an overwhelming wave of shame washed over her. His burst of anger at whatever job he was doing—which was clearly not some random IT gig—was his own demon which hadn't showed its face once in her presence.

One night with him had taught her that she couldn't do this alone. He was right. He might be a stranger, he might have anger issues, but Ruben was her salvation. If he stuck around long enough to see her through this withdrawal, she might make it to the other side. And then she'd be free.

"Yes," she said. "I really do. With you being here, I might see my way through."

He nodded. "Okay. What else do you need from your apartment?"

"My phone, please. And my laptop. I always speak to my sisters on Saturday mornings. It's probably by the sideboard in the foyer. And the food in the fridge. No need to let it go to waste. And anything else you need from my kitchen. After nine months, it must be pretty dire in here."

At this he raised his eyebrows. "Let's not carry your kitchen to mine. I'll bring the food you bought with the champagne. And the champagne only to celebrate with once you're through to the other side."

He left her standing by the open door and she leaned against the doorjamb. She could walk away, and he'd let her go. This was up to her.

Ruben would hold her hand, but it looked like he needed some kind of support too. She couldn't shake the feeling that he was the type of man that would never admit to it. She had her fair share of work-related frustrations, but she'd been able to prattle on about her job to whoever wanted to listen. Nobody she knew ever took a chair to a break room wall in anger or frustration.

If nothing else, she wanted to figure out what Ruben Scott did for a living before they went their separate ways.

10

RUBEN

After five more rounds to her apartment to collect the things she might need, Marlène finally closed the bathroom door behind her.

He missed her presence already. What a mess. He'd given up on seeing her naked back for now. It wasn't the time. It would be a relief to be certain, but he had to respect her too. Every five minutes he'd pray that she wasn't the girl in those images. But then, if she was the girl they'd baptized as Andromeda, the knowledge would open a can of worms he wasn't in the headspace to deal with yet.

What would he do with the knowledge? Having the key didn't mean he should unlock the door, never mind open it—for her sake. Not for his.

He needed sleep but his mind didn't have a pause button.

The last thing he wanted to be was alone in his head. For all that last night had been a shit-show, Marlène's withdrawal kept him occupied, his fried brain busy, and his dread lagging a mile behind him. Bryce's incessant prodding had unnerved him. Yes, he'd been to a psychologist before, they both had. Social workers and all that foster crap you go through. Mentors, educational and school counsellors. Nobody had ever kept him levelheaded like his brother.

The problem was that Bryce hadn't been in France when he needed him. He'd joined a boxing club in the city, but no one there challenged him mentally like Bryce could. He hadn't needed that type of mental and physical exorcism for years and thought his anger outbursts were under control. Ever since he'd been lured onto this investigation, that anger had rippled, from the widest circles made by a stone flung into the water, but he didn't understand where the epicenter was. Somewhere in the calm surface of his life, someone had dropped that boulder that led to this situation.

His job was at stake. That was one thing, but to work on this for so long only to see them fail and a criminal walk away made him physically sick. He'd only been there nine months, but the international team in Paris had been trying to crack the ring for over four years.

The anger simmered so deep inside him, under the thick soup of his daily life and all-consuming work, that a bubble would rarely manage to press its way up and release to the surface. Bryce had helped him manage those handful of times. But now something had turned up the heat and he'd gone from a light simmer to a full rolling boil that threatened to spill over.

Marc was right. He had to sort his shit out.

The bathroom door opened and Marlène came out, hair towel dried, dressed in the very American lounge wear he had dug out of her closet. She was pale and had dark circles under her eyes, but she was still beautiful, and his heart skipped a beat as she walked up to him.

"Feeling better?" he asked.

"Yes, thank you. It really helps with the aches." She reached for the mixing bowl filled with make-up he'd fetched for her. He refused to bring the whole lot, so for twenty minutes he'd fished her list of items out of her bathroom cupboard.

"What now?" Surely, she wasn't going to paint her face. They weren't going anywhere, and she didn't need to cover anything up.

"I—" Marlène clung tighter to the bowl, her fingers turning white at the tips with the pressure. "I can't look like this when I have the group call with my sisters."

When she didn't go into further details, he dropped the subject. He knew nothing of her family and by the look of the clothes in her closet, they were a high-riding upper-crust bunch. Keeping up with appearances might be on her agenda, but it had never been on his. Where he came from, pretense was a waste of time.

Ruben made no comment when she retreated to the bathroom, only to appear forty minutes later, hair blow-dried and looking like she was about to be photographed for the front cover of some women's magazine.

"I had to redo my eyeliner three times. My hands are shaking so much. I gave up putting some on."

He shook his head. He wouldn't know the difference. She was beautiful before, but now she looked striking. "You can always switch the camera off."

She stared at him, wide-eyed. "I don't know. I've never done that before."

The siren's visual she presented was too much to stomach, knowing her inner turmoil, so he fled to the kitchen so that he didn't have to look at her. She was a puppet with strings attached to all the wrong manipulators. The thought made his stomach turn. He needed to get the buzzing question in his head answered or stop speculating so that he could move on. Chances were zero to none. He had to focus on his own issues.

Ruben listened as she dialed in on her laptop to the call in France and soon the small apartment echoed with female voices speaking French. They were talking so fast, he couldn't distinguish separate words, although every now and again he would grasp a one-syllable *oui* or *non* and the effervescent *merde*.

He made her a *tisane*—from her kitchen, not his—and when he took it to her, she smiled at him as she took the cup. A moment of quiet followed as her sisters realized she'd been served a cup of tea by a very male hand, and then a flood of questions and comments made her blush and say *non-non-non* on repeat.

Ruben hovered by her side for a moment, fascinated that she kept the show going despite pinpricks of sweat beading on her forehead. He leaned into her laptop, touched the mousepad and for a moment caught the stunned gazes of the two women on the screen. He hitched his eyebrows at them and calmly switched the camera off.

More giggles followed, but Marlène slumped back on the sofa and mouthed a thank you to him.

"You're welcome," he mouthed back. Let her sisters think they were smooching off screen. Her sisters were sweet, but obviously clueless about what was happening in Marlène's life or her body at that moment.

He couldn't care less about her sisters. He cared about her, and when Marlène shot him a shy smile, his heart skipped a beat.

When Bryce walked in a little later, Marlène was still on the call.

"Friends' chat?" Bryce asked as he dropped the groceries on the kitchen counter.

"Sisters." Ruben opened the bags to find the medication Marlène needed. "I owe you."

"It's nothing. Just promise me you'll sever ties with her, Ruben. Maggie will rise from her grave and come do it for you if you don't."

Whenever Bryce called on Maggie to press his issue, Ruben understood he was serious. Their foster mother didn't need to rise from the grave; just the thought of disappointing her made him hang his head. If it hadn't been for Maggie and her husband Herman, who knew where he'd be right now. "Yeah. I will. Only until she's better, max until next week, then I have to deal with my own shit. And she'll be going back to work in any case."

"Fine." Bryce leaned against the counter and reached for a paper box from one of the grocery bags. "I thought a taste of home would be good now that you're back."

Bryce lifted the lid and the sweet spicy scent of fresh cinnamon rolls escaped and filled him with a pang. He bit down on his jaw to contain the rise of emotion in his throat. He was too tired to deal with homesickness too. "That's home summed up."

"Won't ever be as good as Maggie's, but these aren't half bad." Bryce ran a fingertip along the edge of the box to scrape off some icing and licked his finger. "Hmm. Does this mean you're around for Thanksgiving for a change?"

"I haven't thought about it." Ruben grinned. "I might, actually, be around. You're still trying to perfect Maggie's turkey, or is it still a sacrilege?"

Bryce grinned. "I've made progress. You should come over and taste for yourself."

"Hell yeah, why not." For the past couple of years, he'd always been busy or away on an investigation. Going to Boston for Thanksgiving hadn't been an option. He needed this, even if Bryce's dry turkey was best served to the trash can, uncarved, in one smooth sweep. In the box of four rolls, one quarter was missing, and Ruben smiled. "Coffee? With the other one?"

Bryce dragged in a breath and put the cinnamon rolls on the counter. "I have to catch a flight back to Boston. I need to go visit the deceased man's family and I don't want to do that too late today or on a Sunday. Monday is chaos already. So."

"Right." Ruben closed his eyes for a moment. Bryce had his

own work issues to deal with and shouldn't need to worry about him too. "Thanks for coming."

"Come beat me up soon."

"Yep. Sure thing." The words slipped out easily, but it hit him that this maze had no quick side exit, even though he was lost, had been for some time, and needed a break.

He had to dig to the heart of this issue or give up everything he'd worked toward since he'd woken up in the hospital that morning, stab wounds freshly bound, with Herman and Maggie by his side. Maggie had told him there'd be no bad apples in their basket. There was still time to cut out the rot before he turned completely.

"Your apartment key." Bryce held it out to him and as he reached for it, Bryce pulled him into a bear hug.

"I'm here if you need me."

"I know."

They walked out of the kitchen and Bryce nodded goodbye at Marlène where she was still busy on her call. A young girl's voice came from the screen and a baby wailed in the background.

A last squeeze to his shoulder and Bryce was gone. Ruben closed the door and leaned against it for a moment to take a breath. The rest of the day loomed dark. He observed Marlène for a second. While the camera was still turned on, she had kept her symptoms hidden by covering up with a blanket. With her laptop perched on a stack of books she'd gathered from his shelf, only her head was visible on the screen. Now she slumped into the sofa, exhausted. By the sound of it she was ringing off and could let loose.

Back in the kitchen he fixed her an electrolyte drink. With the CalMag supplements and ibuprofen in hand, he padded over to her as she dropped her head back, her arms hanging limp. Tears streamed down her cheeks, trailing black tracks of make-up behind them.

"Here. This will help for the restless legs and the pain." He sat down next to her and waited.

She hesitated for a second but then nodded. He shook the tablets from their containers into her palm and placed the containers on the coffee table as he worked his way through them. He handed her the electrolyte drink, and she swallowed with a shudder. "How do you know all this crap about withdrawal?"

"Told you this isn't my first rodeo."

Marlène stared at him, and he read her mind. *This was more than what a kid should know.*

She dropped her gaze. "That call was so hard. Exhausting."

Pretending *would* be hard and exhausting, especially if she'd been doing it for a long time.

"They don't know? Nobody in your family knows, do they? And that's why you're in New York? So they never find out?"

She hugged her legs to her chest and tightened her arms around them, curling into a ball. She bit her lip but failed to hide her anguish as she dropped her forehead to her knees. "No, they don't know and I must keep it that way."

This came as no surprise to him. Often family were the last to know about a child's or sibling's addiction. For a lot of people, it was easier to open up to a stranger, like Marlène had with him. He wrapped an arm around her shoulders, and she leaned into him for support.

He was here now, but she needed her family for support too. Despite being close, there was a big disconnect here within her family. Were her parents always this blind? And her sisters always this gullible? The love was there in that call with her sisters, and she wasn't estranged from them, so how had they managed to be so blatantly blind to her problem?

11

MARLÈNE

Being isolated had been her undoing during her previous two attempts to get clean.

Now he was here, and it was just an arm, *his* arm, and a soft squeeze of his hand on her shoulder, that made all the difference.

She was not alone. Not in this, at least. Like she'd done for some years, she'd expended a mammoth amount of energy feigning to her sisters that she was one hundred percent. It was much easier to pretend under the soothing, brain-numbing influence of drugs. Not for one second would she allow them a peek into her world.

Ruben was here and he didn't plan to leave her until she was better. He'd seen her at her worst and there was more to come. Marlène unfolded her body and wrapped her arms around him in a hug he gave right back.

"Thank you," she whispered into his neck, where his scruff scratched her tear-stained cheek.

"You're going to be okay," he murmured.

Already she was going for longer than her previous two attempts, when the lure of her pile of pills was too strong. Now his hard chest, two apartment doors, and a locked suitcase stood between her and her fix.

"What are your sisters' names?" he asked as she loosened her hold on him and let her hands slide down his chest before she sat straight. She wanted to rest her head on his shoulder and stay in the safety of his arms, but he retracted from her body and rested his elbows on his thighs.

"Vianne is the middle sister. She has two little girls; Manon is two and Emily is six months old." Vianne had nursed Emily during the first ten minutes of their chat and Manon had clambered over the sofa like a monkey the entire time. "Anaïs is my youngest sister. So clever. She's a lawyer but she's very broody, especially since Emily arrived. Anaïs babysits whenever she can, so I'm not sure how long her illustrious career is going to last."

Anaïs was planning her perfect summer wedding and asked for Marlène's advice on everything from the flowers to the dress —did she need one or two? A princess dress for the ceremony and then something sexy for the actual party afterwards? The questions were so far out of her life's reach that her heart shredded. She'd had to kill the call as she'd been at breaking point.

"When did you last see them?" Ruben asked.

"I went to France to see Vianne after Emily's birth, but I made a promise to myself: I won't go back until I'm clean." If she ever wanted a paper-thin slice of the life her sisters had, she had to get a grip on her drug addiction. She had until Anaïs's wedding day to do so, seven more months. She needed to get mentally in shape for the wedding too. No way she could face everybody at the wedding without her head screwed on straight.

Her phone vibrated on the coffee table, and she glanced at it. On recognizing the name, her stomach clutched tight, and her gut twisted. He was the last person she should talk to right now. Just hearing his voice would derail her.

Ruben reached for her phone and held it out to her. "Incoming. From Damien."

Regardless of what Damien was going through on his side, she had to be selfish here. Another reason why she had to move away from Paris: to get some distance from her first lover and their inability to let each other go. To talk to him now would set her back not only with her withdrawal, but by months. Every attempt to get clean required mental preparation, and the build-up toward each attempt took time, time she didn't have.

"I don't want to talk to him."

"Right." Ruben put the phone back on the coffee table, where its vibrations cut through the awkward silence. "He's an ex?"

"No, he is...*was* a permanent in my life."

"Until you came here?"

"Until I came here."

"By the tone in your voice it sounds like you should block his number."

Probably. But blocking him from her life wasn't going to erase their history. Her phone stopped ringing and she sank back in relief.

"He isn't your dealer in Paris, is he?" Ruben's gaze trapped hers and her breath stalled.

"I have a script—"

"From a dubious doctor."

"I—" She broke off, not sure if she wanted to tell him anything about her protracted and painful relationship with Damien. She didn't talk about Damien to anybody except Damien. Over the years they'd shared little bursts of frankness, but they'd both suppressed them until everything was back in that mutual cave, that cave they each carried inside of them.

Those pills helped her keep the cave sealed. Talking to Ruben about Damien today of all days would be like rigging dynamite to her gut and lighting a match with the intention to mine deep.

"Did Damien introduce you to this doctor? The one who prescribes you pills?"

She hesitated. Ruben knew nobody in her inner circle and putting this out there would mean nothing to him. "It was actually the other way around."

That summer, now so long ago, when fifteen-year-old Damien had come to the Riviera house with his older cousins for a party. All of them doctors. Friend of friends.

The saying went that anybody knew anybody by six degrees of separation, and it had only taken a couple of years for her to bump into someone with experiences similar to hers. Not that they'd spoken about it when they'd met, or ever, because who the hell did, but that day had been the beginning of her disjointed relationship with Damien.

That day her world had started to shrink to him and her as they'd watched her sisters and the other younger kids like hawks.

"He's your middleman?"

He was in the middle. Sometimes. She kept staring straight ahead, not wanting to blink in case a canvas of her and Damien at fifteen was glued to the back of her eyelids, filling her head with sordid images in black and red.

"Please. I—"

"I don't mean to interrogate you. I want to understand how you managed this." He rolled both hands in the air, as if to encapsulate the whole bloody heap of carrion that was her life.

"I need to lie down." She was in his apartment now, slumped on his sofa, her past the elephant in the room.

Ruben gave a soft sigh but nodded. "I changed the linen on my bed. You'll be more comfortable there."

God no. "Please—don't."

"I'll take the sofa. It's comfortable, like yours."

"Ruben, it's too much." Kicking him out of his space when he'd just got home seemed cruel.

"It's a bed."

"And I bet you want to sleep in it again, after nine months away. No place like home."

"A few more days won't make a difference." He stood and held his hand out to her. "In any case, the TV is here in the living room and if I want to play some video games, I won't disturb you."

The notion that he could be too good to be true punched her in the gut...a gut she'd learned to trust the hard way. "Okay," she whispered, but didn't put her hand in his to stand.

His hand fell away, and she padded over to his bedroom. She paused outside the door and peered in.

The room was the same size as hers and his king-size bed came with a wooden headboard and matching nightstands. Dark blue linen and copper lamps rounded off the male-dominated space. How many women had spent the night here? With him on the sofa?

She wanted to laugh and cry at the same time. She wanted to believe he was good. No, she needed to know, for sure, that he was good. She needed to hear it from him. Actions spoke more than a thousand words, but sometimes all you needed was a few simple words.

Marlène turned and propped her shoulder against the doorjamb. She met his gaze from across the room where he stood, hands on his hips, a frown now narrowing his eyes as he watched her pause. "You okay?"

"What do you mean this isn't your first rodeo? With withdrawal?" She had other questions she wanted answers to, but if he wouldn't tell his brother anything, he'd tell her even less. "There was obviously your mom, but I get the feeling you know more than that." She would hate to put it out there, but maybe he used at some point too. If he had, he now had his life together, and his example should be the perfect motivation to keep her going.

He relaxed his stance and drove his fingers through his hair without blinking. "You need to know to feel safe, don't you?"

"This *is* weird. You have to admit."

"Not weirder than hooking up with a stranger and going home with him."

But that wasn't what they were doing, was it? She'd feel less vulnerable with a one-night stand simply because she knew how to deal with those. Here was this man who didn't seem to have an obvious sexual agenda. She didn't know what to do with him or the situation.

"Probably not. It's only—" Marlène broke off as she picked her words. "You don't come across as someone working in IT like you told me last night and it makes me feel queasy. Over and above the withdrawal queasy, which is getting worse by the minute."

"Right." Ruben's gaze didn't falter when she said nothing, but he didn't smile either. "I'm in IT now, but I used to work for the NYPD. Drugs and human trafficking department."

"Okay," she said.

"Okay?"

"Okay." She turned into the room, closed the door, took the few steps to the bed and caved in.

That explained everything, didn't it?

12

RUBEN

Ruben stared at the closed bedroom door. What the hell had he gotten himself into?

Seeing her on the call, faking life with such animation, had cracked something inside him.

And now he'd lied to her. Not so much a direct lie, more a lie by omission. A little one. Insignificant really, but like an unseen nail on a wall, it could do so much damage once someone snagged her skin on it.

She wanted to trust him, needed to trust him, and this wasn't how you went about winning someone's trust.

He was out of practice with the way he spoke to her. This was what happened when you stayed out of the field for so long, tied to your desk. The lie by omission was one thing, but there was worse: having her in his apartment dissolved the normal barriers there would be between a victim or a suspect and the police. No badge stood between him and her, no uniform, no law.

Without the usual protective barrier of the trade—at a minimum a gun and a bulletproof vest—he was exposed, vulnerable not so much in his body but in his mind. The emotional distance he'd curate with each case was eroding. She was like an orphaned chick swept under his wing, her body's warmth spreading through to his cold heart.

He'd been trained to stay objective and analytical, to remain emotionally distanced from his cases. It was the only way to survive. He had to pigeonhole the solved and sometimes cold cases he'd been involved in so he could move on to the next. Emotional investment was death in his chosen career. Often suicide. He'd lost enough colleagues that way.

On his way here from Paris, he'd had every intention of putting off the meeting with the psychologist until the last week of his leave, but it was obvious he had to sort that shit out as soon as possible. If she was Andromeda, he would ask her for help, and he would need to have a clear, focused mind during the process. He wasn't going to get there on his own.

He needed to sleep, but first he needed to sort out her stash. Even though her apartment key was safe in his jeans pocket, he'd prefer it if she didn't know where her stash was or what he'd done with it. He had some raiding to do too, in the kitchen.

No noises came from the bedroom, so he padded out of his apartment, went into hers and made quick work of her small kitchen, where he found two ground coffee containers with pills hidden under the coffee. Then he went to the bathroom and sorted through the baskets of products, but there was nothing hidden in them.

She was neurotic about her stash, but for an addict that was the norm. With the pile of drugs she transported, the police could already be on her scent. Or not. She had no reason to be flagged. Her actions spoke of an obsessive fear of running out of drugs on the one hand, and a strong, determined spirit to let go on the other. She wanted to quit, and he was sure she would, with support, but the road to getting and staying clean was one that was full of crevices. Like those in a glacier. One slip and you were a goner.

Ruben reminded himself what addiction was—a way to get through the night by numbing yourself with drugs. To keep nightmares at bay, or because you wanted to forget, or to fill the void of what you were robbed of by others. Innocence, a sense of self, love, so many things.

At the thought, images flashed through his mind's eye, and he had to lean against the apartment wall for a moment. He was losing his mind, but avoiding sleep wasn't helping. The nightmares that had been plaguing him of late were new and oddly familiar in a sense, because of his work. He'd always considered himself strong, physically and mentally, but in the past months, he'd only felt a suffocating, disabling weakness that led to his outbreak at work.

It was all in his head.

He took a deep breath, put the last of Marlène's stash in his suitcase, and went to his small storage unit in the apartment block's basement. He hid his suitcase behind some cardboard boxes and his bike and locked the unit again.

Now he could breathe easy.

Or not.

She was alone and shouldn't be.

Ruben rushed to the elevator and had to hold back from hammering the button to get to their floor quicker. He found her flung over the toilet, retching up her tisane, face pale, hair clammy, eyes wide as she looked up at him. "You left."

"I'm back."

"I can't anymore. Every bone in my body aches. My throat is raw." Her voice was so thin he hardly heard what she said.

"You must." He hesitated. "Do you want me to call a doctor?"

"No. Please. No doctors. Ever."

"No doctors. Noted." He hid his dismay. Things would be so much easier if she had some proper medical assistance. "You can't quit this minute. You can't quit this hour. You can't quit today. Only get to tomorrow and we'll see how it goes, okay?"

She nodded, and this time, when he held his hand out to her, she allowed him to help her up. She washed her face, brushed her teeth, rinsed with mouthwash, and reached again for his hand. Wordlessly she stumbled with him to the bedroom and pulled him to the bed with her.

"Marlène—"

"Just stay, please," she whispered, "until I fall asleep."

She was shivering, her body hot and cold, sweating chills. His whole being wanted to sink deeper into the bed, begging his mind to allow him some rest. She clung to his hand as if it was the only thing that kept her going.

"Try to relax," he murmured. Her needs were so much bigger than his right now. Maybe he'd sleep if he stayed close to her. Maybe her presence would ward off the vivid images he feared the most in his dreams. Those of a girl with a scatter of moles on her shoulder, and someone drawing the constellation lines of the Chained Maiden on her back to make sure the tattooed stars would go in the right places, in perfect scale. "I'll stay."

She softened her grip and he got up to fetch a blanket from his closet. He wrapped the comforter over her and lay down next to her, pulling the blanket over him. He didn't push her away when she inched into him; instead, he hugged her closer and let her back rest against his side.

When Ruben woke, his bedroom was dark, and a slice of artificial light shone through a gap between the curtains. Nighttime, city lights, in a place where he felt at home.

He sat up, alert, but his reaction was too slow. He'd be dead if he were on one of those life-and-death missions that his job often entailed. The other side of the bed was empty. His stomach tightened as he listened. He felt for their apartment keys in his front pocket. Soft noises came from the other side of the bedroom door, and he breathed easy as his fingers connected with the keys. He got up to see what Marlène was up to. Something was sizzling and his stomach growled on cue as he paused in the kitchen door.

Marlène stood at the stove with the thick ribeye Bryce had brought smoking away in the skillet. Her hair was wet and curled up in a messy bun on top of her head, some loose strands escaping freely. She wore one of his T-shirts and...only his T-shirt. It was long enough to cover her up to mid-thigh and the domestic comfort of the whole situation made him smile. She sure knew how to make herself at home.

"Hey," he said as he leaned against the doorjamb with folded arms. She had more color in her face and looked better. The urge to step up to her and slide his hand down her back was so intense, he had to consciously stop himself. What he really wanted was to kiss her on the forehead and hug her close.

She looked at him and her eyes lit up. "You're awake."

"What time is it?"

"Almost midnight."

"Well, that's going to be fun, isn't it?" He wasn't getting rid of his jet lag soon at this rate.

"You slept for twelve hours straight," she said with a smile. "I didn't have it in me to wake you."

Out stone cold for a change. He could do with a few more of those nights. "How're you feeling?"

"I managed to sleep and then I took another long bath. The pills you bought also helped take the edge off, so for now, I'm feeling somewhat okay."

It wasn't going to last, but maybe if Marlène could see this through for another twenty-four hours or so, she'd be through the worst of it.

"Anything I can help with?" He stood closer and eyed the

salad she'd made. A piece of buttered baguette she'd been nibbling at rested on the cutting board with the wheel of soft brie.

"Have some," she said with a nod towards the bread. "The steak is going to be a few more minutes."

Their elbows rubbed against each other as she turned the ribeye over, and he tore off a piece of baguette. Neither of them pulled away. This was what you got when you slept with each other, innocently. They had nothing to hide. No uncomfortable dash out of his apartment, no walk of shame. No pretend. She was clean, he smelled of sleep and needed to brush his teeth, but somehow none of this mattered.

He smothered the baguette with butter, slapped on a wedge of cheese, and bit into it with a groan. One thing he'd came to appreciate in Paris was the beauty of simplistic French food, perfected over centuries: bread and cheese.

"I would offer you a glass of red wine with that, but you don't have any," Marlène said as she watched him chew. "You like that?"

"Mm-hmm. Best stuff ever." He glanced at her, and she was staring at him, her gaze homing in on his lips.

She lifted her hand to rub off a breadcrumb from the corner of his mouth with her thumb. Time froze. Her touch was so soft, so gentle, the whisper of a butterfly wing against his skin. But she didn't stop there. Her fingertips traced over his cheek to the angle of his jaw where he bit down at the unexpected, arousing intimacy of her touch. It was the simplest gesture, innocent and yet highly sensual.

She dropped her hand and looked away. "You need to shave."

Shaving was the last thing on his mind. All he wanted was to lean in and run his hand under that shirt of his she was wearing. He wanted to feel the smooth skin of her thighs against his fingertips and graze the soft curve of her ass to find out if she was wearing panties.

His eyes dropped to her chest, the male magnet all women had, irrespective of size. From the hardening of her nipples and those two barbells pressing against the fabric, it was clear that she wasn't wearing a bra.

Fuck.

13

MARLÈNE

She shouldn't have touched him. Not with the touch of a lover.

It had quieted, only their mutual breathing shifting the static air between them. She was trouble. She'd been in trouble. She'd always caused trouble for other people and now here was Ruben Scott. The man who saw straight through her, untroubled by what he found as he read her like a book.

Inside her, something awoke, something she'd suppressed for four long years under the numbing of drugs. Now she feared its stirring, the heat of desire he awoke in her. She hadn't slept with anybody since Damien two years ago, and for someone with her track record, that was unheard of. Lying next to him, breathing in his intoxicating male scent, feeling the shape of his body against her own, shook her in her slumber. This was what Sleeping Beauty felt like when the prince kissed her back to life.

Except she was no innocent virginal princess.

She'd lied to him. Not a direct lie, but more a subtle shift of the truth.

Ruben hadn't slept soundly for twelve hours straight. He'd slept restlessly and, on a few occasions, had muttered incoherently in his sleep, his mumblings anxious as his body quivered against hers. She'd been awake, thanks to her withdrawal symptoms, her legs restless, her heart pounding in her chest. He'd been unaware. In the dark she'd stared at him, her palm on his heart, trying to calm him with her touch until he quieted again.

NYPD Drugs and Human Trafficking. She couldn't begin to imagine the places he'd been, and the trauma he'd experienced through his work. PTSD was real, as she understood all too well. The way he'd crashed into a deep sleep was more than jet lag. It was the sleep of those who undertook a journey too arduous to undertake in the first place.

He was here now, knee-deep in support for her. During the night she'd promised herself that she'd be here for him too, regardless of what plagued him with his work which had brought him to this point. Things had gotten out of hand, and he was home for a reason. She didn't care what it was, but he needed support. She'd give it in every way possible except in the way her body would crave once she'd worked through the initial withdrawals.

She knew herself. She was petrified of what waited once she crossed the first hurdle of this withdrawal. Then the harder work would come. Work that had nothing to do with her body, but her mind—a space she didn't want to spend any time in.

He wore his trauma in the shape of scars from stabbings and bullet wounds.

Her body showed no wounds, but her soul bore the scars, there where nobody could see them.

Ruben reached over her head for two plates in the cupboard and the noise startled her from her inner thoughts.

"Welcome back, dreamer," he murmured close to her ear and a thrill of pleasure spread down her back as his breath ghosted over her skin.

At the current rate, the steak would be over-cooked, and she bet he liked it medium rare.

He stepped away and reached for a dishcloth in a drawer. "I've got some cleaning to do," he said as he wiped the plates down. "Nine months away makes for a lot of dust."

"I can help," Marlène answered, avoiding his gaze. "It's not a lot with our apartments being so small."

Why did she offer? She had to get out of his apartment, or this was going to go places she wasn't mentally ready for. The focus should be on getting clean, not to fall into a fuck-fest with her neighbor to keep that monster busy. With what she'd been going through physically, he'd probably welcome the distance between them. There was zero scope for attraction in withdrawal. But his support was addictive, and she needed to be careful. She couldn't swap one addiction for another, not again —and this time a human addiction of all things.

Sex addiction was one thing, drugs another, but using a human being, someone like Ruben? It was the one thing she would never allow herself to do.

Once he was gone, back to Paris, he wouldn't be here for her to latch on and cling to. Ultimately, she was alone.

"Thanks for this," Ruben said as he took some cutlery from the drawer.

"It's nothing." He'd done so much for her by merely being here. Cooking a meal was the least she could do.

They carried the food to the four-seater table he'd managed to squeeze into his apartment. Her living room set was too big to allow anything bigger than a two-seater flatpack she'd built herself when she moved in.

Now that she had to eat the food, her appetite wavered. She should eat, but she didn't want to vomit it all up again later.

"Only two bites. To start off with. It is after all a midnight feast," he said, an encouraging smile in his voice.

"I'll stick to bread, I think."

"By Monday you should be feeling better."

"This time has been the hardest. Physically." If he hadn't been here, she would've caved in long ago.

"It gets harder every time you try to get clean. Giving up messes with your mind and body that way."

"Maybe I'll be better by Tuesday then." If only she could wind the clock forward.

"We'll see. Want to play a game later?" he asked between two bites.

Her heart skipped a beat. She used to be up for all kind of games. "What kind?"

"Xbox? Not sure how else to kill the time until the sun comes up. I have to manage this jet lag somehow and try to keep awake until tonight."

If she didn't feel so crap and looked like a rag doll that had toyed with a shredder, she might have been keen to introduce him to some other games.

He watched her as he tore off another piece of baguette. "Unless you want to go back to bed?"

Only if you come with me, her mind whispered, but the past twelve hours had been the last time she'd spend in bed with Ruben Scott. "Sure, I'll play something with you. If I'm terrible, we can switch to a movie?"

"I can teach you a few things."

"I bet you can."

"Starting from a zero-knowledge base is sometimes best."

She wanted to be retaught everything from scratch. Wipe her mind's slate clean and have a Ruben Scott introduction to sex. With a body like his, the unforced strength with which he carried her through that past day, the kindness and warmth that radiated from his soul, this type of man should have been her first, and not her go-to to quiet the monster in that cave inside her.

14

MARLÈNE

By Tuesday morning her tremors were better, her restless legs had improved, and although she still woke up in a sheen of sweat, the vomiting and diarrhea had stopped altogether on Monday morning. She'd gone from terrible to passable on the gaming front, and they'd worked through five movies and another order of Go Go Pho takeout.

Ruben had allowed her to nest in his bed, but he never joined her there again, under the pretense of falling asleep mid-movie on the sofa. She wasn't stupid. He also knew where this would end up if they'd let it.

They hadn't left the apartment. Ruben had slipped out for half an hour to meet with someone who had changed his car's battery. Luckily, with his car standing in the apartment block's basement for such a long time, the battery had been the only issue. Now he was sitting at his desk, his laptop switched on, busy checking his email. He'd done the same on Monday morning, but she hadn't paid attention.

"I need to get a few things from next door, but—" She bolstered her courage. "I think I should move back to my place."

He swiveled around in his gaming chair and leaned back to take her in. He'd just showered and wore a dark blue polo and faded jeans. His feet were bare, as always, and she'd quietly fallen in love with them, if that was even possible. Size twelve, pedicured, strong and bony, with a fading summer tan.

"You look better. The color's back in your cheeks." He stood and took the few steps to where she hovered in the kitchen door. "You're welcome to stay for longer, to get through it properly."

She glanced towards his computer and her apartment key that had been lying on his desk since Sunday morning when he'd washed some laundry and had pulled the key from his jeans pocket. It had waited there all that time, inviting her to leave when she was ready. To fetch those pills and fling them down her throat if she wanted to.

Now she wasn't sure she was ready at all. He was here, kept her mind busy, held her tight away from the ledge. Alone in her place she might go mad. For all that New York was filled with people, she'd never lived in a place where people were cubed up in so much isolation.

But she couldn't blame the city for cutting off all humans in her life until she literally stumbled over one who wouldn't allow her to be alone. "You've done so much for me, I—" Tears swelled, and she dropped her gaze.

"Hey," he whispered as he stepped closer to cup her face in his hands. "I'm right next door. Come over any time you want or need to. I have to go out for a few hours today, but for the rest, I'm home." His thumb stroked her cheek, catching a tear midstream.

She nodded and bit her lip to contain her emotions. Her fingers burned to touch him, to grab his shirt, her whole being wanting to pull him closer. "You're going out?"

He hesitated. "I need to go talk to someone. As you know."

So Ruben hadn't forgotten that she'd heard his conversation

with Bryce. "Yes." Talking to a therapist loomed in her future too, if she ever got that far.

He dropped his hands to her shoulders and stroked a path down to her hands and caught her fingers in his. "You're going to be okay, alone?"

There was no answer to that, so she didn't nod or shake her head. "Why are you so good to me?" she whispered as she finally looked up at him again.

Ruben sighed. "When you end up in foster care, you quickly learn that every decision has a two-fork split, one direction towards good, the other direction towards not so good, and sometimes just straight to bad. My life really is that black and white. I try to do good. To stop the bad in this world. If everyone took the fork in the road that led to good, we would all be better off, don't you think?"

He made it sound so simple.

"So, when you can't cope, you make the good choice. Or the better one, at least." He dipped his head to look deeper into her eyes. "You come here instead of going out to find a hit, okay?"

"Okay."

He squeezed her fingers but instead of loosening her grip so he could let go, she dropped her forehead to his chest, burrowed her head under his chin and pulled his hands to her back so that he was embracing her, with her arms the chains that kept them close.

His chest rose with a slow inhale at the intimacy of this stance, and he lowered his face to her temple and brushed his nose along her hairline, his lips cruising her skin but not pressing into something more.

And she wanted it so much.

Marlène lifted her head and trapped his mouth in a hesitant kiss with just enough pressure to allow him to pull away. Instead of pulling away from her, he kissed her back, pressing his lips to hers with soft, sweet tenderness. When he opened his lips to brush his tongue over hers, it was tentative and questioning, making sure she was on board with it too. A soft moan escaped from within her, and he invaded her mouth with a slow turn of his tongue, and she allowed him in, just as she had from day one.

She kissed him deeper, her legs going weak as he responded unhurriedly with a tongue that knew what it was doing. Her fingers softened their grip, and his hands slipped free, only to cup her butt in a sure caress. He pressed her into his body, his growing erection trapped against her thin form. Her hands eased up his sides, and she shifted against his chest, the gentle rub of her pierced nipples against his pecs only making her sink further into sweet arousal.

From the first moment on Friday evening when she'd set eyes on him, she'd sensed Ruben would make her feel like this. He'd made her feel safe, but now he'd ignited reckless desire in her.

When he dragged his mouth from hers with a groan, she blinked and clasped for his chest to keep her balance.

He stared down at her, his face troubled for a short moment before he managed to wipe all expression from it.

"I'm yours, whenever you want me," she whispered.

Ruben covered her hands with his and gently tugged her loose and stepped away from her. He said nothing, seeming intent on suppressing every emotion as he pursed his lips together.

"I'll be good, very good," she whispered. "For you and you alone."

There it was. The open invitation to use her as he pleased. At the end of the day, she was just a common whore.

"No," Ruben said hoarsely as he turned away from her. "There's no need for a thank-you fuck in any of this."

His rejection stung and tears pushed up afresh. That wasn't what she had in mind. For the first time in years, she wanted to make love to someone. To him and with him. Only *him*. Her words had come out all wrong. And Ruben wasn't the type to take what he wanted and use women.

Marlène strode to his desk and fumbled for her apartment key, glad she was unable to look at him as he stood with his back to her. This was a walk of shame of a different shade altogether. En route to his front door, she scooped up her laptop bag, mostly because it was right there as she passed it. She slipped away to her apartment without another word but closed his door much too hard for her liking.

15

RUBEN

"Fuck."

Marlène slammed his apartment door, and everything shifted off balance. She'd turned him on from zero to one hundred within a minute of pressing her body against his. It was hardly a surprise, as he'd become more aware of her as minutes had ticked into hours, and then into days. He'd forced himself to keep his distance, but now—

There was no way in hell this was going to end well.

He took a long moment to will his erection into submission and dragged his hands through his hair. Her kiss had been a drug. He wanted more. His hands wanted to roam over every inch of her skin, his lips wanted to follow in their tracks. He wanted to melt into her with every part of his body and be consumed by her. He wanted to make her feel the way she made him feel—*alive*. After nine months on this godforsaken job, it was all he wanted: to feel alive again and have his life back.

She most probably wanted the same—to get off drugs so that she could feel alive again and have her life back.

This wasn't good, but he'd done the right thing, hadn't he?

He'd clung to the good side by saying in a harsh voice that he didn't need a *thank-you fuck*. Did he use those ugly words? To *her* of all people?

It had slipped out unchecked, before he'd gotten his head around the situation. It was a knee-jerk reaction. He'd buried those memories, but they'd forcefully resurfaced at her words. Time and again after they'd extracted human trafficking victims from their situation, the offer of sex as a simple *thank you* was an ill-disguised plea for drugs. Sometimes it was an honest offer and an honest thank you, which disturbed him even more. This was the only thing these women had to give. It was the only thing they knew.

It was fucked up. You save someone, the next month they're back where you dug them out with a pimp. Not because they wanted to be there, but because the system kept failing these women. They never got the leg up that they really needed. How else did you stay alive? The world had an unlimited supply of men who'd use, abuse, and sell women to other men who couldn't get enough. Supply and demand, a simple equation he'd tried to rupture for years.

He was a good guy, wasn't he? He wasn't the guy who lusted after something he couldn't have. He didn't force himself onto women and he sure as fuck didn't sleep with someone who was possibly under investigation, by him of all people.

The uncertainty was half his problem. He could be going through this mental flogging for nothing, and things could have gone places. Naturally. Between two people who'd started to feel more for each other.

There were two ways to find out. See her naked back or ask her directly about her past. The latter opened the way for a conversation he wasn't ready to have. Getting off the plane from Paris on Friday he would still have had it in him, but now, after spending all this time with her, his thoughts were jammed, his body was strung tight with need. He'd developed feelings for her. More than protectiveness. More than admiration for her spirit and courage. Something, currently undefined, that weakened his resolve.

As for that *need*, he'd just rejected her offer to get naked which she'd handed to him on a silver platter. *I'll be good, very good. For you and you alone.*

Her last words sent him into a tailspin. She'd done this before? Nothing about her situation now indicated that she'd prostituted herself out at some point in time. Maybe she'd been one of those girlfriends rich men leased on the side. She was beautiful and would fit the bill. But she had an ex and another *permanent* in her life she didn't want to talk to right now. Plus, she had a daytime job at a renowned magazine. And money. By the look of the heirloom furniture in her apartment, it was old money.

He couldn't be sure.

Bottom line: he didn't know her at all. Despite spending all this time with her, living with her, Marlène Desrosiers was still an enigma. So much for his investigative skills. Spending time in the shitshow that was the dark internet swamp had all but killed his ability to be in tune with humans. He should get out more.

Ruben glanced around his apartment. He'd upset her so much that she'd forgotten her belongings. Everywhere there were signs of her. The scent of her luxury soap still drifted from the bathroom. A pair of discarded sleeping socks was balled up next to the sofa. Two coffee cups where there would usually only be one. Every bit of this filled his empty life with what he missed the most in Paris: normality.

If nothing else, he needed to damage-control this situation. He gathered a few things she might need, taking care to leave a few behind. She had slammed the front door on him, but he would keep the back door open.

Arms full, he knocked on her door. It was quiet for a long

minute and his heart started to pound. Had she already done something stupid? But then footsteps sounded behind the door and paused. She was hopefully looking through the peephole.

Marlène opened her door an inch, then wider once she saw her things gathered to his chest.

"Thank you." She reached out to take her clothes from him.

"Marlène—" Her eyes were red from crying and regret twisted his gut. "It came out wrong."

"Where are my pills?" she asked, as if she didn't hear his comment.

"They're gone."

"What?" Her eyes widened as her breathing hitched. "You fucking asshole."

The look on her face told him everything—he'd managed to find all her secret stashes.

"Listen, what happened earlier—I didn't mean it."

"Which part? The *thank-you fuck* part or the kissing part?"

The words sounded even uglier coming from her mouth, with its cupid's bow upper lip and kiss-swollen bottom lip that he wanted to tug and suck between his own.

He couldn't lie to her, not again. "The thank-you part." He swallowed and took a step closer. She took a step backwards, deeper into her apartment, eyes wide. He mirrored her movement, wanting to reach out to her and touch her. "It's just that we don't know each other—"

"You've spent days with me. You've seen me at my utmost worst. You know I'm terrible at video games—"

"And that you cook a mean steak. All that doesn't matter. I want to get to know you at your best." Beautiful and gorgeous and full of laughter. How she'd been before drugs got to her and helped her slip away into a hole, a hole he was trying his best to drag her out of. "Go on a date with me. Please."

Her eyebrows shot up as her eyes widened. "A date?"

"Yes, the thing people do when they want to get to know

each other." She kept staring at him as if she couldn't understand where he was coming from. "Let me take you out for dinner. Please."

"I can't and I don't want to go anywhere looking like this."

He reached for her cheek, where wisps of blonde hair had loosened from the knot on her head. With a gentle sweep, the softest caress he could manage, he gathered the strands behind her ear. "You're beautiful as you are. You only need a few more days before you feel yourself again. How about Friday night? Would that be enough time?"

Marlène closed her eyes as his hand lingered, his thumb on her cheek, his fingers slipping into her hair. She didn't pull away and by the way her breathing faltered he understood where she went in her head—where he wanted to go too. Hands back on her body. Kissing and not stopping until he was slowly making love to her.

When she looked up at him again, she merely nodded before pulling away. "Okay, a date. To celebrate. On Friday night. What time?"

"Seven?"

She nodded and hugged her bundle of clothes tighter.

"You'll be fine until then? On your own?" He dreaded that she'd go out on the street to find a hit. Or even worse, have a dealer on speed dial for situations like these.

"I don't know," she whispered. "I'll try. I need to try."

She was so brave in this moment. Admitting to her weakness, her dependence, her fear. He wished he could lock her up in his place and keep her safe from herself, but at some point, she needed to do this on her own. The worse side of the physical withdrawal was over, but for her the mental struggle had just upped a level.

"I'm going to make an appointment for the thing I need to do. This afternoon I'm meeting up with my Little Brother. For the rest, I'm home."

"Little brother? You didn't mention you have another brother?"

"A foster kid I mentor. I haven't seen him since March and, well, you know—"

"No, I don't know."

"See? Date night."

This made her smile and seeing the light break through made relief pulse through him.

"You're welcome to hang out at my place whenever you need to." Maybe he'd cut her a key in case she needed a change of scenery without leaving home.

Yep, he was fucked. He was much further gone than he realized. "I'll check in on you when I'm back, okay?"

She groaned a sigh. "I should stop calling you an asshole, shouldn't I?"

There it was—her admission that he was right disguised as an apology.

"It would make for a nice change."

"Oh, go away already! But only so that you can come back."

He wanted to lean in and give her a forehead kiss and a long, deep, thorough hug, because she sure as hell needed it. Instead, he raised his hands in defeat, took hold of the door handle, and pulled it closed behind him.

Ten minutes later, when he left his apartment, he had a spring in his step for no reason whatsoever.

16

RUBEN

The tall teenager that stood inside the school basketball grounds had grown at least a foot since he'd last seen him.

"Caleb!" Ruben dragged his fingers over the fence to catch his attention.

The boy turned and his eyes lit up as he spotted Ruben.

"You're back?" Caleb asked as he jogged up to him.

"Yep, for now. Let's go grab a burger. I got the go-ahead, and the principal has okayed it."

"I missed you, man," Caleb said as they walked along toward the main building.

"Yeah, I missed you too."

"Let me grab my backpack and we can go." Caleb disappeared into the school building and reappeared minutes later at the entrance.

"How long's your break?" Ruben hadn't done this for a while and going for a quick lunch with his Little Brother seemed like a foreign concept until he'd decided to reach out on Monday.

"Forty minutes."

"Perfect." He pulled the boy in for a shoulder hug but then he let him go, too conscious of perceptions.

"How was Paris?" Caleb asked as they walked into their go-to burger joint mere steps from the school.

"French." Ruben scooted into a booth the waiter had pointed them to and picked up the Perspex menu on the table. Caleb knew he was a cop and still worked in investigations of sorts but knew better than to ask more questions. "Tell me about you? How's school, life in general?"

"Yeah, it's all good, man."

"Yeah?" This was how it was going to go. A lot of *yeah*-ing. He remembered too vividly being this age. Awkward, out of place, with hormones shaking you like maracas and no beat to be found.

Caleb fisted his hands together, shy, and not looking him in the eye. Damn. He should have been here and helping this kid out for the past nine months. Now it almost felt like they were strangers. They talked about the menu for a minute, then ended up ordering the same as always.

"You got the shoes I sent over for your birthday?"

"Yeah, they were great."

"Bet they didn't last long by the look of you."

Caleb shrugged. "The kicks were good for 'bout two months. The other kid in the house wears them now."

At least there was that. Nothing went to waste here. The waiter arrived with their sodas and burgers, and they ate quietly. Between bites he tried to lure Caleb into conversation.

"So, schoolwork?"

Caleb wobbled his hand mid-air. "It's going. The math teacher makes me sweat, but whatever."

"It's because you're good at that stuff."

"Yeah."

"You need extra help with any of it?" Ruben had been good at math too but didn't get the support he needed as a kid. With time on his hands, this was one area where he could make a difference. Once back in Paris, he would pay for extra math lessons for Caleb if that was what it would take.

"The school's good. Teachers are okay. So, yeah."

Great. Just great. "Pull your weight, okay?" He would hate for Caleb to waste his obvious talents because of circumstances that were less than favorable. This side of the city, nothing came easy, nothing was gifted. Everything was blood, sweat, and tears. "You're going to show me your report card for the first term when you get it?"

"Sure, if you're around."

Ruben bit down on a groan. Who knew where he'd be in a month's time? He might be in Paris back at work, he might be here, wondering what the hell just happened. If he wasn't present, it would be best to source Caleb a new Big Brother. This wasn't fair on the kid.

"I might be going back to Paris, not sure for how long. At the moment, nothing's confirmed."

"Yeah, whatever, man."

"Real talk now, kid, you're staying away from the pot and all that crap?"

Caleb blew a deep breath out, sending a whiff of masticated burger his way. "Trying my best, sir. You know how it is."

Yeah. He knew how it was. There was no such thing as the straight and narrow here. Not with drugs available on every street corner. "What about girls?" The last thing anybody needed was for Caleb to knock up a fifteen-year-old schoolgirl for the fun of it.

"Nah, they scare the living crap out of me. I'm good with the wood. Na'mean?"

At this comment, Ruben looked down to hide his smile. He was surprised he got that much out of the kid. All clammed up and then frank as fuck. "How's your family, all going well there?" Ruben asked. He made the question sound casual, almost as a by-the-way, and not as the opening to a conversation that could lead down some dark paths.

As a foster kid, Ruben had counted himself lucky. He'd ended up with good people, but he'd be the first to acknowledge that those were few and far between. By the rounds Bryce had done before landing in the same home as him, there were some horror stories out there. As a mentor he had many objectives, but the biggest one for him, even more so now, was to make sure Caleb wasn't being abused, physically, emotionally, sexually.

People hurt kids in so many ways, it made him sick to even think about it. He put his half-eaten burger back on his plate and picked up a fry. He dunked it in ketchup but let the fry droop from his fingers. He couldn't do it. He couldn't find the words with which to subtly ask Caleb whether wrong—illegal—things were happening to him at his foster home. The kid had been with the same foster parents for two years now, so at least things were working out, or so it would seem.

Caleb sat across from him, eyes downcast, one last bite of his burger between his fingers. Then he shrugged. "Yeah. All's good."

"Really?" Ruben leaned in, dropping his fry, and pushing his plate away. "You know I'm here to listen, right?" Inwardly he cursed. A kid needed time to warm to a stranger, to have the relationship grow in trust so that they would speak truthfully. Being away for nine months had eroded the headway he'd made over the eighteen months that he'd known Caleb before Paris.

Now Caleb sat across from him, silent, jaw working, and the warning lights in him were flashing blue and red. "Look at me, Caleb," Ruben urged softly. "What's going on?"

"Nothing." Caleb shoved the last bite of his burger into his mouth and wiped his hand with the paper napkin.

Ruben leaned back, not taking his eyes off the boy who still avoided his gaze. Caleb had been abused by his dad, who was now in prison for armed robbery. His mom had skipped town, leaving the kid with neighbors, and had wound up dead two months later from an overdose in Florida. Next of kin: none.

Caleb was a master study in the making, and if things were happening at his foster home, how was this kid going to cope without help?

"I gotta go." Caleb picked up his soda and slurped at the last sip with the straw. "Class starts in ten. Thanks for the grub."

"You're welcome." Ruben stood as the boy scooted out of the booth. "Same time, same place next week?"

"Yeah, sure."

Ruben wanted to draw him in for a bear hug, but Caleb was already stomping off. His limbs were too long, his frame too skinny, and the burger he'd inhaled in ten minutes probably filled the hollows in his knees, having dropped straight through his stomach.

"Right." Ruben sank back into the booth. He was starting from scratch here. The whole time they'd been skidding around issues, not really talking. He needed to phone the nonprofit and make a plan here. As he pulled his phone from his jacket pocket, a new message beeped.

Your appointment with Dr. Graham Foster has been confirmed for Wednesday at 9 AM. The address for the consultation rooms followed.

How the hell? He'd planned to make his way to the Interpol offices that afternoon with the intention of figuring out where to start.

Fuck Marc Lindquist already. Ten times from here until Sunday. Somewhat under duress while still in Paris, they'd spoken about therapy, and he'd agreed to see someone once back in New York. Marc had said he'd *find a therapist without a waiting list with his connections*.

Great. Marc wanted results. Marc wanted him back on the

job. For a second, he felt some relief. He hadn't been permanently booted. Not catching a criminal was one thing, a case going cold was another. But the worst was watching from afar how a whole investigation collapsed, knowing criminals walked away free and he would be partly to blame.

Graham must have had a cancellation. No chance in hell you just strolled into his rooms a week after your boss sent an email to someone in the confidential mental health maze.

At least he'd be seeing Graham and not someone new. He had no clue how ethical that was, but he couldn't care less. With Graham, he could skip all the preliminary discussions.

Let the digging begin. Tomorrow. At nine. Sharp.

17

MARLÈNE

Marlène didn't do dates.

She met people in places and fucked them, alone, or with others. Whatever they wanted, whatever the mutual mood demanded. Whatever she learned about them along the way was coincidental.

She drank champagne in chic French bars and private swingers clubs. She held Damien's hand, and he held hers as they navigated the Parisian underworld of desire. At that point, she worked at an interior design magazine but had applied for a position at a fashion magazine. On the day she'd learned that she'd gotten the job, she'd gone out with Damien to celebrate.

Damien had been in the process of finding investors for his night club, and when they'd randomly met James that night, at a wine bar where the English crowd hung out, it was as if fate had guided them there by the hand. Damien was perfecting his English; James was working on his French. She was in the middle, translating. But it turned out you didn't need to be fluent in anything to fuck.

They made a curious threesome—James, Damien, and herself, those initial drinks and dinners they'd had together.

James had caught on quickly and he'd been cautiously curious. Damien, the good-hearted soul he wanted to be, had seen something more budding and had cut her free and allowed her to try the couple thing. She'd wanted it so bad too, something so mundane and normal, always out of reach. Now here was the boyfriend she could introduce to her parents, her sisters, the extended family! Marlène had finally stumbled upon *The One*.

She'd loved it, all of it, but she couldn't do it. Initially it went well until something inside her raised its head. The monster. From within the cave. She needed to entertain. She needed to be sure James was entertained and not looking for distractions elsewhere. It was an art she'd perfected, sex service similar to what you'd appreciate from your waiter at a three-star Michelin restaurant. Long ago she'd learned that the best way to keep a man entertained was to deliver what he needed before he even anticipated that he wanted it.

James's demons fed her own, and they could have gone on like that forever, if it weren't for Damien with his heart of gold.

She couldn't leave Damien behind—he needed her, and she understood why. He had a monster too, in a cave. One that was always hungry. Damien had started to use cocaine, he'd popped pills, he had the whole gambit of drugs going on at some point. She knew it was stupid, selfish, sacrificial, and that James would leave her for it, but drugs gave her something James couldn't: a mind-numbing sense of peace. Nights without terrifying dreams. They weren't nightmares, where things were surreal. These were real, terrifying dreams of things that would happen to her sisters if she didn't stop them from happening. That they were all grown up and out of the danger zone didn't help with any of her troubles.

Only drugs made the monster lie low.

Marlène pressed away from her apartment door. She'd all but collapsed against the door once Ruben had left. His request for a date freaked her out. He was the gentlemanly type, and she didn't know what to do with him. These were uncharted waters for her because she didn't meet him on her usual playing field. She'd stumbled and spilt soup over him. Not her usual MO.

Dressing for dinner wouldn't be a problem. He wouldn't recognize her from the disheveled train wreck that had invaded his apartment over the weekend.

But there was a much bigger problem on hand: Ruben wanted *to get to know* her, except nobody ever *got to know her*. She walked into her bedroom, ignoring the desperate disarray of her apartment. When she'd stumbled back here after their *thank-you fuck* conversation, she craved to descend into oblivion and searched like someone possessed for one pill. Except Ruben had tossed her drugs and if she wanted total oblivion, she needed more than opioids.

He was good for her. He really was. And she'd promised she would be good for him in return, even if it was only platonic support.

But Ruben wanted more, needed more, and so did she.

Marlène opened her closet and stared at the designer contents. Where would he take her? It would be somewhere special. She flipped through the row of dresses, her hand lingering on the soft velvets. It was fall after all. He would have to give her a hint of where they'd be going, otherwise she might overdress.

She had to admit that the idea of a date with Ruben made her heart race, butterflies getting busy in her stomach. She couldn't recall ever feeling this way. At the memory of his kiss, her legs caved in, and she dropped back onto her bed, staring blindly at the ceiling before closing her eyes. The way his hands had squeezed her butt, firmly, possessively, pushing her against him, had her all wet with longing. Her hands slid over her body, wanting to revive the traces of his touch.

No. Not this, not now. She would wait for him and not get off simply because her body was begging for it.

She needed to prepare for this date business. Women would fret over every detail of their attire and make-up, but that part she had under control. To navigate the conversation would be a different story. Over the past few days, they'd talked as you do when you invade someone else's space. She'd been out of it most of the time and it all seemed like empty chatter now.

If only she could phone one of her sisters to ask for advice, but it would be awkward coming from her. At thirty-three, you should have this nailed, *non*? Marlène groaned as she got off the bed to look for her phone. As she went through the apartment, she rearranged the mess. Her immediate bloodthirsty craving had subsided with the date distraction.

Now she couldn't find her phone. She'd left it in Ruben's apartment. With all her other things. *Merde.* Her laptop bag stood in the corner where she'd tossed it when she came from Ruben's apartment, so she reached for it instead.

Soon she had her laptop up and running and she settled on the sofa with a fresh cup of coffee. She typed *Questions to ask on a first date* into the search engine and a plethora of articles flooded the screen. She opened an article and smirked as she glanced over the questions. They were so superficial, dipping into a job interview style of questioning. *Politics*? Who talked about politics on a first date?

She scrolled lower and her gaze snagged on sex questions. Orientation: how do you define the word *sex*? Did people ask these things on *first dates*? This wasn't so different from what she was used to, but this situation was different. This was Ruben. He wouldn't need to ask; he would instinctively know. He already knew her in so many ways but this—he wouldn't ask these questions, would he?

Heat spread in slow pinpricks of dread as the questions dug

deeper: her first time, her tastes, things she wouldn't do in bed. She bit on her bottom lip to contain the grip of emotion crushing her throat. She would have to lie about all of it. She let the laptop slide off her thighs to the sofa and curled into a ball, hugging her legs tight, too drained to deal with the memories.

She tried to breathe through the emotions, suppressing them, wanting anything to soothe the anxiety, but nothing would help her now. Opening her eyes was worse since she was surrounded by the isolation that her life had become. Alone and pathetic.

In the deadly quiet, a knock on the door startled her. She wiped at her cheeks and stood, still shaky. Ruben was on the other side of the peephole, waiting. To let him see her like this *again*.

She opened the door, without any pretense. *Here, this is me, most of the time. When I'm clean. Alone and thinking too much.*

"Hey. I—" Ruben took in her face, concern in his eyes.

"God, I'm so sorry. You see me like this all the time." She turned and walked back into her apartment.

The door clicked closed and his footsteps came towards her. "I don't see you like this. Marlène." His hand was on her shoulder, with a squeeze that urged her to turn around. "It's okay. I know there's more to you than this, so much more. And that you're fighting for that part of you right now. You are a warrior, in a brutal, messy battle."

She couldn't meet his gaze as his words triggered a cloudburst of tears, sobs like thunder ripping through her. He was thinking of her addiction; she was thinking of everything that caused it. But he saw more in her than *this*. No wonder she was falling for him.

He pulled her closer and she buried her head into his chest, under his chin, where it felt so safe, her palms on his chest, her arms trapped against him in his secure embrace. He didn't let go until she'd done her worst to his shirt. "Have you eaten anything?" he asked softly.

She shook her head, all snotted up and disgusting.

"Maybe you should?" He wiped at her cheek with his thumb, then reached for her hand. "Come here. I'll make you something." He settled her on the sofa and reached for her laptop to catch it from falling to the floor.

The screen lit up to reveal her last search, the *150 Questions You Can Totally Ask on a First Date (and probably should)*. He sat down next to her, a smile toying on his lips as he placed the laptop on the coffee table, not closing the screen.

"A hundred and fifty questions will make for a very long date. And you'll need notes to keep track," he said, teasing in his voice. He hitched his eyebrows at her. "May I?"

She couldn't blush deeper or look worse than she already did. There was nothing there he shouldn't be seeing. "Go for it."

Ruben scrolled the article. "Politics? Passion killer 101."

Marlène chuckled.

"Job? Off limits. Family? Ugh, you don't want to hear my sad story. Religion? Jesus Christ, they really want you to break up before you can even get along." He glanced at her, and she met his gaze. "You're not nervous, are you?"

She shook her head then lifted her shoulders, not committing to a verbal answer.

"Are you doing a refresher course here then? Because you should know I haven't been on a date in more than five...six? Hmmm, yep, six years."

"Why not?" A gorgeous, sexy guy like Ruben was single and shouldn't be. He didn't strike her as a player, and he definitely wasn't into the things she was into in France. *It takes one to know one.*

"The job always interferes." He closed the laptop screen with a sigh. "So maybe, just maybe, I'm nervous too."

This made her laugh and he smiled at her, resting his head against the sofa.

"What if you ask me something I can't answer?" she whispered.

"What if you ask me something *I* can't answer?" he whispered back.

"We need a safe word." She watched as he settled his hand between them, fingers relaxed, veins a roadmap running over the back, all of them leading to his heart. His beautiful, big, strong, beating heart.

"Sounds like a plan." She slipped her hand beneath his, into the warm hollow formed by his palm.

Ruben closed his fingers gently over hers and the last of her anxiety lifted. "Later," she said. "We'll use the word 'later.'" Because she might not tell him things on this first date, but maybe she would tell him, later.

"Sounds good to me. Later it is then."

They sat for a moment in the quiet of mutual agreement and Marlène wondered at the calm that settled over her with him here. He hadn't pulled his hand away, and without noticing, they had nestled closer, shoulders touching, heads inches apart.

"How was your meeting with your Little Brother?"

"I don't know," Ruben said with a sigh. "I'm worried about him. You know that thing kids do when they don't trust you, don't know how to talk to you? Or if they even should? I thought he was glad to see me, but in the end it was awkward."

"I'm sorry. You'll see him again?"

"Next week. I should spend time over the weekend with him too, but we didn't talk about it."

"Maybe things will be better then. He'll open up."

"I hope so. Foster kids come with a lot of challenges. Lots of things went wrong in their lives and lots of things can still go wrong in their lives. I want to help him navigate through it, but when I'm not here, it isn't fair on him."

"Life is hardly fair. And that doesn't only apply to foster kids. It applies to all kids and any kid on this planet."

Ruben searched her face in the way that he did, a cartographer at work. "Very true." He let go of her hand to reach into his jeans' front pocket. He pulled out a key and pressed it into her palm. "For you, a key to my place. Use it now; use it later. Whenever you don't feel like being alone."

The metal was warm in her hand. "I don't think I'm ready to be alone."

"Just because you could be, doesn't mean you should be." He stood and held out his hand for her. "In any case, the food is in my fridge, and I promised to make you something to eat."

She placed her hand in his and got to her feet. They didn't let go as Ruben led her back to his apartment. She'd follow him anywhere, and for the first time, she'd chosen good over bad on a second-by-second, minute-by-minute basis in her life. She'd experienced what he meant.

Going off the rails had always been a split-second decision that, in retrospect, she sometimes hadn't seemed to have made for herself. Going in that direction was easier, habit, ingrained, and had been groomed into her ages ago.

She was swerving in the opposite direction, if only she could stay on course.

18

RUBEN

Ruben left Marlène in his apartment, still sleeping in his bed. He was tempted to kiss her goodbye, but each of them was encased in a paper-thin glass bubble which they were careful not to shatter by coming too close, physically.

That was saved for their date night. A rule, unwritten, unspoken, but holding steadfast. Another night on the sofa where he was constantly aware of her presence, mere yards from him behind a closed door. Sleeping was going to be tough, but he was used to it. At least until Friday night. Then he'd sleep soundly next to her.

He smiled at the memory of them navigating living together. How the hell any of this just happened, he still didn't understand, but he was grateful for it. He wasn't alone, he had someone to look after and be with, he had a goal in this godawful, month-long void Marc had bestowed upon him like a God: look after his neighbor and get her through the worst.

The last thing he'd wanted was to come back to New York and hole up in his apartment, alone, busy in his head, solving a puzzle for which he no longer had access to the pieces.

Marlène seemed clueless as to her improvement since the

weekend. As her withdrawal symptoms eased, she was eating better, her color had returned, and her sleep seemed to have improved. She must still feel wretched, but another week and she'd be though the toughest physical part of withdrawal. Maybe even earlier. Going forward, she would need more support mentally and he already dreaded not being there for her. He needed to sort everything out and he'd start by talking to Graham.

He rushed down the steps into the subway to make his way across town. Dr. Graham Foster's rooms were in a bigger practice where half of Manhattan probably tried to come to grips with life from a sofa.

The commute took half an hour and as he stepped into the reception of the practice, he did a double take. This was the last type of place he'd ever thought his best friend from the police academy would end up in, but looking back, it all made sense. Life was weird that way. He signed in with the receptionist and filled out the routine admin forms.

"Graham's already here?" he asked the receptionist as other people sat down in the waiting area. He was nervously anticipating seeing someone he could talk to in the confines of patient-doctor confidentiality.

"Dr. Foster clocks in at seven-thirty every morning, come rain, hail, or shine," the receptionist said. "I'll let him know you're here."

Ruben took a seat and quietly sighed in relief that nothing was department related. Minutes later, he heard the familiar off-beat sound of Graham's footfalls in the corridor, one step a split second out of time with the other on the hardwood floor.

Graham peered into the waiting room. "Ruben Scott?"

Ruben stood and met his gaze.

"This way, please," Graham said, and Ruben followed him, quiet, heart in his throat, beating wildly.

Graham held his office door open for him and as soon as it

closed behind them, they shook hands. They pressed each other close for a second, in quiet acknowledgement that they both had covered some miles since they'd seen each other last, but a lot of their past miles they'd traveled together.

Both chuckled as they pulled apart.

"How's the leg?" Ruben asked as he took off his coat.

"Brand new," Graham said, taking his coat and hooking it on the coat stand. "Got a new prosthesis two weeks ago. It's shiny. Wanna see?"

Ruben glanced down at Graham's polished Oxford shoes. Nothing gave away that his partner had lost half a leg in a drug bust-related shootout that nearly cost him his life. After rehab, Graham hadn't returned to mundane office work. He'd experienced the system for himself and had vowed to make a difference within the police force. His head and heart had been in mutual agreement, and he went back to college to become a psychologist. His thesis on post-traumatic stress disorder earned him a doctorate.

"I'll skip, thanks," Ruben said with a smile. "How're the kids? Melissa?"

"All good, growing up fast." Graham indicated the sofa and wingback chairs. "Sit, please."

Ruben padded over to the sofa and sank onto one side of it. Graham picked up a notepad from his desk and came to sit in the wingback nearest to him. He crossed his legs, and his trouser hitched up an inch to reveal a colorful, funky sock that covered a too-thin metal ankle.

"Is this a social call? You never followed up with me on the drinks we were supposed to have," Graham said once he'd settled.

Ruben met his gaze, trying to relax, but everything that had happened had filled him up and compounded inside. He was at bursting point.

"I ended up in Paris. Signed up with Interpol on Marc

Lindquist's team and well, nine months later I'm here." Talking to a shrink. So how did it pan out for him, really? "And no, this isn't exactly a social call."

"Okay, Ruben, I ethically—"

"Don't tell me you can't see me. Please." Ruben groaned. "I have to get some things off my chest. Today."

Graham searched his gaze and acquiesced with a sigh. "Okay. Marc Lindquist obviously doesn't know that we're close friends, because technically—"

"No, and I'm not going to tell him."

Graham put his notepad to the side with a sigh. "How's Marc doing?"

"Frustrated as fuck."

"Yeah?"

"He—" Ruben broke off. This was becoming tricky. "Are we consulting yet? Can I speak freely? Confidentially? As a patient?"

"Client. Yes, of course, since you walked into the practice, even more so since you walked into my rooms. You need to understand that I'm not keen on this situation professionally, but we can talk. As *friends*."

Ruben exhaled, unaware that he was holding his breath. As friends. He'd take it. He wasn't going to talk this easily to anybody else. "Right. Where do I start?" Graham gave him a moment, not interfering as he scrambled through his thoughts. "You know how I was working on the human trafficking ring we busted in Texas. We worked extensively with Mexico and some South American countries where victims were trafficked from. And within the States too."

"I read about it in the papers. I never saw your name linked to the case."

Nothing new there. He was the shadow man, working behind the scenes, hacking, infiltrating, gathering data, images, coordinates, anything digital to help crack a case. "We worked

The Neighbor

on the ring for over two years. I came in for the drug trafficking, ended up busting the human trafficking syndicate in the process."

Graham nodded. Ruben paused, his head flipping through images of the case, how they managed to finally pry it open and what it revealed, at the bottom of the barrel once they emptied all the other shit out.

"You know how these things work. Layer upon layer, each one harder to infiltrate. During the final days of the Texas bust, once we made arrests, we broke into the last layer."

Graham studied Ruben, waiting.

"You know what it is."

"I do?"

"Child pornography. Exploitation, abuse, photos, videos." All those images he couldn't wipe from his mind.

"Okay."

Ruben swallowed, his gut twisting. "That was fucking hard." Impossible honestly. He didn't have the stomach for it, and him, a seasoned detective who had dealt with *shit*. Bodies, limbs, heads, women tied to beds, bloated, half-eaten corpses rotting for days under a bright Texan sun. He'd seen it all, but this—

Graham merely nodded.

"Well, one thing led to another, and next thing Marc is in New York asking me to join his team in Paris. He's been working for some time with Interpol, on a ring on the dark web that seems to work out of Paris, but it could be anywhere in the world. The content comes from everywhere. And with digital technology, the field is constantly changing." Ruben shook his head, his frustration like a constant ringing in his ears. "We have experts in every field weighing in on our process. Hackers. Tech firms. We even have France's biggest cybersecurity firm sending us another pro to work with the team to help us break the ring. But the goalposts are up in the sky, never mind on the field. It used to be a one-eighty-degree game, now it's a freaking sphere. Do you understand what I'm saying? It's insane, the amount of content coming from all corners—" He swallowed again, feeling the odd pressure of tears squeezing his throat. "Nobody can keep up; the world is ablaze, and we're armed with a fucking watering can."

Graham said nothing, waiting.

"Every case we crack, every pedophile we manage to catch, is like shaving a slice off the tip of the iceberg. With a fucking potato peeler."

Graham leaned in to push the tissue box on the coffee table an inch in his direction.

Ruben felt for his cheek and wiped at the wetness. "Fuck. I'm sorry."

"It's okay, Ruben." Graham waited for him to finish wiping at his tears. "Seems like you're frustrated too."

"And angry. So fucking angry. It's eating me alive. At all hours. I can't switch off. I can't walk away. I've never had this before, where I'm being consumed, totally, by what I'm working on."

"That's not healthy. But then, none of it is."

"You know where I come from, you know I've got anger issues. You know I've been managing it for years, but this is more. I don't know what to do with it."

"Hmm." Graham shifted in his seat. "What exactly happened in Paris that Marc thought warranted you seeing a psychologist?"

For a long moment, Ruben considered what a waste of time this was. "I shouldn't be here. We're this close to a breakthrough and yet—" He fisted his hands with a groan because he was avoiding the question. He didn't know how to explain that his frustration and his anger at work had become more than their failing to have a breakthrough. "I broke a wall with a canteen chair. Until Marc contained me. It was late at night, and we were alone at the office."

Graham nodded but dropped his gaze.

"And now I know exactly what you're thinking."

"You do?"

"Yep, you're thinking at least it was only a chair and not a guy like that fucker we caught with his underaged 'girlfriend' during that drug bust in the Bronx."

Graham huffed and met his gaze again. "That was a long time ago."

"We were rookies."

"Yeah," Graham said with nod. "But you're wrong. That's not what I'm thinking. I was wondering if any specific thing or image triggered you?"

"A photo dump. Every now and then someone will dump a few photos, older ones. From the seventies, eighties, nineties. Pre-internet. They're not hard to spot. Faded, old, printed photographs. Some pedophile's collection that has been thumbed so many times, the gloss is matte. Sometimes they're more recent. Artistic. From the time where traditional film co-existed with digital." Ruben raked his hands through his hair. "Fucking artistic, do you hear me? As if child exploitation is an art." Graham shifted in his chair. Ruben groaned. "The fucking French. Art in everything."

Graham made a non-committal sound that was neither a hmm nor a ha.

"Yes, okay, no one's sure it's a French pedophile."

"Any photo specifically that affected you?" Graham asked.

"I don't know. Could have just been a long nine months without a breakthrough that got to me."

"Yeah. That could happen." Graham pushed his glasses up his nose and shifted in his seat. "How long are you here for?"

"Four weeks. That's if Marc takes me back on his team. He won't, not unless I sort my *issues* out."

"I see." Graham stroked a hand over his mouth. "This type of anger often comes with a trigger that's deeply wired to the source of negative energy. It could be anything, even something you're hiding from yourself. It could take some time to figure it out."

"You know my story." Ruben suppressed a sigh of frustration. "I'm starting to think that this is more than that."

The nod. Again. "Are you exercising? Eating well?"

"I jogged in Paris, did weights, some boxing."

"Still box with Bryce? He's in Boston, isn't he?"

"I haven't, nope. Not for a long time."

"Go see him and beat each other up. That usually helped."

Fuck. When people knew you too well. "When? How? Bryce is busy."

"Yeah, he won't be too busy for you. Take the train. Box. Come back in time for dinner."

"Jesus Christ."

"You need your brother, Ruben. He gets you. He cares for you. Everybody needs that."

Ruben bit down on his jaw, grinding his teeth against the swell in his throat. Graham was right. Bryce had been his anchor for so long, and there hadn't been enough time between his last case and this one to recalibrate, to make the mental shift he needed to leave a case behind. If he could go back and change anything, it would be to avoid the Texas human trafficking bust that dragged him to this last outpost of human depravity.

"As a friend, I'd prescribe you 'homework' for this week," Graham said. "A boxing match with Bryce and all the other days at least an hour of exercise."

"Right." How this was going to help he had no clue. The shit was in his head, not his body.

"Sex life?" Graham asked.

"What?" That was point blank.

"Are you seeing anybody? When last have you connected physically with someone?"

Ruben looked away, shaking his head with a groan. "You try having sex with those images in your head. I've lost interest." It was true in Paris, even earlier, since they'd cracked the ring in Texas, and he got into investigating child exploitation.

But it was no longer true. Not since Marlène Desrosiers stumbled over him in the corridor outside his apartment door, and something in him had stirred awake. A woman, a beautiful, spirited woman, filled with her own demons, awoke him as she scooped pho soup off his chest with such gentle care, her face flushed in consternation as she bit her lip. The notion made him want to weep.

"Yeah? That's not ideal."

"And the next thing you're going to tell me to get laid." His options were limited as it was, and he wasn't the type to go find a prostitute. He knew where those came from, what they'd been through. And now this. He was in the worst loop of human crime and exploitation and unless he got back into the dating scene, he wasn't going to get laid.

He was going on a date with Marlène. On Friday night. With every intention of getting intimate with her at some point. He'd been fantasizing about touching her soft skin, brushing her lips with his thumb, and following the path with his tongue, more, lower, to those breasts and the barbells he wanted to suck into his mouth. And his mind didn't stop there. He was so screwed.

"Well—"

Ruben leaned forward, resting his elbows on his thighs. "Tell me, Dr. Foster, how do you go about dating, never mind having sex, with a woman who you suspect is the girl in the photos you saw back in Paris? You're not sure. But you need to know because the notion is driving you fucking mad. Here's a possible voice to a photo. Many photos. They only speak of silent crimes. But now, here's an actual human being who went through that hell maybe two decades ago, and it could be her?"

19

RUBEN

Graham stared at him, a frown slowly creasing his forehead as if he was having a hard time understanding what Ruben had said. "What do you mean? I don't understand."

"I met someone. My neighbor. Totally by accident." He didn't want to go into Marlène's stumble, her withdrawal or drug use here, because it wasn't related to his specific ethical dilemma.

"Okay," Graham said, his tone encouraging.

"One of the older photo collections we've been working on these past months is of a girl, between the ages of ten and thirteen. Someone dumped several different photo sessions of the same girl. She has a distinctive pattern on her left shoulder blade. Three moles in a row, spaced out, with more scattered about, forming the natural start of a star constellation, but—"

"A constellation?" Graham had schooled his face back into an emotionless blank page and waited for him to continue.

"With a bit of help from a tattoo artist, yes. There're photos of someone drawing lines on her skin, a tattoo artist then tattooing extra moles in place, to mark her."

The Neighbor

Graham's eyebrows rose half an inch. "What? Tattoos on a child?"

"It's a common practice in human trafficking. Leaving your mark, ownership inked into skin."

Graham shook his head in disbelief. "I thought that was cartel and gang related."

Ruben rested his head for a moment against his hard thumb knuckles, pressing into his forehead to ease his distress. He sat straight and breathed in deeply. "Yeah," he sighed, "it's a gang-related practice. With this we don't know. It's the first time we've come across anything like it and some of the team have seen a lot of things."

"I can believe that. How big is the tattoo?" Graham asked.

"That's just it, the tattoos themselves are so small, almost insignificant. It isn't a Japanese *horimono* that covers the whole back and more. The tattooist made a few simple dots to replicate the look of a natural beauty spot on her skin. Unless you know it's there, you wouldn't notice it. The whole process would have taken mere minutes once they drew the constellation on her skin, but it covers a big part of her back."

"I still don't get it," Graham said, puzzled. "How many dots? A constellation? Of what? Orion's belt?"

"Andromeda. The Chained Maiden." Ruben pulled his phone from his jacket pocket. "You mind?"

"No, go ahead."

Ruben opened his internet browser and searched for an image of the Andromeda constellation. "This." He faced the screen to Graham. "On her back. No lines. Stars only, black against the sky white of her skin."

Silence crept into the room as Ruben watched Graham studying the image of the night sky, lines connecting stars, the penny dropping. "It's Greek mythology, isn't it?"

"Yep," Ruben said. "Our pedophiles like their Greek stories and gazing at the stars."

Eventually Graham looked up and breathed into his hands. "How old did you say?"

"Anywhere between ten and thirteen. Girls develop at different ages."

"Well, that's messed up. Caroline is eight. Only two years until she's ten."

Ruben nodded. Visualizing shit like this happening in your personal life always made things more real and terrifying.

"It's messed up, all right. It took us a few days to figure out what they were doing. With the curve of her back and her shoulder and the constellation extending to the skin under her arm, it wasn't clear from one image. We don't know why. She just sits there, in the images, naked, letting them do it." Ruben swallowed, his throat tightening again. "The passive ones are worse, in so many ways. It's as if they've given up, as if they've worked through all the emotions to end with acceptance."

Graham dragged a hand over his mouth and shifted his legs to put both feet on the floor. "And this is your neighbor?" he asked. "Why do you think she could be the girl in those photos?"

"I saw part of her back, with her moles. It's as if they've been branded on my brain. You can't unsee what you've seen, and they were there as she bent over to put something on her coffee table."

"And the tattoos? You've seen them? On her?"

"No. I'd need to see her complete naked back."

Graham shook his head in denial. "What are the chances?"

"I don't know. What are the odds genetically, for two women to have the same scattering of moles that could be the building blocks to the Andromeda constellation? None? One in a million? One in fifty million? I don't know. But she's French, and that narrows it down for me. Significantly."

"How do you know the girl is French?"

"Other clues the specialists put together by studying the photos in detail. It could be as simple as a clothing tag that gives it away. A book on a bedside table, or a can of Coke."

Graham drew in a deep breath. Ruben sensed this was something he'd never dealt with before. Funny how in the world there was always something new, something surprising, and yet he'd seen too much to think that this had been the first time something like this had happened to someone.

"And you are seeing her? You're dating? I assume you haven't had a chance to get naked with her?"

"No, we aren't dating. We're just neighbors." Ruben groaned. "You can understand I have several problems here." Never mind the one where he was going soft on Marlène with her fighter's spirit and teasing retorts, where other parts of him were going hard.

"I do."

"Here's a chance where I can put an adult face and an adult voice to a girl who was abused and exploited. She would know who took those images. We could finally nail the bastards down. Lock them away for life."

"You can't assume, Ruben. Sometimes the eye only sees what it wants to see, and not what's really there. And even if she is this girl, you can't ask her to talk about trauma like this in passing."

That was the other thing that ate him alive. How did he even start the conversation with Marlène?

"Have you ever had a client that went through something similar and spoke about it?"

"I've had cases. Too many. It isn't something people open up about easily. It takes time, lots of patience. Sometimes an adult can't remember it even happened, but the body holds a map of memories all on its own." Graham shook his head with a sigh. "There's stigma attached to it for various reasons. Shame for one, but it messes up people's lives in ways they don't even begin to understand."

"Right." Fucking fantastic. "What do I do? If I can't talk to her about it? If I can't ask her outright if it's her, or not?"

"Do you have a photo you can compare her to? Do facial recognition or something high tech?"

"Yes and no. It's in the database, which I currently have zero access to. I can't check if those photos have any other hints that it's her because those are images of a girl, and she is all…woman."

The silence between them stretched as Graham looked at him, unnerving him to such an extent that Ruben dropped his gaze.

"You're not falling for her, are you?" Graham asked.

"No."

More silence. *Liar liar liar* juggled in the air between them.

"Good," Graham said. "Because, technically, if she *is* the girl in the photos, then she's a victim. And you're the police force investigating her case. She might be an adult now and no longer underage, but I don't need to tell you this. Bottom line, whatever you do, keep your side clean and professional."

If Graham had spelled it out word for word, his meaning couldn't have been clearer. He wasn't to get Marlène Desrosiers naked, not under the pretense of his investigation, or attraction. He couldn't even engage with her in a one-night stand to satisfy their mutual budding desire.

"I only want to protect her."

"That's who you are, Ruben. Remember that."

He closed his eyes, willing away the images that flitted uninvited through his head, but he couldn't. This urge to protect the young and the vulnerable had always burned in him, but it was only since busting the Texas child exploitation ring—something he'd never been involved in until Texas—that this need in him had exploded like fire that had tasted oxygen. When Marc came with his job offer, he grabbed it as if his survival depended on putting these assholes behind bars.

"Ruben?"

When he opened his eyes again, he felt disoriented in the quiet of Graham's office.

"You need to talk to someone, professionally, and it can't be me." Graham lifted his hands, indicating it couldn't be helped. "We're friends."

"I'm not interested in talking to someone else. I'm not even sure what I'd be talking about to a shrink."

"You, of course. We didn't talk much about you, did we?"

"I wasn't avoiding talking about me. There's nothing to talk about when it comes to me." Ruben shrugged. "This is what I need, just to get things out in the open and throw ideas around, confidentially. The nature of my work limits the number of people I can talk to."

"Yeah, I get that." Graham stood. "I'm serious about Bryce and the boxing. Even if you only go for a beer afterward."

Ruben shrugged. "It isn't as if I have anything else to do."

"I'll see if I can source a psychologist in our practice that can see you."

"I'd rather just do this, if you don't mind," Ruben said, suppressing a groan of frustration. "Off the record."

"Yeah? Off the record?" Graham smirked. "It's not your ass that's going to get busted if things go wrong."

"They won't go wrong." Ruben held out his hand as he stood. "You have my number."

They shook hands and Graham led the way to the door, where he handed Ruben his coat. "I'll let you know who I can set you up with."

Ruben walked out and nodded to the receptionist in passing. The exhaustion of the past forty-five minutes settled over him like the coat he pulled on. Graham might want to set him up with someone else, but he'd fight that battle the next time they spoke. He was talking to Graham or to no one.

Back on the subway he stood and swayed through his thoughts.

He couldn't help Marlène and avoid her in the same breath.

He couldn't be there for her if she was locked up next door, alone and isolated, like him, for days on end.

He couldn't feel anything for her even if she was the last woman on the planet and he was already halfway there.

As he took the elevator to their floor, he knew he had to steer in the direction of good; only problem was, good and bad seemed to be the same thing, interwoven, one thread dependent on the other, and not to be untangled without ruining everything.

20

MARLÈNE

Marlène looked up from where she sat on the sofa as Ruben walked into his apartment. It was surreal waking up without him being home, breathing, moving, making the Ruben noises she'd come to know over the past few days.

Beyond the regular hum of traffic, the occasional honking, and the sirens of emergency vehicles that infiltrated even this high up in the apartment building, the quiet had been eerie. She didn't like being alone like this. Nerves frayed because she was sober, nothing to do, her mind busy, working its way into a frenzy of one infinite circular thought, like a dog chasing its tail. How quickly he'd become the habit that kept her sane.

She set down her phone beside her as their gazes met across the room "Hey."

"Hey."

Those dark circles under his eyes persisted and the lines bracketing his mouth cut deeper than usual today, but he lit up with a small smile when he saw her waiting for him.

"That wasn't fun, was it?" she said softly. He'd told her he'd be off to a shrink first thing in the morning.

"Nope, but necessary."

Marlène looked at her phone and picked it up again. Anything to avoid the truth of that statement.

Ruben flopped to the sofa next to her, inhaled deeply and huffed out a sigh. "Who knew it would make you so hungry?"

She hugged her legs to her chest and turned towards him to study his profile, his regal nose, steep forehead, and his dark hair that fell backwards in a soft wave. "I can make you breakfast?"

"You've eaten?"

"Only coffee."

"That isn't food."

"Depends on who you're asking."

This earned her a smile as he turned his head towards her. "And how much cream you've put in it."

She hid her smile by biting on her lip. "Only enough to make it count as breakfast."

He studied her intently for a few seconds, taking in every feature of her face one by one, his gaze lazily resting on her lips. "You're looking so much better."

"I—" She broke off. Where did she even start to thank him? He'd done everything for her—a total stranger. So much so that he might restore her faith in humanity. "I'm feeling better. I wouldn't have been able to do this, come this far, if it hasn't been for you."

"I'm glad I'm here."

"Thank you. For everything." She wanted to reach out and touch him but didn't dare.

"It's nothing." Ruben ran the back of his fingers down her cheek. As if he'd caught himself doing something he shouldn't, he balled his fist and pushed it against his thigh. "Feel like bacon and eggs? Toast? Jam? The whole nine yards?"

"Sure. I might even manage to keep it all down."

"Would make a nice change," he joked as he got up. "Come on, we need to talk."

He made his way to the kitchen, and she followed with her empty coffee mug in her hand.

Ruben wanted to talk. She dreaded that he was going to ask her to leave. Her heart pounded in her chest as her mind raced. A session with a shrink might lead to that. He needed his space. Here she was, invading his much-needed break from work, and he had his own demons to deal with. That had been clear from day one.

Marlène put the mug in the dishwasher and watched as Ruben took the eggs and bacon out of the fridge. She leaned with her butt against the counter next to the stove.

"I need to go to Boston." Ruben took four slices of bread and popped them in the toaster.

The statement was so out of left field she wasn't sure she'd heard right. "Boston?"

He glanced at her. "Yep, to see Bryce. Doctor's orders. Apparently, I need to get rid of my restless energy."

Ruben didn't only have restless energy during the day, but he was restless at night too. She was desperately trying to catch up on her missed sleep from the weekend's withdrawal and still felt exhausted. He seemed to function fine on four hours of sleep a day, if that much.

"How, in Boston?"

"Boxing at our old club. Bryce and I both boxed as teenagers. Sometimes we still do." He reached for a pan and started the toast at the same time.

"When?"

"Today. After breakfast."

Marlène widened her eyes. "Okay." A sliver of dread quivered through her. She was going to be alone. The thought sank in deeper, and a slow panic rose in her. Not a good thing. She reached out to dig her forefinger into the belt loop of his jeans, wanting to hook on to him and make him stay. "That sounds...awesome."

He glanced down to where she had anchored herself to him, then let his gaze travel slowly up the contours of her body. She blushed. This morning she'd had a shower and then pulled on her oldest, softest, wash-worn skinny jeans and one of his T-shirts she'd adopted as her own. He hadn't made a comment and she just kept wearing it because it was comfy. A warm hug that smelled of him. She hadn't bothered with a bra in days and now his eyes rested on her breasts and her nipples, which were hardly covered by his old T-shirt's thin fabric.

He reached over and slipped his hand underneath her T-shirt, warm fingertips skimming the skin on her waist, searching, until he found a belt loop of his own, and hooked a finger through it. Her whole body burst ablaze with the sensation of his touch on her bare skin, from chills spreading to her breasts, hardening her nipples, to her sex, where she pulsed with need. "I think getting out will be good for you. And for us. Help us keep things contained."

Marlène dropped her head to his shoulder, unable to resist this off-center hug they found themselves in, unable to look at him now, in awe of her reaction to this simple touch.

"You want me to come with you?" She had no clue how that was supposed to contain this *thing* between them. They needed distance, walls, doors, between them, not a trip to Boston.

"Yes."

She hesitated. "I'm not sure I'm ready to leave the apartment."

"Can you be ready in half an hour?" He tugged at her belt loop and their bodies collided gently. "You've showered. You just have to grab a few things. We'll be back tomorrow."

"Not in that way. I'm not ready mentally."

"Hmm, you've got to do it. The sooner the better."

He was right, and she hated that he was always right. Stupid shrink. Most probably planted all of this in his head in forty minutes flat. She glanced up at him, at his lips that were so close to her own, she only needed to go onto her toes and lean into him to kiss them. If only he knew what she'd been, he wouldn't be so hesitant to fuck her senseless. She chuckled, but it sounded like a constricted groan caught in her throat. "I'll go pack. Where will we be staying?" A hotel room, all to herself. No temptation in sight. No drugs, no Ruben. No nothing.

"At Bryce's. He has a really, *really* nice place." Ruben circled his thumb now, teasing her skin, torturing her with deliberate intent.

Non-non-non. "Bryce hates me."

"No, he doesn't. He doesn't know you. He dislikes your addiction. If he has an issue with you coming along, he can deliver a few out-of-line punches." Another soft trail of his thumb. She burned to get up on the counter and open her legs for him, peel off his shirt and kiss those scars. "Bryce must need to let off steam too, with what happened at his work and the fatality." He paused his hypnotizing touch. "So, you see, I'll need you around to patch me up afterward."

"Ugh. Men. So bloodthirsty."

The toast popped and she let go of his belt loop at the same time he extracted his hand. Ruben didn't know her either, but deep inside her, there was a budding need to let him in, one she didn't understand. She'd never felt like this with James or anybody else before. It was petrifying.

"Go get ready. We'll eat first and then we'll hit the road." He got busy cutting a square of butter and scraping it off into the pan.

She missed the warmth of his fingers, but Ruben had dismissed her.

Maybe, if she could get her head around it, she might let him into her world. What didn't kill you, made you stronger. Apparently.

21

RUBEN

Ruben still questioned his sanity as they hit the freeway to Boston. He was hoping Bryce would be the stabilizing force that came between him and Marlène, and yet, this whole situation was reckless.

They were adults and his own resolve to resist her was being stretched too thin. Marlène respected that he wanted to keep an arm's length between them for now, but she wasn't shy in making sure he knew what she wanted. This restless energy he had to address—thank you, Dr. Graham Foster—had evolved. To be honest, he needed to get laid. Hard. Fast. Slowly. Repeatedly.

More than a week away from his work and the images were no longer at the forefront of his mind. Even those of the girl in the black-and-white photos had faded into the background with Marlène ever present. She had helped him in her way, to such an extent that he'd forgotten there could be a link between her and the girl. Everything was becoming inconvenient.

He checked the time. They'd be at Bryce's apartment in about four hours. He'd sent a message to let Bryce know they were on their way, but his brother hadn't responded yet. Bryce wouldn't mind. Between them, they had an open-door policy and Bryce was currently single. No chance in hell he had a woman at his place mid-week. The man was way too much of a workaholic for that. Bryce liked his world compartmentalized. Wednesday was boxing night. It always had been.

"You good?" he asked. Marlène had curled up in the passenger seat and had brought a pillow for napping and a plastic bag for vomiting. Both rested on her lap.

"I'm fine." She stuffed the pillow against the window and leaned into it.

"Still tired?"

"It's exhausting."

"I know." His phone rang. An unknown number appeared on his car's dash screen, and he pressed answer, without thinking.

"Ruben? It's Graham. Is this a good time?"

Uh. No. "I'm in the car with someone, driving to Boston, but sure, go ahead."

"Okay. Listen, I have a few recommendations for other psychologists at our practice. I know you're press—"

"I don't want to talk to anybody else." Ruben glanced at Marlène, but she kept staring out of the window. "I don't have time to start from scratch and rehash the same history with someone new. Honestly. Graham. Help me out here. I only have a few weeks, a few sessions to keep Marc happy."

"Yeah." Graham sighed through the line. "I hear you, but professionally I can't do this and with your mental state and the work you're do—"

"I can't discuss that now," Ruben cut in again. "Just book me one more appointment and we can talk then? If you still feel you can't do this, fine. It's four weeks, Graham, not even. C'mon."

"Oh, for fuck's sake. Come tomorrow at six. It's after hours."

"Thanks." Ruben smirked. "You won't regret it."

"Yeah. Totally. Asshole. Until tomorrow." Graham rang off and Ruben pressed his back deeper into the seat, feeling somewhat triumphant.

He wasn't rehashing his life story again with a new shrink. Graham knew him and if he wanted to dig to the bottom of his anger issues, he couldn't waste weeks or months getting comfortable with someone new. And then allowing said shrink to rake around his head for some inexplicable explanation why a heroin junkie's orphaned child landed up in foster care with anger issues. Nope, he wasn't doing it.

"He seems sweet," Marlène said drily and shot him a glance.

"Sugar-coated from top to bottom."

Marlène chuckled and all he wanted was to reach across the console and take her hand in his, rest it on his thigh and hold on to her.

They sped along and at some point, she seemed to nod off. When his phone rang again, she stirred and he killed the call just as he realized it was Marc, phoning from France.

Shit.

A minute later it rang again and with a hushed *sorry* he answered.

"Ruben."

"Marc. So nice to hear your voice."

"Same here, dickhead. How are things back home?"

"I'm driving with someone in my car to Boston, so keep it family friendly, will you?"

Marc smirked. "Right. Only checking in to see how things are going. You've managed to see Graham Foster?"

"Yeah. I've spoken to him. Seeing him again tomorrow night." At least that wasn't a lie.

"Good. Good."

A strained silence followed. Ruben had so many questions

—how things were going at work, had they made progress, had the team made a connection with the team in Madagascar where lately, 'seats' to live streaming were being auctioned off over the dark web. A hundred dollars could feed a family for weeks in that place and you only needed to have five people watching the live stream from overseas to make 'a killing.'

Had Marc had a successful meeting with the French cybersecurity firm that had offered to place another professional with them to help them break the ring? Ruben was supposed to attend that meeting. Had anybody completed background checks on all these people like he would have?

But foremost in his mind was Marlène. He suspected she was feigning sleep next to him, listening in. She would know who Marc was, a colleague at a minimum, or his boss and team leader. He burned to ask Marc to grant him access to their system and database again from there, so that he could have another look at those artistic images, black and white, of the girl being tattooed. Her face was only ever in profile. It messed with his head.

"I'll keep you posted," Ruben said. "I'm planning to be back in Paris at the end of this month."

"Yep. We're missing you like a sore tooth so make sure you do what you need to do to make it happen."

"Right." Ruben smiled but didn't fail to read between the lines. Marc was serious about him seeing someone. "I'll catch you soon."

They rang off and Marlène shifted in her seat and opened her eyes. "Don't you just work with a bunch of charming *fellows*."

He laughed at her feigned British accent. Her English pronunciation leaned in that direction more often than an American accent. "Marc's my team lead. He's a background superhero. Fighting villains in the underworld."

Too late he realized he might have given away too much,

but Marlène shrugged. "All boys want to be Superman at some point."

"Pretty much."

A phone rang again, this time from her purse at her feet. Marlène reached down and retrieved it with a sigh. "Does everybody have to phone right now?" She glanced at the screen as the phone rang and rang.

Unlike him, she didn't answer, but dropped the still-ringing phone into her purse and placed it back on the floor. Eventually the person gave up or the phone went to voicemail.

"Scam?"

"Damien. He should leave me alone, but he doesn't seem to get the message."

"Send him one?"

"No. I don't want to open any avenue of conversation with him. He likes hearing my voice. He'll message me as a last resort."

"Still sounds like you need to block him." *And if he was your supplier, you should*, he wanted to add.

"Soon. I will." She sighed. "Soon."

What the hell was she waiting for? The guy was clearly black mold in her life. Best ripped out. But this was part of her journey, obviously, and there was no slide down, fast and easy, to the end of this ride. Nope, she'd have to take every arduous step by herself and make these decisions on her own. The only thing he could do was to hold her hand, help her along the way and allow her to lean on him.

So, he did. He reached over for her hand and wrapped his fingers around hers. She didn't pull away as he rested her hand with his on his thigh. This was normal, so beautiful and just normal, he couldn't bear thinking of it shattering to pieces.

22

MARLÈNE

Bryce didn't know she was coming along with Ruben. That much was clear as he opened the door to his rooftop apartment in an old Boston harbor-side suburb. His eyes widened just enough before he schooled his face into indifference. He stood away from the door so they could walk in. "Welcome."

Ruben mock-punched his brother in the gut in greeting and Bryce retaliated with a chip to the back of the head as Ruben walked inside, as if his brother was being a naughty little shit.

"Save it for the ring, boys," Marlène said. She had to stand her ground now, or Bryce would think she was a pushover.

The men laughed.

"You're coming along to watch," Bryce said as he took her bag from her.

He was trying to punish her for being here already. "*Non-non-non.*"

"*Oui-oui-oui.*" Ruben took her hand and led her past the open plan living area with its modern brown suede set to the glass doors that opened onto the terrace. "Check out this view."

It was late afternoon and the sun had set. The view over the harbor was breathtaking with a pale orange glow that thinned into the night sky. Wind cut cold to her bones, and she shivered.

"Yep, be glad you're not here in December. In November, the wind is only warming up."

"That's anything but warm!" She tugged Ruben back towards the door and into the apartment, where her eyes met Bryce's. His burning gaze dropped to their hands, showing disapproval with a single killer glare.

Marlène glanced around the apartment if only to avoid Bryce's eyes. On the glass coffee table, architecture magazines and a closed laptop held flat a roll of architectural plans. A gas fireplace ran along the wall and a beautiful piece of modern art hung above it.

"Best get going if you want to be at the club by six," Bryce said. "You can settle downstairs. If I'd known—"

"Don't worry about us, we're cool," Ruben cut in. "I'm going to change." He let go of her hand and picked up their bags where Bryce had left them at the stairs that led to a lower floor.

She didn't want to wait alone with Bryce, who was dressed in sweatpants and a T-shirt, but she could hardly run after Ruben like a puppy and show her hand even more.

"Make yourself at home," Bryce said as Ruben disappeared down the stairs. "Can I make you a coffee to take along?"

"I'm good, thanks. We had coffee on the way here."

Bryce took a step in her direction, and she suppressed the urge to take a step back. He was tall and muscular, intimidating as he glared at her, taking her in from top to bottom.

"What *is* your problem?" she whispered.

"I don't have a problem. As long as you don't mess with my brother."

"I'm not messing with him. What's it to you in any case?"

"He's the only family I have. And I won't let a freaking addict turn his head."

She swallowed at the low growling anger in his quiet whisper. "I'm done with drugs. And I'm not turning his head."

"Whatever. You don't see how he looks at you."

But she did. Ruben's gaze had been all too consuming, from day one. She shook her head, no snarky retort ready to level Bryce to the ground.

"I'm just making sure we're on the same page. If I get a whiff of drugs around Ruben, I will haul your ass out of his place, pluck you away whether you're on top or underneath, and make sure he ends it with you."

"*God.*" She breathed. "What the? This—" Her voice broke. *Merde.* Why must she still be so fragile? Why must he be such an asshole? "He works for the police. Drugs and human trafficking. Don't go on as if he's never been surrounded by bags of white powder."

Bryce took a step closer and between them there was less than a yard of breathing space. "And that's what you think? This is what he told you?"

She nodded. Everything Ruben did for her over the weekend had made it clear that he was an expert on drugs. As for the human trafficking part...she didn't want to go there in her head.

"Is that *all* he told you?"

"Why else would you take such a dislike to me?"

His gaze softened and he cursed under his breath. "He hasn't told you, has he?"

"What?"

"Ruben was...ah *fuck*—" Bryce dragged his hands through his hair and huffed a sigh as he looked away. "I'm not telling you."

"What?" she hissed. "You can't throw words like that at me and then clam up with the excuse that you're not telling me. You've made it pretty clear that Ruben's business is yours, whether it really is or isn't."

He nodded. "True that. How long have you two been dating?"

"We're not dating."

Bryce shook his head, but this riled her up even more. If Bryce wanted to treat her like shit, she deserved to know why. She was trying to turn her life around and this wasn't helping. She'd had enough of men fucking her over, fucking her around and in general, just fucking with her.

"We only met last weekend for the first time. So?" She raised her eyebrows in question.

"It isn't my place."

"No, it isn't your place," she echoed back and stepped away from him, wanting to leave his apartment. Be anywhere but here.

"He was born addicted," Bryce said on an exhale. "His mom was a heroin junkie who couldn't kick the habit for her own baby."

Marlène recoiled at the words as if they were a sucker punch straight to her heart.

"She got pregnant by some random trucker who drove through town once." Bryce didn't break eye contact with her. "I thought you'd known each other for a long time with the way things were when I was there on Saturday."

Her breathing stalled as every reason for Bryce's concern finally made sense. Ruben's expertise was seeded at conception. Tears burned behind her eyes, and she had to look away.

"He spent the first five weeks of his life in withdrawal in the hospital." Bryce sighed. "Yeah, that's how fucked up it is. So… You understand now why I'm like a momma bear? He's my little brother."

"Yes." She fingered her tears away and swallowed hard. This wasn't the moment to have a meltdown. She would digest this later.

"I sometimes think he chose the drug and human trafficking unit to surround himself with evidence why trying the shit would be a very bad idea."

She bit her lip to curb her emotions. "Okay."

A beat of silence stretched for a second too long. Marlène looked up as Bryce's gaze flickered to the side.

"Nice." Ruben stood at the top of the stairs, mere yards from where she and Bryce had had their exchange. His face was drawn, a muscle ticking in his jaw. He'd heard most of it, if not everything. He'd scaled the stairs so softly, but maybe they'd gotten much louder towards the end. "Now that we've got *that* out of the way, are you both ready to go?"

She was shocked into silence. Bryce had the grace to look flustered.

"Your acoustics rock, Bryce." Ruben stepped closer to take her hand as he searched her face. "You good to go?"

"Yes." Inside, she was dying for him. Ruben looked at her with such unfailing tenderness that all she wanted to do was to wipe his story away and start with a perfect, pretty one instead.

"I'm in for a beating," Bryce quipped as he turned and led the way to the front door.

"We'll see. Probably." Ruben's tone held no mirth in the comment.

Marlène couldn't wait for Ruben to beat Bryce up. That was an overshare of note and not authorized. As they got into the elevator, she let go of Ruben's hand and hugged herself tight, wanting to squeeze the knowledge out of her system.

At least she could scratch one question she should ask on a first date off her list. No need to poke around to find out who Ruben's parents were and how he came into the world.

23

RUBEN

Ruben could count on his two hands the number of people who knew his birth history. Bryce wasn't one to overstep boundaries, but this time—

The drive to the club was tense with Marlène quiet in the back seat and Bryce grim next to him. It had taken only two minutes to grab his kit and by that time, Bryce and Marlène's interchange had echoed down the stairs, allowing him to hear every single word.

His fists itched to connect with Bryce's jaw, but the anger in him wasn't fueled by what Bryce had told Marlène. It was more like...she didn't need to deal with his shit too. Not now. Maybe never.

"Let's see what kind of shape you're in, little brother," Bryce said as they banged the car doors closed.

"All I know is you're going to look like hell once we're done," Ruben said as he rounded the car to catch up with Marlène. He wanted to guide her in the dim streetlight to the club's dodgy one-door entrance, but she'd shoved her hands into her coat pockets and walked abreast with them all in silence.

Cars and motorbikes filled the parking lot outside the club

and as Bryce opened the door, the heat and sweat of heavy exercise sliced into the November chill.

His heart rate revved as he followed Bryce into the club, greeting people as they made their way to the back where Bryce had a ring and a session booked with his private coach.

"We'll be about an hour, I think." Ruben pulled up a chair for Marlène. "You can sit here and watch me sweat."

"Thank you. Please draw blood."

Ruben shot her a wicked grin. "I'm tempted."

Marlène smiled back at him and sat down, her hands still hidden in her coat pockets.

Bryce waited next to the ring, rolling his shoulders in a slow warm-up. Ruben joined his brother and soon they were done with the stretches and getting into the squats and jumping lunges. By the time they'd done burpees and stomach crunches, he was sweating, and his wrath had somewhat diluted.

Ruben shot a glance at Marlène. She'd pulled off her coat and was keeping an eye on them, not bored at all.

They geared up with mouth guards and protective headgear, then strapped on their boxing gloves. Soon they were in the ring, shadow boxing. The coach then took each of them one-on-one for instruction, and as Ruben caught his breath, he studied Bryce. His brother was in excellent shape, easy and light in his footing, shadow boxing as if this were a real fight. When it was his turn, his body yelled that he'd let himself go over the months he'd spent in Paris. He was still in good shape, but he used to be able to go for hours, not huffing like this after a mere half hour.

"You boys going to do some sparring?" the coach asked.

"That's what he came for," Bryce said, shifting his weight from one leg to the other, never standing still. "All the way from New York."

"And someone asked for it," Ruben threw in.

"Right. Seven, nine, or twelve rounds?"

"Seven," Bryce said. "It's all we have time for and in any case, Ruben isn't in shape for more."

"More like you're shitting in your pants, brother." Ruben grinned. "I have some pent-up energy that'll make up for it."

With a nod, they chose corners. The coach, now referee, looked on as they greeted each other on the battleground by tapping their gloves.

"Easy on the face," Bryce said. "I have a funeral tomorrow morning."

"Same here, I have a date on Friday night."

"Need to look pretty, huh?" Bryce was skipping away from him, getting into his corner. "With whom?"

Ruben nodded in the direction of Marlène. "My neighbor."

"Ah, for fuck's sake. She told me you're not dating," Bryce muttered.

"Not yet."

"I put my foot in it good and proper, didn't I?"

"Yeah, I'd say so."

With both in their corners, the coach indicated that the timer was on and they could get busy. They circled each other, testing the waters, Ruben careful to avoid that first hit. His brother's eyes looked sharp, if a bit apologetic. What had been said couldn't be unsaid. Maybe Bryce had taken a load off his back.

The first punch came hard and fast, and he barely had time to block it, but with the opening punch out of the way, Ruben gave it all he had.

He had plenty, but Bryce wasn't holding back and by the end of the third round, several circles of pain pulsed in his abdomen and ribcage.

The coach came to his corner. "He's pissed off because you're not going at him hard enough. Bryce can take it, so give it to him. Let go."

The Neighbor

Ruben dropped his head, still waiting for his breath to catch up with his heart rate. A soft touch on his leg made him look out of the ring to where Marlène stood by his corner.

"I can't watch this. Every punch... I can't watch him hurt you like this."

He wanted to chuckle but took in her tense stance, her frown and concern in her eyes. "I'm good, it isn't bad. Really. We've done this a thousand times." Ruben glanced to where Bryce stood, ready for the next round. "Max sixteen minutes to go. Do you want to go wait outside, in the car?" It would be cold, but women getting lost between the rings, offering an unwelcome distraction to the testosterone-dense gym, wasn't done.

"No, I—"

"Time!"

"Look the other way."

Ruben got up with new determination. He would fight for her, if not for himself. In him, an itch of anger sprouted. Did his brother not understand that Marlène needed support and not judgment? Regardless of his birth, Marlène was going through withdrawal, not him. He knew Bryce, sometimes too well. His brother's standards were sky high, unattainable for most, never mind a woman who might have been messed with in the most horrific ways possible.

With his first hit, the energy surged through him, building and bursting out in rapid succession. One minute in, Bryce clinched him close. "Hell yeah, Ruben, now you're getting it out. Go for it. Harder," he hissed as they circled, chests heaving, sweat sticky on their skins, shirts drenched.

"You want more?" Ruben huffed back. "Good."

There still wasn't a clear winner, but their fifth round was done. Ruben's chest heaved with exertion as he looked for Marlène outside of the ring. Her chair was empty. She stood back against the wall in the shadows, her arms clutched tight around her waist.

He crossed the ring to where Bryce was wiping off the sweat with a towel. "We're leaving. Marlène isn't well."

"We've got two rounds left?"

"Those aren't happening."

Bryce glanced around until he spotted Marlène's hiding place. "No showering either?"

"Nope, we'll do that at home."

"Right."

Ruben squeezed through the ropes, jumped down to the ground, and bit down on the Velcro strap of his glove to peel off one after the other. He tossed them in the direction of his gym bag as he strode over to Marlène. "Grab your coat, we're going home."

She glanced up at him, eyes rimmed red. Shit. She'd been crying and wiped at her face with shaky fingers.

"Is this trembling withdrawal or something else?" He searched her face, cursing inwardly that he hadn't paid closer attention to her.

"It's everything. Your story. And something else. Something I hadn't thought about in a long time and that all this—" She broke off and gestured to the ring, her bottom lip quivering. "Just memories that drugs helped to numb, if you know what I mean."

"Okay."

She swallowed, her bottom lip quivering. Ruben took a step closer, his eyes searching hers. When he gently ran a thumb along her lip, wanting to dilute her distress, she thankfully didn't pull away. "If I'd known this place could trigger you, I wouldn't have brought you along."

She leaned into his touch and gave a shaky sigh. "If *I'd* known, I wouldn't have come along."

He cursed softly. She'd come so far these past few days, and to dunk her into a trigger zone was unforgivable of him. He was sweaty but all he wanted was to pull her closer. Instead, he squeezed her shoulder. "Sorry."

"I'll be okay. I just don't want Bryce to see me like this."

He dropped his hand. "Screw Bryce. He isn't as holy as he seems." He reached for her coat, which was draped over her chair. "Here." He held it open for her to slip on, wanting to give her time to compose herself. "Wait here and let me get my things sorted. Are five minutes enough?"

"Yes." She hugged her body tightly, protective. "Thank you."

He went back to gather his things and then struck up a conversation with the coach on a few pointers to buy her some time. When she came closer, eyes downcast, he took her hand in his. Bryce said nothing and they made their way back to the car and drove home in silence.

"I'm going to shower and get some takeout," Bryce announced as he opened the apartment door. "Everybody good with Chinese?"

"Sure." Ruben was grateful that between those moments at the boxing club and the car ride home, Bryce had caught on that time alone might be on the cards for Marlène. "Let me show you your room." He guided her by the small of her back to the stairs, shooting Bryce a last glance and mouthing, "Take your time."

When they reached the lower floor landing, he paused. "Study." Ruben opened the door to Bryce's perfectly organized work life. "Man cave, with home gym." He opened the second door where a massive TV hung on the wall and gym equipment stood against the opposite wall. A punching bag hung in one corner. The usual black living room set that he planned to bunk on was no longer there, and the room looked empty. That was an unexpected wrench in the works, but he schooled his face and carried on. "Bathroom. I'll be going in here shortly. And bedroom."

There was only one bed, albeit a big one.

"Thanks."

"You'll be okay?"

She gave him a weak smile. "I might go make myself a drink."

"I'll be quick."

He watched as she scaled the stairs, still burning to pull her into his arms. This woman had more going on than he understood, and he hadn't even scraped through one layer of her yet. He wanted to ask her so many things, but he'd paused all his questions, preferring to be in the moment. Deep down, half of him didn't want the answers anymore. The more he got to be with her, got to know her, the less he wanted to know about her past, dreading what it would do to their relationship, whichever shape it was shifting into.

For now, she was just Marlène with a small chance of her being that girl in the photos. He'd rather have that than deal with the truth.

24

MARLÈNE

Marlène opened Bryce's freezer to look for ice. She found a clean dishcloth, wrapped some ice cubes in it, and tied the lot with a rubber band she found in a messy drawer. It was nice to know Bryce had one of those too in his expensive black granite and steel kitchen.

She needed to busy her mind with anything other than what had happened at the club. She'd forgotten about it. For years. The memory had been squashed and suffocated under the weight of other memories until, at the hard pound of a gloved fist against Ruben's ribs, it had drawn a wheezy breath and came back to life. She bit her tongue and sniffed, as tears still sat shallow with the flashbacks that flickered through her mind. It had happened only once, and that was why the memory had faded.

She went through Bryce's cupboards to find some tea and stumbled upon an old box of chamomile. She'd love something stronger, rock hard, to be honest, but drinking was the worst of addictions and with her tendency to fall into anything on offer, she should steer clear of alcohol with its easy accessibility.

Bryce didn't have an electric kettle, so she poured some water from the faucet into a mug and heated it up in the microwave.

From the adjacent master bedroom, which was situated on this floor, the tell-tale sounds of someone digging in a closet for clothes came through the thinner walls. Bryce had finished with his shower, and she didn't want to see him. Not when she hadn't had time to get her head around what he had disclosed about Ruben. Once she'd made the tea, she hurried back downstairs, mug and cold compress in hand. Bryce had been pounding into Ruben's shoulders and stomach; there was bound to be some bruising, and this could help.

As she reached the landing, Ruben came out of the bathroom and steam clouded out of the door to the ceiling, filling the space with the scent of fresh-cut pine. He wore grey sweatpants but was holding his shirt, a towel slung over his shoulder.

"I'm still trying to cool off."

He didn't need an excuse. She'd been burning to see his naked chest since that first night, to touch it, to stroke over his scars with a gentle caress. But now, that need had multiplied exponentially. Since Bryce's revelation, she couldn't help thinking that Ruben had been scarred before he'd even been born. Seeing Bryce punching him to boot upped her anxiety and that must have triggered her.

As she glanced down his torso, every hit Bryce had made was glowing red. Poppies between the trenches of his muscles and scars. His exposed shoulder looked bruised where Bryce had delivered his hardest hook several times.

"I got you this." Marlène raised the cold compress. "It should help."

"Yeah, sure. Thank you."

She walked into the bedroom and put her tea on the nightstand. He followed her as he towel-dried his hair into spikes, then tossed both the T-shirt and towel onto a convenient chair.

"Sit here," she said, pointing at the bed's corner.

The Neighbor

He complied with a groan and a soft chuckle. "Bryce didn't hold back."

She wasn't sure if he was talking about the information Bryce shared without permission, or the beating they'd both taken in the boxing ring.

"I'm sorry for bringing drugs into your life," she whispered, her voice almost choking on the words. She knew how bad it could get, for Damien did the same to her. If it weren't for Damien, she would never have tried drugs.

Ruben looked up to where she stood with the compress in her hand, shy to touch him now, knowing that deep down, his body had the same fucked-up blueprint as her own. Once an addict, always an addict.

"I probably would have told you at some point. Sooner or later."

Depends on where this is going, she finished his sentence in her head. "But it would have been on your own terms."

"Yes."

To think that had happened to him. She had felt horrible over the weekend and couldn't imagine how terrible it would be for a newborn, to go through withdrawal first thing, with no reference to what it meant to be a normal human. "I'm so sorry."

"I'm okay. But Bryce is right. I probably did join the drugs unit as part of my continuous exorcism." He raked his fingers through his wet hair, gathering it away from his face. "Keep your friends close. Keep your enemies closer."

"It's one way to deal with it, I suppose."

"Funny how you can't see that in yourself, but to someone else it's crystal clear."

"Either way, you're brave, so very brave."

"So are you."

"No." She didn't need someone else to point this out for her. She'd been running. For a long time, she was as immobile as a baby, until she could sit. Then at some point she crawled, and then walked, but once she started running, she couldn't stop. Breaking that twisted bond which had tied her up hadn't been done overnight. But she'd been running for years now, and still it seemed she'd put no distance between herself and her past.

He held out his hand to take the compress from her, but she stepped up to him and ignored his gesture. She recalled the men's well-matched physiques circling each other, both of them pure muscle, testosterone, and roiling with pent-up energy. "I think Bryce feels and looks equally sore. You didn't hold back in the ring either."

"But nobody's prepared him a cold compress." He smiled at her, and her heart warmed.

"Let me do this for you." She placed the compress on his shoulder, and he closed his eyes with a groan.

"This is good?"

"Yeah. My skin still feels hot from the shower."

She inched closer and her leg brushed against his. There was an easy quiet between them that came with shared knowledge, shared secrets. She didn't step away to break the contact and he relaxed his leg against hers.

"Do you want to talk about what happened earlier?" Ruben stroked his hand up the side of her thigh to her hip, a gentle gesture that stole her breath. "About what triggered you?"

"I—" Her mind had only been on him and his trauma until that first punch rattled her to the core.

She could brush him off.

She could lie.

She could use their safe word. Time would pass and *later* could turn into never. She had so many ways to cop out of the truth and yet, if she was going to redefine herself, drill through all those layers to find the person underneath them all, she had to be honest. If anybody deserved her honesty, it was Ruben. He'd revealed so much of himself over the past few days, and she was tired of clutching her secrets close. Letting go of one secret couldn't hurt anybody.

"A man hit me once just like Bryce punched you in that first round. I'd forgotten all about it. The sound...the memory came back to me as if it were me being hit." She'd felt it, the crack of her rib, the pulse of nerves that rushed with the message to her brain that *that* had actually happened.

Ruben tightened his clasp on her hip. "Fuck."

"It was bad. But he only hit me once and I never saw him again." It was true, but Ruben didn't need to know how old she'd been when all this had happened.

"Where did he hit you? And why?"

"Here." She placed her hand under her breast where her ribcage sloped down towards her side. "Do you even need a why?"

"No, I don't," he said on a sigh. "I feel like a fool for asking."

A lot of men didn't need a reason to beat a woman, but they could all justify it afterward. She'd been crying and it hadn't *worked for him in the moment*. It had been a punishment, delivered swiftly. She'd never cried again. Not until now, when it was all she wanted to do.

At least Ruben understood this. He had worked on humanity's shadow side. He wouldn't need any further explanation. His hand slipped underneath her sweater, warm on her skin, asking to touch her where her hand rested so she made space for his palm underneath hers. She held on, wanting to soak up his protective touch as if it would erase the memory.

"Tell me who he is, and I'll go beat him up. I'll get him locked up for you if you want. I have a lot of friends in the police force."

"You're really sweet, you know? Recover from this pummeling first." She chuckled, but the sound shattered into a sob. She didn't know her assailant's name. "It's too long ago now, so many things have happened since then. I'm okay."

"You were, until this evening."

This was the start of the withdrawal's aftermath, and it would be the worst. She'd known it from the start. The long, lonely ditch in which she crawled had an exit if she could only look ahead and stay the course. The light at the end of the tunnel that always seemed within reach but never came close. One day, surely, she'd step out into it.

"I'm okay when you're with me," she said. It was the truth. To say it out loud surprised and scared her. His presence had come to mean so much to her in such a short time. She felt safe with him, and he treated her as if she was something sacred to be cherished.

His fingers shifted and his thumb stroked her skin, brushing against the underwire of her bra. "I'm not going anywhere."

The slow rhythmic circles of his thumb grazed the curve of her breast. Her arousal, which ebbed away only to tsunami back whenever he touched her, reverberated through her body as she suppressed a plea for more.

As if he heard her all the same, his thumb circled higher, his fingertips caressing the side of her breast in equal slow motion. She closed her eyes and her breathing slowed down in anticipation of him touching her nipple through her bra's thin fabric. She gasped as he finally brushed over the hardened pebble, his touch easing over one side of the barbell piercing first, then over her nipple to drop off on the other side. Each subtle movement sparked a blaze straight to her sex, which contracted in wanton arousal.

"Can you come if I touch you like this?" he whispered.

She sucked her lip as Ruben wasn't stopping. With each round he upped the pressure a mere fraction, and with his other fingers caressing the side of her breast, it was as if they were buried in her with his thumb slowly circling her clit. Her body was that connected, and he was driving her to the edge. "Yes."

"Do you want to?" His voice was deep and heavy with desire.

She nodded and he tugged her hip to pull her down to his leg, making her straddle his thigh. She let go of the compress to hold on to him, his skin now cold where the ice had rested, her hand too hot.

"I want you to come like this," he whispered against her ear, his breath sending chills down her neck and to her breast. He pushed down on her lower back and the curve of her butt, making her feel the pressure of his thigh, quietly instructing her to rock her heated sex against him. "Can you do that for me?"

"Yes," she moaned, almost there, her fingers digging into his hair to pull him closer.

His other hand slipped underneath her sweater while his lips grazed her neck and the soft skin behind her ear. Her nipples puckered even more, almost painful now with need as both his hands stroked and teased her. He kissed a slow trail to her mouth, and she curved her back, pressing her breasts into his hands.

Ruben kissed her then, slowly, and her open lips melded with his, their tongues searching each other out, eager, caressing deeper. His kiss was a drug, zoning out everything except him, her, and the intense build-up in her body. She moaned as his fingertips still stroked her breasts, only intensifying the ache between her legs with each glide of his thumbs over her nipples. His lips and fingertips were working together to take her ever closer to the tipping point.

"Come apart for me, sweetheart," he whispered and at his words a powerful orgasm rippled through her and she cried out against his lips, the relief almost too much. Her body trembled and his thumbs stroked gently as he kissed her again, this time slower, making sure to pull out every last shudder.

Marlène leaned into him, pressing her face into his neck. He gathered her to his chest and lifted her legs to wrap around his hips. She pressed kisses to his neck, wanting to taste him, make him feel like he made her feel, have him come apart too. With his erection pressed against her drenched sex, long and so freaking hard, her whole body begged to have every last inch of him buried deep in her so he could take her there again.

"That was a first." She had to admit it, to him. He'd done something to her no man had ever done before. She hadn't even taken any of her clothes off.

"Yeah?"

She smiled and nibbled at his earlobe. "Let me," she murmured in his ear as she rocked her hips against his length. "Let me take care of this for you."

"Marlène—"

"Please." Her lips were begging for it not only with words. She brushed a hand down his chest towards his erection, but he covered her hand with his.

He groaned as he maneuvered her to the bed to lie on her back. He leaned over her, regret in his eyes. "I shouldn't have done this. We shouldn't do this."

"Why?" He wasn't going to allow her to reciprocate?

He was too quiet, too contained.

"Not now." At some point earlier, a door had closed upstairs, and she'd registered that Bryce had left. He might be back soon. "Later?" She reached to stroke his cheek with her fingertips, wanting to kiss him so bad. He still said nothing, and the realization rose up in her, incredulous. "Never?"

Ruben looked away towards the door. "I don't know."

This was a second first. "Ruben?"

He stood and adjusted his straining cock which, at the tip, had spread a wet blotch on his pants. From the upper floor, the sounds of Bryce's return echoed down the stairs. She sat and wanted to take his hand in hers, but he stepped out of reach.

"Fuck." He cupped his hands to his mouth and sighed into them, staring at her before closing his eyes and blocking her out.

Physically, she was all mush from her intense orgasm. Emotionally, she wasn't in a space to deal with this rejection. Bryce might have arrived home, but there was more to this than his brother's presence.

"I can't do dinner." The last thing she wanted was a cozy dinner for three, with Bryce of all people.

"You're not hungry?"

"Not for food." For him, yes. For an explanation, less so. She needed to be with him, in his arms. She needed more. Of him.

"You need to eat." He swallowed and, in that moment, revealed the immense constraint with which he kept himself in check.

What was going on in his head? "I was planning to."

"Okay. I'll bring you something."

"Please. Don't."

Ruben nodded as he made an indecisive turn towards the door and back to her. He stroked a stray hair from her cheek. "Forgive me."

With two steps he was at his suitcase and plucked out a fresh pair of jeans and a T-shirt. He disappeared into the bathroom and when he came out a minute later, she still sat frozen on the bed where he'd abandoned her.

"Go to sleep, I'll see you in the morning," he murmured and softly closed the door on her.

Here was a man who didn't use her. Didn't expect her to entertain. Who wanted absolutely nothing from her.

And all she'd wanted was to give herself to him, no holds barred.

She'd forgive him anything if he'd let her.

25

RUBEN

Ruben scaled the stairs slowly, adjusting himself in his jeans and making sure his shirt hid his arousal. He shook his head as he paused for a moment. He'd almost lost control. And he would have come in ten seconds if her lips had sealed over his cock.

He had to get a grip. If it weren't for Bryce's untimely and yet timely arrival, he would have caved in and let Marlène work her magic. Because magic it would be. The way she kissed...the thought of it now made him want to reach for his cock. Ideally, he should jerk off and get some release, but he could jerk off for days and it wouldn't be enough.

All he wanted was her soft warmth against his skin, her lips on his own, her moans muffled in his neck as he rocked into her, deep and slow to keep her on edge for hours.

He needed *her*, more than he needed an orgasm.

Ruben groaned. This wasn't helping. He took the last few stairs and Bryce looked up from the kitchen island where he was unpacking the takeout.

"I got some chow mein, sweet and sour pork, shrimp with garlic, and chicken with cashew nuts."

"Were you hungry or what?" Ruben said as he sat down on a barstool. He pulled a container closer and popped the lid to inhale the scent of garlic and shrimp. Anything to distract his mind.

"You're not?" Bryce had three beers on the counter and handed him one.

"Yeah." If only he could focus on the food, he might survive the severe case of blue balls. He cracked open the beer and chugged back half the can in one clean gulp.

"Marlène's coming?"

She was, not too long ago. "No, she isn't hungry."

"Wants to stay in bed, does she?" Bryce smirked. "I'd hoped you'd get some. You obviously rocked her world."

"Jesus Christ."

At this, Bryce hitched his eyebrows. "Not?" His hands stilled and silence sliced through the apartment. "Okay. What's up? I thought I beat the shit out of you, but you look like you're about to ignite."

Ruben groaned a chuckle. Fuck. Bryce knew him too well.

"Didn't I give you enough time?" Bryce muttered. "Sorry, dude, how much time do you need?"

"Shut up already. This is so fucked up; I can't get my head around it."

"Look, I'm sorry I told her about your mom and your birth. I only want to look out for you."

Ruben leaned on the counter and rubbed a knuckle on his forehead. "That's the least of my worries. I already forgot about that."

"What is it then?"

There wasn't much he could tell Bryce that wouldn't open a can of worms. "Um, to sum it up, my work is interfering with my sex life?"

"Okay. Jeez. In what way?"

Ruben shook his head. He couldn't talk about it.

"You're not having issues—" Bryce jerked a hand up and down. "You know, getting it up?"

"No, asshole, that's not the problem."

"Phew. My worst nightmare."

Not quite. Not anymore. Not for him.

"What's the problem then?"

Ruben shook his head and took another sip.

"You're talking to someone, aren't you?"

"Graham Foster. He says hi. Told me to come see you and beat the crap out of you."

"Nice. Told you to get laid too, I bet."

Ruben laughed into his beer. "Why does he think sex is the baseline solution for all problems? Is it a therapy thing or is it a Graham thing?"

Bryce reached for some bowls and forks. "I dunno? Maybe the way into your head is through your dick?"

They both cracked up laughing and after dishing up, Bryce handed Ruben a bowl of Chinese food, filled to the brim. "Now seriously, what's going on?"

He hadn't been ready to talk to Bryce on Saturday morning, but maybe he could now tell him about his work. "I've always been able to distance myself enough from work to keep going, but Paris was too much."

"What are you doing there? You can tell me. I'm not going to tell anybody else."

Ruben knew this. Bryce was solid and he trusted him more than he trusted himself. "We're homing in on a sex ring. Trafficking and child exploitation."

"Fuck."

"Yeah. I thought I could deal with it, and we're making progress, but—" Admitting that it was too hard didn't come easy. He'd only recently started admitting it to himself. Saying it out loud would make him feel like a failure.

"You should've come home."

The Neighbor

"In retrospect, yes. Probably." He poked at a shrimp with his fork. "While I was in Paris, it seemed stupid not to spend my time off in Europe. See the sights."

Bryce cracked open a beer and took a sip, all the while staring at Ruben. "How is it that you got into this type of work? I mean, why not stick to New York and drugs? There's enough to do there."

"I dunno, this work sought me out. I sure as shit wasn't looking for it." Inside him, a whisper circled that maybe, just maybe, that wasn't entirely true. His whole career had spiraled in from the outermost circle to this point, the epicenter. It couldn't get darker, more degrading, or more violent than this. Over the months, it had cracked him like an iron maiden of visual torture, until he snapped.

They ate in silence for a few minutes until a sigh from Bryce made him look up.

"You're only human, Ruben. You know that, right? You need to live a little too, you know, have a life. You've been trying to find your way for so long, but I don't think this latest gig is it. Especially not if it starts messing with the good things in life. They're so few and far between, don't let work mess with it."

"Hmm. Yeah." What's been seen, can't be unseen. Bryce wouldn't understand this. You defined your work, and then, one day, you looked in the mirror only to realize work had defined you.

"I have no issue with Marlène, and I fucked up. She knows how to stand her ground. There's a lot to respect right there."

"Yeah."

"Please, stay as long as you need to, or want to."

"Thanks. I'm seeing Graham again tomorrow, so we'll be heading back first thing."

Bryce nodded. "I have the funeral in the morning and am still trying to catch up on my work backlog."

"What's happening in your man cave? The sofas are gone?"

"Yeah, slight timing glitch. I donated the old ones, and the new ones aren't coming till next Monday. I didn't know you'd be here, otherwise—"

"No worries." There went the sofa he'd intended to sleep on. Maybe he should give up the pretense and sleep in a bed for once. Next to her. Wrap her warm body in his. Keep her safe. Keep his nightmares at bay.

His muscles talked to him now. After the session at the club, he was exhausted. Not much could go wrong when they were both asleep.

They finished eating and once they'd packed away the leftovers, Bryce collapsed on his sofa and pulled his laptop closer. There went another sleeping option, but he wouldn't ask Bryce to move to his office so he could sleep in his living room.

"I'll see you in the morning."

Bryce nodded and Ruben felt his gaze on him until he disappeared down the stairs. In front of the guestroom door, Ruben hesitated. He was only human. With human needs.

And she was a woman. A beautiful fighter. Passionate. Generous. With needs of her own.

He wasn't stupid. The need between them would only escalate, unless he removed himself physically from her, like he would soon enough. He could keep his suspicions to himself, and even if they turned out to be true, nobody would be any the wiser. Nothing would stop him from going back to Paris to crack this godforsaken case. This neighbors-with-benefits thing he and Marlène blindly stumbled into had a solid expiration date.

Ruben pushed the door open, and his heart swelled with longing. Marlène slept under the covers, in the middle of the bed. In the soft moonlight coming from a gap in the curtains, he could see from her exposed shoulder that she wore his old, wash-worn T-shirt. Why was that such a fucking turn-on?

Because it was normal, and all he craved was normal.

They'd slept next to each other before, so this wasn't exactly new.

He caved in, stripped to his boxer briefs, and slid underneath the covers. She was close, so close and warm and soft. Ruben turned on his side and as his hand grazed her hip to nudge her closer, his palm met naked skin where the T-shirt had scrunched up. His breathing stalled. She wasn't wearing any panties.

If he hadn't told her he'd see her in the morning, implying that he'd sleep elsewhere, he'd swear she was teasing him. He turned his back on her, careful to not wake her.

He burned to spoon her, but he'd never fall asleep with that sweet butt pressed against his cock.

26

MARLÈNE

Ruben was here, where she needed him the most.

She'd been drifting in and out of sleep, still trying to understand what had happened earlier. But now he was here, his hand warm on her hip, his fingers stilling as he brushed her naked skin.

He wasn't supposed to be here, and after the conflicting signals he'd been shooting her way, she hadn't been sure she'd even want him here. But now, with his body next to hers, she understood how much she needed him to be close to her. She didn't stir, scared that he'd want to leave if he knew she was awake.

She still didn't understand what went on in his head, but it was no surprise to her when he turned away to his other side.

Back to back, it was almost like a wall stood between them. She couldn't stand it. "Ruben?"

He groaned a sigh. "Did I wake you?"

"No. Why are you here?"

He didn't respond immediately, and she rolled onto her back, brushing her arm against him.

Ruben didn't speak, but his chest rose and fell with strained breathing. "Because I need you to hold me."

In the dark, she stared at the back of his head. "Okay," she whispered. "What's going on?" She'd been so stuck in her own misery that she'd been blind to his struggles. He was going through something hard and didn't share any details with anybody. For all she knew, he didn't understand what he was going through himself. She turned towards him and pressed into his back. "Do you want to talk about it?'

He kept his back to her, but tenderly gripped her hip and pulled her closer. She slipped her hand over his side and to his chest and for a moment they just held on to each other.

"Later. Please." He hesitated. "Maybe. I have to sort out my head first."

That hurt. When he asked about what had triggered her at the boxing ring, she'd also stood at a fork in the road. Trust him with her past, or not. Now, instead of opening up to her like she had to him, he closed up.

Later. Or never.

But this was the agreement they had, and the least she could do was honor it. She traced a line along his spine with her nose and pressed a soft kiss to a shoulder blade. "Okay. Later."

"Thank you." He took his hand from her hip and clasped her fingers in his, holding her hand close to his heart.

His grip eventually relaxed, and his breathing took on the rhythm of sleep, but still she stared into the dark.

Her withdrawal insomnia had improved but with him here, like this, she couldn't sleep for worrying about him. It was coming, for sure, that moment when his body would jerk, caught in a nightmare. This time, she wanted to fold him into her embrace and chase those visions away, whatever they were.

When he stirred against her, she woke in a daze. She'd fallen asleep and during the night, they'd turned. She was in his arms now, his erection pressing into her bum. For a moment she waited, barely breathing, to see what he'd do next. When he rocked into her again and muttered something incoherent, she shifted to look at him.

Marlène smiled. Ruben was fast asleep and having a very nice dream, indeed. She'd love to make it all real, if only he'd allow her to go down on him. She put her hand on his chest. "Ruben, you're having a dream," she whispered and pressed an innocent kiss on his shoulder.

His eyes flickered open, and he huffed as he became aware of her leaning into him.

"Hey," he managed, slow to awake to the fact that his raging erection rubbed against her thigh. "Shit. Sorry. Did I—"

"Shh, it's okay. You're dreaming, but for once it seems to be a good one."

Her hand smoothed over his chest and slipped down his stomach and along the elastic band of the briefs he slept in.

"Marlène—" He groaned as she grazed her fingertips along the ridge of his erection that strained and twitched against her palm.

She looked up and in the first dawn light their gazes met. "You always know what I need. Please trust me to know what you need, too?" She was begging, because she wanted to do this so much, for him.

He didn't stop her when she went on her knees and dragged down the comforter to expose his cock, straining against his briefs, eager to take him in her mouth.

"Marlène...fuck." He sounded more awake by the second and now he sat up, his hand in her hair, his grip seeming unsure as to whether he wanted to pull her towards him or push her away. "We shouldn't do this."

"Why not? Are you married and this will be cheating on your wife? Do you have a girlfriend you haven't whispered a word about? Some bug you don't want to pass on?"

"No." He breathed and for a moment they stared into each other's eyes, gauging, searching.

"Then say yes."

"I don't want to take advantage of you."

Her heart swelled and her throat tightened. Nobody has ever said that to her. She pressed her forehead to his and for a moment they just breathed as she grappled with her emotions. He cradled the back of her head in his hand, his fingers gently stroking and slipping between the strands of hair. He was so careful with her, as if she would break. It only upped her longing.

"You're not taking advantage of me," she whispered. "I want this. With you. With nobody else. Only you." She'd never had such a deep urge to give herself to someone. Everybody always took, whether she had something to give or not. Nothing about the way he'd treated her had made her feel cheap and used. Ruben was so different, he only gave, never expecting something in return.

She'd been crushing on him, but she might already be head over heels. She swallowed with the need to taste him, her sex wet with the thought of pleasuring him.

"Take this off?" she whispered as she ran a finger under the waistband of his boxer briefs.

"Yes." With a tortured groan, he pushed them down his legs, freeing his cock. She moaned as she took in his size. The thought of him filling her slowly, then ridding her as hard as her body was begging for, wet the inside of her thighs.

She gazed at him, her hands back on his body, caressing their way up his thighs to his cock. As she took his shaft in a firm grip, he snatched a strained breath. He eased onto his back as he exhaled, and the tension seemed to seep from his body.

Her rhythmic strokes made his hips rise into her hand, chasing for more. Her lips closed over the tip, and she drew him in deep. She stopped before she could gag, fisting him harder at the base to get a better grip on all of him. Ruben gently buried his fingers in her hair to stroke the base of her neck. The touch was so intimate and caring, she paused for a minute as tears swelled afresh. She should have known he'd twist this around, make her feel as much as she made him feel.

He looked down at her to stroke her cheek with his other hand, tracing a line where her lips sealed around his cock. The touch was so erotic, the wonder in his eyes almost too much, an intimacy she'd never experienced before.

She took him in deeper, feeling him widen her throat as his breathing hitched. He was close, his sack pulled tight against her fist, with each thrust going further as she warmed up to accommodating him. She held steadfast when he gathered her hair, knowing he wanted to pull her away and not come in her mouth, but she craved having him complete inside her. With an intense moan his body stiffened as he came, and she stilled, allowing him the pleasure to do so in her mouth.

"Fuck," he murmured as he lifted her away.

She met his gaze, which was hazy and lost in lust, and the pleasure of having pleased him rippled through her. She wiped her mouth with the back of her hand, hiding a smile.

"That was explosive," he murmured, somewhat dazed.

Marlène leaned over and took a sip of the cold chamomile tea that stood on the bedside table as his hand slipped up her thigh. Yes. More. She wanted him to touch her now, let his hand roam and his fingers penetrate her. She leaned into him and kissed him, soft and slow as he cupped her cheek. He reached for her mouth and wiped at her bottom lip with his thumb. "You wicked, wicked sweet girl."

His words ripped through her as if she were made of paper. She stilled with eyes closed, her heart clutching tight, ready to crack. He was not like them. He was different.

He was her ultimate fork in the road.

But she couldn't. Not yet. Not now. Not here. Later.

Always later.

She drew in a shaky breath, a tremor running through her at how close she was to breaking. This. Exactly this was what those pills kept at bay.

"Marlène." He reached out for her, but she pulled away.

"Call me anything you like, Ruben," she whispered. "Do your worst. Call me a cunt, a whore, anything really, anything except a baby or a girl."

To hear her trigger words coming from him was proof that she'd never escape her past.

"Marlène—" The anguish in his tone was almost too much. "I'm sorry—"

"No. I'm so sorry." She raised a hand to stop him from coming closer. How could he even begin to know, begin to understand... She eased off the bed and bundled her things together for her shower. She was out of the bedroom before he could stop her.

27

RUBEN

Ruben stared at the bedroom door as Marlène shut it behind her, a boulder pressing down on his gut.

He'd fucked up. Badly. On so many levels.

Those words had hurt her, and the last thing he wanted to do was hurt her.

And he'd caved in, completely, under her warm, sensual touch. He didn't even have the excuse of being half asleep. By the time she went down on him, he'd been wide awake, unable and unwilling to stop her. He wanted her. He needed her. The human in him had begged and nothing in his weak-ass manbrain could force him to stop her.

She'd wanted him. Until the moment he called her a *wicked sweet girl*.

The boulder turned. Those words had triggered her, and he suspected why.

What was a twenty-eighty chance hours ago had just flipped into forty-sixty territory.

He slumped back into the pillows and pushed the heels of his palms to his eyes. How much more could he mess up in one morning? Maybe he shouldn't get up until...*later*.

That freaking word.

He wished he could put everything off forever. Go live in a vacuum with her, where they had no past, no future, only the here and now, in which they clung day by day to only each other.

How much could he really live with, in himself? He'd been in the pristine white of the moral grey zone he'd found himself in, doing good, but he was making black scratches that changed the color of this landscape.

This was why Bryce disclosing to Marlène that he was a heroin baby didn't eat at him much. He probably knew something of her that was a secret too. That nobody knew and she never spoke about either.

Nausea hit him from nowhere. He had to do something. Anything. Look at his options and decide on a plan of action.

He could ask her for the truth and see if she'd give it to him. Later. Could he wait? Possibly for a lifetime?

Or he could cut her off, go back to Paris and never see her again. Carry on with his job as if she hadn't happened. She was so close to pulling through on her withdrawal. Could he do that to her? She was reshaping his plans, tilting the scales. Paris wasn't paramount anymore.

Or he could dig to the bottom of her secrets, without her knowing, and never say a word. Investigate her, as was his forte. Privately. For himself, and then see what happened.

Nothing good could come from any of those options.

He swung his feet to the floor and raked his fingers through his hair. With her in his apartment, in such an intimate space, an investigation wasn't an option. And he wanted her close and safe, and to help her stay clean. But keeping her with him would lead to only one thing…them taking what had started in the past few hours here in Boston to the next level.

With a groan he reached for his jeans and put them on, followed by a discarded T-shirt. Barefoot, he strode out of the bedroom and up the stairs to where the nutty aroma of coffee drifted. He needed some of that to clear his post-blowjob brain fog.

As he walked into the kitchen, Bryce looked up from the fridge where he was reaching for a carton of half-and-half. "Sleep well?"

God, yes. Better than he'd slept in years. He nodded and rubbed his hands over his face.

"Woke up well too, by the look of it."

Screw Bryce. What would he know about it? Had they been noisy? Maybe. He hadn't been paying attention. Marlène had blown his mind. He scooted onto a barstool by the counter with a groan. No tiptoeing around the subject now. "Can you fall in love with a woman just because she gave you the best head in, like, ever? Like in your entire life?"

Bryce grinned at this, averting his gaze. "Probably. I'd like to imagine that we strive for more."

"Jesus Christ." Ruben smirked at Bryce's word choice. "*We?*" Who the hell did his brother think he was, in any case? He was screwed up in his own special way, but Bryce, always striving for more and all, had karma on his scent like a bloodhound. "You know what you've got coming, right?"

"No? Enlighten me."

"Your match. And she is going to be totally off limits because that's what you deserve."

"Hmm." Bryce laughed, even if it was rather dry. "I have no problem with Marlène. I told you so yesterday already." Bryce reached for another cup and put it under the coffee machine's nozzle. "Pick your poison. Strong, medium? Black, white?"

"Double espresso?"

"Done." Bryce popped a pod into the machine. With a rumble, the coffee dripped into the cup and Bryce turned back to the fridge to get the eggs and bacon. "How's the body feeling?"

The Neighbor

Ruben had hardly noticed, but now that his brain could move on from other parts... "Slightly stiff, but I'm okay."

"Same here. You still give as good as you get." Soft footsteps fell behind him and Bryce's gaze looked past him. "Morning. Would you like some coffee?"

Ruben turned towards Marlène, trying to keep his expression neutral, but his heart pounded and his pulse skipped. She clambered onto the stool next to him, sliding her hands over the counter.

She looked beautiful. Fresh. Unrattled. She wore make-up, but her hair was gathered on top of her head in a loose knot, a few wisps brushing her temples. Soft and feminine. If she wanted to make him fall deeper, she was doing great.

Marlène shot him a glance, her eyes telling him nothing; her sweet smile held no secretive tease about what they'd done this morning. "Hey."

He reached for her hand, wanting to touch her, to make sure she was okay. She let him do so, but only for a second before she stood and went around the counter to Bryce.

"Coffee would be great. Can I help with this?" Her voice was cheerful, with no tension in her stance.

"Sure," Bryce said. "You'd like bacon and eggs too?"

"Seems to be the standard with you two," she said with a smile. "Sure thing."

This Marlène was his Marlène, yet she was different. Easy, unfazed, light.

Was she over her withdrawal or was this an act?

He swallowed as she brushed a rogue wisp of hair from her cheek, the slight tremble in her fingers the only indication that she wasn't fine. If he hadn't spent days with her as he had, he would have missed it.

She was the queen of pretend. Smoothly natural.

Was this for Bryce's benefit, or for his? She didn't need to fake it in front of him.

Marlène looked up and met his gaze head-on, but her eyes were empty. Fuck.

Those few times he'd seen her outside her apartment door, late at night, always light and easy. The call with her sisters had been a forty-minute-long act. She'd been going through the hardest part of withdrawal, on screen, and even though he'd cut the camera, she would've kept up the pretense if she'd had to. And now, after what had happened in their bedroom—she'd been doing this for years...

Acting came to her as naturally as breathing.

Playing the part wasn't for his benefit alone, but for everybody around her.

And probably even for herself. Everything was okay, wasn't it? Always.

He'd zoned out of her conversation with Bryce, and by the time she pushed a plate of fried eggs and bacon in front of him, it was too late to catch up. He was sunk too deep into his thoughts and ate in silence. He would have five hours in the car with her. She couldn't escape. He could try and open her up, petal by petal, seeing if she'd let him inside her and to what she'd been hiding from the world.

"I'm ready to go if you are," she said. "Once we've eaten."

He wasn't ready. He was falling for her. He didn't want to know. Once things were there in black and white, they couldn't be unwritten.

"Ruben?" She touched his arm. "You okay?"

"Yeah. Thanks for the breakfast. I'm going to shower and then we can hit the road."

The last thing he could do was act as if nothing had shifted in him, between them, and he needed to get away from her.

He could hardly look his brother in the face either and rushed off.

In the shower, he opened the water as wide and hard as it

would go, and finally let tears crack through the surface. When had he become this freaking weak?

The gnawing certainty that she was the Chained Maiden was a slow suffocation. This was too much. She was too much.

But there was more. Something was birthing, trying to break out and reveal itself to him.

If he could run from it, he would, but it had grown into him, and he couldn't escape it.

He didn't want to know what it was.

Graham.

He needed to speak to Graham.

28

MARLÈNE

Ruben had been right. Getting out of her apartment had done her a world of good. Up until this morning, that was, when his words hit her gut like an iron fist. Now they were on the interstate back to New York, and in the car, it was quiet and tense. Ruben was trapped in thoughts of his own, appearing calm, but by the tapping of his thumb on the steering wheel, she could tell he was anxious. To get home? Or because of her words to him?

Her head was still coming to grips with the last conversation she had with Bryce while they were cleaning the kitchen, Ruben downstairs in the shower and packing his things.

"How are your withdrawal symptoms?" Bryce had asked.

"They're so much better. Fingers crossed it won't be long until they're gone for good."

Bryce had stared at her for a long moment. "Sometimes you are stronger when you do something for someone else's wellbeing, rather than for your own."

Oh God, that had been true, always for her. "I'm quitting for myself." For the first time, this was all about her.

"Yes. Well, my brother is falling for you and...and I'd hate for him to—" Bryce had broken off and puffed out a sigh.

Still, sweet heart of mine. Ruben was falling for *her*? "No drugs. I know."

Bryce had nodded. "Okay. Good. Well, if you want to be with him, focus on staying in recovery for him when that siren call becomes deafening. Because it will come. And it *will* be deafening. And you know it."

She wasn't sure if that had been Bryce's vote of confidence, or a final warning to stay away from Ruben. She needed time to understand what she wanted here. Everything had been bogged down with her withdrawal and she was only starting to think clearer now.

"Ruben?"

"Yeah?" He glanced at her, his thumb pausing.

"I—" She swallowed. How did she break off whatever they had without shattering to pieces? She didn't want to break it off. Maybe she wasn't ready yet in her mind for this, or for what it would take to be his. "I'm going to take a few days."

"Okay. Going anywhere?"

"My apartment." She would laugh if her stomach wasn't twisted tight.

"Good. It's the right move."

He thought so too. They'd taken things too far, too soon. And yet, it all felt so right. Righter than anything she had ever felt before. "I'm sorry about this morning."

"Which part?"

"What do you mean?" She glanced at him, not understanding.

"Let's see. The blowjob? Or telling me not to call you those words and walking away, leaving me gutted? With no explanation. Or acting during breakfast as if nothing happened and pretending that you're fine? Boston has been a massive trigger tour for you, hasn't it?"

Trigger tour? In Boston? Wait until she was back in France. "I'm sorry. About all of it. I shouldn't have pushed—"

"Fuck, Marlène. We don't need sorries, and we don't need any more regrets."

Why was he so freaked out about a simple blowjob? If he knew how many men she'd blown, he'd feel like a number. But a man didn't like being a number. No, a man wanted a girl to be so deep into him, as if he were the only God.

Maybe this wasn't about her, but about him. "I know you're stressed about your work. I'm here, you can talk to me, even if it's confidential. You need only give me the broad strokes so I can support you. I want to help you, like you helped me." She swallowed a breath. "Unless you're an assassin and would need to kill me if…if I uncovered your secret."

He didn't laugh.

Well, crap.

"I'm talking to someone. I'm seeing him later today. And I don't even know if my *issues* are work related. What I'd like to know is what your issue is with the words *baby* and *girl*."

The silence in the car stretched. The hum of the wheels on the tar became almost deafening.

"If I wanted to talk, I would have gone to rehab," she finally managed. Or not. She bet once there, excavating that cave would kill her.

"Right." He took a deep breath and rubbed a hand over his forehead.

Miles went past and she hated being like this with him. He'd done so much for her, and she didn't want to give him even a speck of herself. This was why she and James had failed. This was why Damien had a stronghold on her soul.

"If there was anybody I would choose to talk to," she whispered, her voice breaking, "I'd choose you."

He inhaled at her admission, but it wasn't with relief that he let his breath release again. "Yeah. Thanks." He didn't reach over for her hand as she hoped he would, to give her a comforting touch.

She was so close to tears, but she fought them back. "I just need more time."

"I'm going back to Paris and might not be here by the time you decide you're ready. Maybe it's best if we don't let this get out of hand."

"Yeah. Okay."

He turned on the radio, as if that would distract them, and for the rest of the trip they drove in silence.

When they arrived at the apartment block, he steered his car into the underground parking lot and carried her bag all the way to her apartment door. "Do you still want to go on our date?" he asked once she unlocked her door.

She bet he'd had his fill of her. One last night was all she would have with him. One perfect night to dress up and say their final goodbyes.

"Yes please. We can talk about first date stuff."

"By the look of that list you had, first date stuff is petrifying."

There he was. Her Ruben. She gave him a shy smile. "We'll be okay."

"We will. Yeah." His gaze dropped to her lips, but he turned away to his own apartment door. "I'll see you around. Pick you up tomorrow night at seven?"

"Sure. Thanks."

He paused for a second, his eyes no longer on her. With a frustrated groan, he dropped his head back. "You know I'm right next door if you need me."

"Yes. Thank you." She needed him, but in a deeper sense, more than she ever needed someone before. Ruben understood her, as nobody else had ever understood her. "I'll knock if it comes to that."

"I'm not here for a couple of hours tonight."

She'd been there when he made the psychologist appointment in the car. He wanted to make sure she was going to be fine, twenty-four seven. That someone could care so much almost made her weep. "I know."

"Okay."

"Okay."

They were like teenagers talking on the phone, and neither of them wanted to be the one to end the call. She tore her gaze away from his and pushed open the door. As she closed it behind her, she collapsed against it.

Ruben Scott was a beautiful, gorgeous, warm-hearted, strong man. He wanted to know her, both inside and out. She could open up to him, let him into her cave of secrets to see eye-to-eye the monster that lived in her.

If she survived letting him in, talking to him, and allowing him to see who she really was, she had no guarantee that Ruben could live with it. She wasn't sure they could survive her trauma and be together after her revelation.

A man like Ruben Scott would be beyond irate. He had anger issues. And knowing her past would hurt him, so badly, and the last thing she wanted was to hurt him.

What if she told him and he turned his back on her, telling her he wished she'd never opened up to him? Once he knew the full truth, he might feel he hadn't asked for the knowledge and couldn't live with her past.

Everybody she loved she'd locked out like this. She cared too much for them and couldn't let anyone be privy in her shameful history. Distributing the weight wouldn't make hers lighter, it would only burden those she loved, with a burden no one knew how to carry.

And somehow Ruben was slipping into that zone, where she wanted to protect him from the worst, because she'd fallen in love with him.

29

RUBEN

Ruben slumped onto the sofa and dropped his head into his hands, breathing into his palms as Graham settled into the wingback closest to him.

"How are you?" Graham asked.

"I might have to lie down."

"Go ahead."

He toed off his shoes and swung his legs onto the sofa. He'd hardly straightened them before he shot up again to stalk around the room.

"Ruben." Graham's tone was neutral, but with a soft tinge he would never have associated with someone who'd worked in the police force. "Breathe."

He couldn't recall getting here, being lost in drifting, erratic thoughts. His work, Marlène, their intimacy, a triangle of choice he was trapped in. He needed to make a decision.

"My shoes. I should've kept them on?"

"No, please. Be comfortable."

He dropped to the sofa again. "I went to Bryce's. Boxed. Ran ten miles today."

After he'd gotten back to New York and Marlène had gone her separate way, his nervous energy hadn't eased. He had to go for a run and even now, with everything he'd put his body through, a buzz still hummed in him.

"How're you feeling?"

"I'm fucked. I'm going to stumble into sex with her, but it's more than that. I'm crushing like a freaking teenager."

Graham said nothing, sitting quietly, waiting for him to... what? Carry on? Give more details?

"Last night things got out of hand, if you know what I mean." Ruben groaned. "She went down on me this morning." He had to close his eyes on the memory and swallowed. "My homework's all done."

"Good."

When Graham said nothing more, Ruben stared at him, leaning in. "Is that all? Can we talk about the mess I'm making of this?"

"You might be crossing a line, but you're not sure. Does it bother you that much that you feel like this?"

"Yes." Ruben paused. "No. That isn't it. It feels so right. Have you ever had that? Where things between you and a woman are so right, so in tune—" He broke off. Even now, the memory of Marlène's hands on his body fueled an erotic fire in his veins. "But my gut's clenched tight, as if something wants to burst. The tension. Graham, help me here. I can't carry on like this. Do you think it's an ulcer? Should I go for a check-up?"

"You should eliminate any physical reasons, so yes, go see a doctor, but you're here now. You came to see me about your recurring anger issues."

Ruben shook his head with a sigh. That was Paris. This was now and more immediate.

Graham shifted in his chair. "Now that you're here, as a friend," he said as he made quotation marks with his hands, "I'd like to do some work with you. Some relaxation, just to see where it goes. You need to be on board, though, because if you're not ready, it—"

"Yeah, sure. Let's do it." Whatever it was, he wasn't walking out of here until his head had dialed down. He needed to sleep, and Marlène wouldn't be next to him tonight.

He could make plans with Marlène. He could hack into the Interpol system to find those photos of Andromeda. He could go in from the front end like any other pedophile and search for her. With those photos on screen, he could confront her, tell her everything. No, confront wasn't the right word. Expose. Yes. Expose himself as the two-faced fucker he was being. Fuck, he could even have a sneak peek at her back and decide where he wanted to take this once he knew for certain.

Either way, this was killing him.

But his anger. There was no back end or front end to it. It wasn't like the surges he was used to. This was all over the map, like a constant ringing in his ear. Somehow this worried him more. What would he be capable of if he lost it, with this build-up in his body? He had to get it under control.

"Okay," said Graham. "I need you to understand that this work could make things come to the forefront."

"Today?"

"We're only starting and first you need to get a feel for it," Graham said, clearly unwilling to commit to an answer.

Great. Touchy-feely. His favorite part. "That's fine." He wasn't sure what he was signing up for, but he needed to do something that took him forward, not backwards.

"We'll be doing a visualization meditation, to see where you're at in your body," Graham said. "Approach this with curiosity and no judgement. It's okay if your mind wanders. You don't need to do anything. This is just a first try."

Meditation of all things. Whatever. "Okay," Ruben agreed on a sigh.

"Lie back, or sit, whichever you prefer, and try to relax. Close your eyes, follow my prompts. Okay?"

He nodded as he leaned back into the sofa, but as his shoes were already off, he settled on his back with his feet up, sinking deeper into the padded seating. His body buzzed though, caught in an adrenaline high. He closed his eyes and waited for Graham to start, but it was a good five minutes before Graham spoke up and told him to breathe in deep and exhale. By that time, his frame had molded into a comfortable position, and if it weren't for the twisted roll of barbed wire in his gut, cutting him up inside, he might have been able to relax. That's what ten miles of running would do to a guy.

Ruben followed Graham's soft instructions, and after the third breath, he let go of the rebellious thoughts in his head. Mainly that this was dumbfuck stupid and he'd never get anywhere by lying here like this. If nothing else, this could help him sleep tonight.

Soon Graham instructed him to relax one body part at a time, starting at the crown of his head, down to his toes, each limb and digit at a time.

"Now imagine you're going to go deeper," Graham murmured, "and you can communicate with me by tapping your right hand's forefinger. Can you do that?"

Ruben tried to move his body, but the only part willing to move was his right hand's forefinger. It rose and dropped, the movement taking more effort than he'd anticipated.

"Good. Now you're going to do a body scan. You don't have to do anything, just feel. Imagine going through your body, just like you did with the relaxation. If you come to a place in your body where you experience discomfort, or some sort of positive or negative emotion, raise your finger."

He wanted to open his eyes, but found his lids were glued closed and even if he wanted to move, his will had depleted.

Graham started at the top of his head, guiding him to feel each part of his head, his ears, his forehead and temples, to his face, giving him a moment to acknowledge every feeling that may be trapped in his bones and skin. He moved lower, to his neck and shoulders, where he felt Bryce's battering from the boxing ring. But it wasn't pain. It was merely physical bruising. Graham guided him down his arms and fingertips, and then to his torso. When he mentioned his stomach, his finger, by its own volition, tapped up and down as if pressing a piano key again and again.

"Good," Graham's soothing voice came to him. "A lot of energy appears to be here. No need to do anything with it. Just let it be. Be curious about it. What does it feel like? What color is it? What shape is it? Does it feel light? Does it feel heavy? No need to verbally answer. Feel it."

Then Graham guided him lower to his hips and down, but before he could get to his thighs, pain tightened in his butt and groin, and his finger shot up and froze.

"Notice the sensation being there. Let it be, breathe through the sensation. Just like before, be curious about it. No need to do anything with it."

He didn't want to be there, not caught midsection in his body where the guilt of the past days spent with Marlène seemed ingrained. He lowered his finger and Graham continued to his thighs, down his legs to his ankles and feet. Graham led him back up, linking all his body parts together, making him feel and sense the whole.

"When you're ready, bring your attention back to the room, feel your body lying on the sofa. Feel the smoothness of the leather, the warmth of the leather, and when you are ready, slowly open your eyes."

He wasn't ready. Not yet.

But within him, something had shifted and rearranged, like

furniture in his inner world. He wasn't sure he liked this new layout. He didn't know what to do with the sensations and feelings this session had unleashed or where to go with them. They were foreign and out of place.

Ruben took a last deep breath and gradually opened his eyes. He lifted his hand and smoothed it over his forehead, nose, and the scratch of stubble on his jaw. He managed to sit up straight, surprised his body was obeying commands. For a moment there, he'd panicked, thinking he'd lost all control. Glued to Graham's sofa, chained to his voice and instructions. So open, vulnerable yet safe and weirdly calm despite what he'd experienced in his body.

Graham sat in his wingback, giving him time to adjust to being back in the present. Ruben didn't know where he went, but he'd been gone. He turned his gaze to the clock Graham had on his wall. It was seven already. He'd been horizontal on Graham's sofa for an hour, and it hadn't even felt like a minute.

"What does that mean?" Ruben whispered as his eyes locked with Graham's. Not that he wanted to know. Not really.

"That you are allowing yourself to heal."

"Is it the guilt for having had something I shouldn't have had? With Marlène?" He'd never been strung so tight with emotion over a woman before. He'd have to break it off with her before his conflicting needs strangled him, because that was what it felt like.

"Ruben." Graham said his name in a tone so neutral, it wasn't swinging in any direction. "Let's not judge this. It's a feeling, remember. It's there for a reason. Try not to overanalyze what it may or may not mean. It just is."

"You can't leave me hanging like this."

"I'm not leaving you hanging. I'm letting you go home to rest." Graham stood. "I can do the same time on Tuesday. Will that work for you?"

He'd been places. He'd experienced things in his early life. That had always been the source of all his issues. But this, this was new. And he didn't want to know.

"Yeah, sure. I'll see you Tuesday."

30

MARLÈNE

Absence made the heart grow fonder. More like he was the only thing she could think about since they separated yesterday.

This anticipation was new to her. She'd never been on a date before where the outcome wasn't pre-defined. She had no clue how tonight was going to end. Her anticipation had built over days, never mind hours. Now, as she fastened a pearl stud to her ear, her fingers were trembling. Was this normal?

She'd wanted normal, hadn't she?

Normal suddenly seemed overly complex.

For someone who was so used to acting, these nerves were foreign. She hadn't been able to fake it with him since day one, and even yesterday in the car he'd called her out. *Or acting during breakfast as if nothing happened and pretending that you're fine?*

Ruben, for all that he worked in dark spaces, didn't need to know everything about her. Over the past two days, once they'd gone their separate ways, she'd come to that conclusion. The easiest and safest thing to do—for him and for her—would be to let him go.

Why did the mere thought hurt already?

He'd be back in Paris soon enough and her lease here was up in ten weeks' time. She'd been planning to extend, but that depended on her work contract. If they did renew her contract, she might look for somewhere else to live, so that she never needed to see him again. New York was big enough for that.

Her off-the-shoulder black dress was an easy go-to. It fit tightly over her butt and ended above her knees, being demure enough to go anywhere. She'd spent the afternoon curling her hair and pinning it into a loose bun at her neck, soft and feminine, leaving her shoulders and neck exposed. She had no clue where they'd be going, but that was irrelevant. Ruben should remember her like this, at her best and confident, not clinging to the toilet and vomiting her guts out. The back was maybe a bit too exposed considering the weather, but with a coat, stockings, and heels, she'd be warm enough if they didn't spend much time standing around outside.

When his knock finally came, she hushed her heart. It was one night only. She'd been here before, like a thousand times, but never like this. In love, poised to rip herself from him in the morning, body for one, but for the first time, soul too, if this date went beyond dinner.

God, it was going to hurt.

Maybe he'd save her the heart-wrenching effort and leave her by the door after their date and take it no further. Or have sex with her and go back to his place, merely one apartment on, and treat her like the whore she was.

She opened the door and found Ruben standing there, obscured by a bouquet of beautiful multi-colored roses. Her breath caught. Heavens, there were at least thirty of them, and they weren't mere long stem hot house flowers. These were heirloom roses, simply gorgeous with their scent that perfumed the air.

"You shouldn't have," she said as a blush heated her cheeks.

The blooms were different, and she would love to know where he sourced them from, because this took planning. The gesture was so unexpected and sweet.

"Hello to you too." He smiled, his gaze taking in her face.

"Come in." She held the door open for him and he walked inside.

Marlène closed the door and took the flowers from him, taking a moment to smell their perfume. "Wow. They are so gorgeous. Let me put them in water and then I'm ready."

"Sure."

He followed her to the kitchen where she propped the flowers in the sink. "You might need to help. The vase is on the top shelf, and I can't reach it without a chair."

She opened the cupboard and pointed to her underused glass vase. He stepped closer, his subtle fresh shower scent drifting over, wrapped in his body heat. No cologne. Only pure, clean, straightforward Ruben. She wanted to straddle him already.

For all that her thoughts had been predominantly occupied with having to let him go, the undercurrent of needing a week of pure, un-paused sex with him raged on. Maybe that would cure her of this infatuation. If he told her now he had no restaurant reservation and no plan beyond these flowers, she would lead him straight to bed.

He reached for the vase and brought it down to the counter. "There. Anything else?"

Marlène rose on her toes, slipped her hand around his neck for quick purchase and kissed him softly on his lips before he could realize she was homing in. "Only that," she murmured as she pulled away, the pressure of the kiss still warm on her lips, her pulse going wild. "Thank you. I can't recall the last time someone gave me flowers."

She stroked her hands down the lapels of his thick woolen jacket, and he caught them before she could pull away.

"You're breathtaking." His gaze brushed back up from where it had strayed to her breasts, to her collarbones and neck. She held her breath, eager for him to reciprocate the kiss, for her lips only pleaded for more. His eyes swept up to hers, pinning her down, searching. "You've been okay?"

She swallowed, disappointed, and yet he cared so much. "Yes." Mostly.

Ruben lowered their hands and stepped away from her. "Let's fill this with water." He got busy, leaving her standing, butterflies wild in her stomach.

"How have you been?"

He didn't answer immediately. "I'm good. I missed you."

She closed her eyes, another hairline crack splitting into her heart. He was so frank. She'd missed him too. So much. Her apartment was an empty box in which she'd floated around, a lost dust bunny. "Your shoulder?"

"All good."

She arranged the flowers, and he carried the vase to her coffee table.

Marlène followed him into the lounge and reached for her coat inside the entrance coat closet.

"Let me." His hand warmed hers for a split second before he took her coat and held it for her. She turned her back to him, raising her arms, and he slipped it on, slowly, with such tenderness, that when he smoothed his hands over her shoulders, she leaned back into him.

"One date." He breathed into her ear, sparking a rush of goosebumps down her neck and straight to her clit. When had sex become so complicated for her? It had always been easy and uncomplicated. This was so much more. A messy game that was only going to leave her in pieces.

"Yes." She turned into him, and his lips caressed her temple and her hairline as he slid his hands down her arms. "Where're we going?"

"Somewhere we can work through your list of questions." His fingers grazed her palms and with a last caress he let go of her fingertips.

"Can't wait," she whispered, caught off guard by his tender physical flirtation. Her hand was on his chest, and she leaned past him to the foyer table to pick up her clutch. "I'm ready."

He held the door for her and waited for her to lock her apartment. Once she'd put her keys in her clutch, he took her hand and her fingers slipped between the solid, warm strength of his.

They took the elevator and her fingers quieted from her early nerves in his steady hold. She took a deep breath as the doors opened on the first floor. This was it. He led her straight to a black taxi that had been waiting and she shot him a glance. Ruben had planned this, to a T.

When he held open the door for her, she chuckled. She should have packed an extra pair of panties. "What else do you have up your sleeve?" she asked as he scooted in beside her.

"Just the usual."

Nothing about him was usual. When the taxi stopped outside two adjacent doors to two restaurants, she knew they were going down into the underbelly of the building and not staying on ground level. Ruben led the way to the door, which bore a sign that would have been inconspicuous if not for the blue neon light it was made in, reading *Piano Piano*.

In the old days, you could learn a lot about someone without snooping. A CD or DVD collection, books and photo albums were on display, so revealing. She'd spent time in his apartment, and bar knowing that he played civilization-themed video games with earphones and didn't mind watching movies she chose, she didn't really know his other tastes. Unless she trespassed into his phone where he stored his life, or stalked him on social media, or even worse, investigated him on the internet, she didn't know much. She took him at face value on what he'd told her about himself, and as such he'd crawled into her heart.

"You like piano bars?" she asked as they descended the stairs.

"Yes. Good music. Not too loud if you choose the right table. Good food if you pick right, excellent wine, if you pay, and a chance to dance, if the lady is willing."

She chuckled. She was willing. All she wanted was to be in his arms.

They reached the bottom of the stairs where a doorman waited, and after giving them a cursory inspection, the doorman swept a heavy velvet curtain to the side.

The venue was a sensory seduction. From the lighting, soft and intimate, to the music coming from a sole grand piano on an elevated stage, to the cozy tables for two where couples were sipping wine. It was all leading to only one thing.

She wasn't sure she'd be able to wait until they got home for Ruben to touch her intimately, because the need to be with him had been pressing inside her since boxing night, when all he'd done was to ignite the flame in her.

31

RUBEN

Ruben had needed to stop himself a hundred times over the past two days from knocking on her door to check in on her. He'd waited in vain for her to come over and had listened restlessly for any proof of life coming through their shared wall. Marlène's side had been quiet, and in the silent stretches he'd freaked out. When a dull sound came through, he'd breathe in relief.

Seeing her like this was a soothing balm on sunburnt skin. Holding her hand anchored him in his confused emotions that Graham had unearthed during their last session.

Whatever that visualization bullshit was, he'd concluded that the tightening he felt in his groin and butt hadn't been her, or what they'd done at Bryce's apartment. Nothing that right, that good, and that pure could incite such opposite sensations.

Looking at her now, as she eased out of her coat for the waiter to take, Marlène had a healthy glow, so different from when they'd first met. How he was going to keep his hands off her, at least until they were back home, was going to be interesting.

One night. He had to remind himself that this could only be

The Neighbor

one night. For her sake, he had to let her go. She was in the second phase of withdrawal, where she fought, weaponless and weak, those demons that made her take up drugs in the first place. She had to adjust to coping, emotionally and physically, first without drugs and then without him. Once back in Paris he wouldn't be there for her.

For one night, he was going to turn a blind eye. He was going to embrace this beautiful woman and feast on being in a normal orbit where things just happened, one after the other.

Her dress with its low-cut back was his first green light. When he'd helped her with her coat, his eyes had roamed free over her creamy skin. He was so used to scanning and capturing data in what little he saw that it took only a second to realize there'd been nothing there. No dark stars continuing the constellation that plagued him. The cut wasn't low enough and he needed to see all of her back, but he would. Later.

What if she asked him to stay? And not go to Paris? He couldn't allow his fantasies to sweep him away like that.

Ruben held her chair for her, and they sat down across from each other, at the back of the restaurant away from the piano. He'd wanted a booth, but he'd reserved too late to secure one. In a way, this was better. In a booth, they'd sit so close their legs and hands would brush against each other all night. To ease a hand under the tablecloth to her thigh, and deeper, to her sweet pussy, would be no challenge.

Even with this calculated distance, he had no clue how he was going to get through dinner without touching her as he'd wanted to. Since the minute she'd opened her door in this striking black dress that merely accentuated her womanly curves, the elegance of her collarbones, and the intoxicating swell of her breasts, it had been all he could think about. His hands on her body. Her breath on his skin. That rhythm under which their bodies would capitulate.

God, he was fucked.

"Wine?" he asked, as he reached for the wine list.

"I'd love some red."

"Perfect. Do you want to share a Chateaubriand?"

"Sounds amazing."

When the waiter returned, Ruben ordered a bottle of Bordeaux and the Chateaubriand. He reached over and splayed his fingers over hers where she rested her hand on the table, fingers restless. "Thanks for coming."

For a moment she looked down at where his fingers captured hers. "We all need to get back into the game at some point."

Except this wasn't a game for him. It had never been. Women weren't toys, hearts weren't pawns. "Are you nervous?" After what they'd been through, he'd hate for her to be nervous with him.

"No." She broke into a soft laugh and bit her lip as he turned her hand around to circle his thumb in the concave of her palm. "Your hands. It's been more than two years and the way you touch me..." She finished with a soft moan as he paused. "It's so sweet."

Her gaze lifted and his breathing stalled as he took in her flushed cheeks, then down to her neck, where a little pulse seemed to skip under the smooth skin. Then lower, where her nipples pebbled against her dress's fabric.

Fuck. She was aroused. By this simple touch.

"Don't tell me you can come from me just doing this?" Ruben resumed his soft stroking of her hand, skating circles over her delicate skin with his fingertips. He vividly recalled how her body had trembled with release when he'd caressed her breasts the other night. It had been so sexy and walking away from her that night had been one of the hardest things he'd done in a long time.

"Ruben," she breathed. "You. This. It's the only thing I can think about."

His mouth dried at the thought as his cock strained against his fly under the tablecloth. She was the only thing he could think of too; in the wash with all his other fucked-up thoughts, she was the one thing that bobbed to the surface the most. This sensual woman, in his arms, and how he wanted to make her come again and again. Fill her up with him and fog her brain with love and lust, eliminating those demons.

The waiter arrived with their wine, and they pulled away as if they'd been caught in the act.

He cleared his throat as the waiter poured him a taste. "We have one hundred and fifty questions," he said as he put his wine glass down after tasting. The waiter poured for her, and their eyes met across the table as they clinked their classes with a *salut*.

"Right." She gave an exasperated sigh. "You go first."

He had so many questions, but now he no longer felt the urge to rush right to the end. "Tell me about your family." She had an unfair advantage over him when it came to personal history.

"Hmm, well you've heard all about my two sisters. My father's a heart surgeon. One of the best in the world."

"Wow." *Wow*. Was this her access point to prescription opioids? The thought made his stomach turn and he tightened his grip on his wineglass. It wouldn't be the first time a parent fucked a kid over by introducing her to drugs. He had to force his mind away from the whirl of dark thoughts. He didn't want to dig there tonight.

"I know, right?" Marlène chuckled. "He's amazing. All brains, somewhat distant and in his head, more worried about his patients than anything else."

It sounded like she loved and admired her dad. "And you weren't ever interested in studying medicine?"

"Oh, God no. We have more doctors in the family, but I don't have the stomach for what they do." She dropped her gaze. "My uncle is a pediatrician and works with my dad. I'm my mother's child and into pretty things. She's a model."

"A model?" This was news but didn't surprise him. Marlène was striking, her skin flawless, her green eyes big and wide apart, her lips full of allure.

"She's been working in the industry for almost forty years. At first in front of the cameras and then behind, and now she's somehow revived her career and is doing campaigns aimed at older women. When you're in France she's sort of everywhere. The subway, bus stops, magazines. It's weird seeing her like that."

Did his brain mess with him on their first Friday night? Marlène had looked familiar, and he hadn't been able to put his finger on it. If she looked like her mom, his subconscious, after spending months in France, could have meshed the two faces together, giving him the feeling that he knew her from before. Marlène hadn't been familiar because of Andromeda's photos. A second green light.

He took a relieved sip of wine. Those moles on her back had been work following him home. He'd been so messed up when he came home from France.

"You look like her?"

"Totally. The blonde is fake, obviously." She ran a finger along a soft curl, her eyes teasing. "But you know how the saying goes...blondes have more fun."

His eyes skipped to her hairline. He never thought about her hair color and whether it was fake or not. The blonde suited her. "You never took up modeling?"

"I don't like the camera on me." She dropped her gaze. "It's more a mental thing than anything else, you know? My mom wasn't keen for us girls to jump in headfirst. She knew the industry and wanted to keep us safe." Her hands were restless again, but she smiled. "Plus, I'm too short for the catwalk so my mom nudged me into more sustainable parts of fashion."

"The beauty product side?"

"I don't think it was intentional. She wouldn't even allow me to play with her make-up or try on her clothes. She always said I shouldn't grow up too fast. So, you know what a rebellious teenager does? She gets into make-up and clothes. I studied journalism and ended up working for several magazines over the years. When the opportunity at this fashion magazine came along and I actually got it, I was over the moon. They offered me a temporary contract in New York, and it was the right time. I'm so lucky. This is how I ended up where I am. See? Living the dream."

But she'd told him she was bored.

Marlène took a sip of wine. "Now, my turn. You never answered me when I implied that you're a government-employed assassin yesterday morning. I'm really worried."

He broke into a deep laugh. He couldn't take his eyes off her. The wine had rouged her cheeks and lips. All he wanted was to kiss her and taste the Bordeaux on her lips.

"You have quite the imagination on you." He reached for her hand. She was too far. He needed to be closer to her, so much closer.

Ruben stood and scooted his chair around the corner of the table to sit next to her. As he settled, he leaned in, taking a slow inhale as he traced his nose from her temple to her neck, where a floral scent lingered. "If I tell you I'm CIA, what are you going to do to me?"

32

MARLÈNE

God. He could do anything to her right now. The warm tip of his nose on her temple, the heat of his shoulder as he leaned into her and grazed her arm, made her libido explode.

She hadn't expected this intense swell of desire that bounced back so quickly once the opioid fog had lifted. Damien had urged her to use with him so that he could reach climax, but for her, using had had the opposite effect. Her libido, which she hated very much, had for once shut up and sat quietly in the corner.

Peace. It was all she'd wanted. Peace so she could deal with the shit in her head, and the imprints on her body, and the recurring flashbacks that hit her out of nowhere. But the drugs kept those at bay too.

For almost four years, she'd been able to distance herself from her inner world. Before that, it had been James and swingers' clubs, and before James, it was hook-up after hook-up, Damien in tow or not.

Emotionally, she had too much work to do and no energy for it. She'd thought she'd be able work through, file, and archive all those memories in that cave while on drugs, but she

The Neighbor

hadn't. Drugs had only pressed pause. It had been naive to think she'd be able to get clean and walk away cleansed.

Ruben's knee rested against hers and she eased her leg underneath his where it was warm, safe. She needed him close, like this. He calmed her, his mere presence a wall between her and the outside world, his soft words a barrier to her destructive inner self. How she was going to keep going without him, without free-falling into relapse...even the mere thought was too hard to bear.

Maybe it was him. Maybe this desire for him wasn't from the need to still her unwanted, mind-fucked cravings. Maybe it was the purity of falling in love that did this for her. Did other women feel like this when they fell in love?

If he was her cure, she needed him to stay and not go back to Paris. She still hadn't answered him on his spy question because the sensations that he let loose in her body overwhelmed her. Now she breathed, taking in the male scent of him, the heat glowing from his body, his big strong fingers that took hold of hers again.

"Honestly, what I could do to you, doesn't interest me," she whispered as he lifted her hand to his lips. "I'm more interested in what you could do to me."

He shifted his foot, trapping her leg with a low chuckle. The movement nudged her legs apart beneath the table. "I think we should stick to our list of questions."

"Deflecting."

"Maybe." He pressed a soft kiss to her wrist, right there where her veins surfaced. "I believe it's my turn."

She leaned into him, watching with a quickening pulse how he kissed and nibbled a trail to the soft heel of her palm.

"Ask me anything. Ask me...everything." As she breathed the words, the urge to tell him everything shot up from nowhere, bursting in her like a firework. He'd seen her at her worst, what more could shock a man who busted drug cartels and rescued women from sexual slavery? Was this why she trusted him? No, she trusted him because he had a moral code he loathed swerving from. Good and bad. Black and white. Things must be so easy for him.

"What I've been burning to know, since noticing...and touching your—" He inhaled and as he exhaled, his warm breath spread a chill down her arm. "Fuck," he murmured, his gaze pinning hers. "Just the memory—"

"Go on," she whispered, pressing her leg deeper under his, loving the way she was entrapped.

"Beautiful breasts." His gaze dipped down, and lingered, sweeping over the low cut of her neckline.

"Yes? They're not fake, if you were wondering."

"That much I gathered."

"Good." Any man who'd had his hands on a few would know the difference.

He gave her a side glance, his eyes wandering down to her nipples, one at a time. Those treacherous little peaks tightened more, squeezing the metal they were pierced with. Did Ruben even know what he was doing to her?

"So," he started, his focus returning to her hand. "Do you have any more piercings I can look forward to?"

"Oh my." Her breath caught as Ruben's lips continued their journey, progressing to the center of her palm. He pressed a soft kiss there and followed on with a slow lick with his tongue, a bottom lip sliding in its wake.

"That's not an answer," he murmured into her hand, his mouth moving over the valleys and hillocks of her ring finger that curled over his lip.

"No, if I did—" *God.* He sucked the tip of her ring finger, making an electric current shoot through her body directly to her clit. "If I did, I'd be coming right now." She stroked his cheek and urged him closer to her mouth, where she caught his lips in a hungry kiss. He answered back leisurely, calming her down while upping her arousal at the same time.

"Hmm." He pulled away, lowered their hands to the table and shifted in his seat. "Slow down."

His hand disappeared underneath the table, clearly on a mission to adjust things downstairs.

"You're uncomfortable?" she teased.

"You think?" The look he gave her told her everything. He'd like to have her on the table, legs spread, eating her out until she raised the roof. Except they weren't alone, and Ruben wasn't into the games that she used to play. Years ago, she would've been happy to partake in the display and entertain, but this tender, measured, sacred seduction had her teetering on the edge much more than anything she'd ever experienced, whether in private or at a swingers club.

"I think we should skip dinner." Her voice was husky with arousal, her panties soaked through to the upholstered seat.

"And go home?"

"Yes."

"But we've only covered…two? Two questions."

"I don't care about the questions. Feel what you've done to me." She bit her lip, wishing he'd move his hand from his sex to hers.

As if he'd read her mind, he leaned closer and with soft fingertips, smoothed down her thigh to her dress's hem, letting his fingertips follow the hem's border to dip lower, to the soft curve by her knee. But he didn't trace up her thigh as she wished he would, and she swallowed a soft moan of frustration.

"You need to eat," Ruben murmured. And there it was, the slow, intentional stroke of his hand up her inner thigh, pools of touch expanding over her skin, making her burst into chills of heat. The delicate brush of two fingertips up and down her slit made her glow and pulse. "So that you have energy when I take care of you later."

She'd stopped breathing, so close to the precipice. Ruben extracted his hand and it appeared above the table where she'd been crumpling the white tablecloth in her fist. He covered her hand with his. "Can you do that for me?" he murmured.

Marlène nodded, closing her legs, trapping the orgasm that begged to surface. "And you want me to focus on questions?"

"Yes. All hundred and forty-eight of them."

She relaxed her hand and pulled a face. Ruben's lips twitched.

"Come to think of it, you haven't even properly answered my first one. You, Ruben Scott, are not playing fair."

He smirked and picked up his wine again. "I'm not a gun for hire, but I—" He broke off and her breathing stalled again.

"What?"

"You don't want to know how many people I might have offed in the line of duty, had incarcerated, or plan to put behind bars." He groaned a sigh. "My job is a real passion killer. Can we leave it there?"

He was all good cop, there was no bad in him.

"Okay. I'll stop pestering you. Shoot me another question."

"Okay." His lips twitched. "No piercings. Any tattoos instead?"

Her stomach, which had been aflutter with their flirting's sweet anticipation, gave a snarky twist. She took a long sip of wine and licked her lips, not sure how to reply.

"Maybe," she murmured, teasing him.

"That's not an answer."

"No, but playing tattoo hide and seek is much more fun, don't you think?"

The look he gave her left her pussy tightening. One night. This was going to be one to remember. Ruben Scott was going to fuck her until she saw galaxies tonight, never mind stars.

33

RUBEN

Tattoo hide and seek? What the hell? She wouldn't give him a straight answer. Being served a spoonful of his own medicine served him right. He was anxious for his last green light, the final go-ahead to take this evening where his heart, body and mind needed it to go. She'd side-stepped giving it to him completely.

The food couldn't arrive soon enough. Now that Marlène had teased him to the point of combusting, he needed to get his hands on her skin, his eyes on every inch of her, and seek until he found the evidence.

They ate in relative silence, the tension between them not abating. She'd pushed her leg underneath his again, and throughout dinner, the touch burned. He had many fantasies about how this night was going to pan out. He'd like to take his time, have this one evening to treat her how he would love her to be treated for the rest of her life, make her understand how much she meant to him.

Once the waiter cleared their table and the wine was finished, he reached for her hand. "Dessert?"

"No, thank you."

"Then dance with me," Ruben asked. He wanted her in his arms already.

"I'd love to, but not here. If you don't mind?"

"No?" The piano man was playing a slow number, and a cello and bass had joined in, deep notes plucking into a rhythm that set the tone for what was to come.

"At home. Where we're alone. I don't want people looking at us."

Ruben nodded and lifted his finger to ask the waiter for the check. He wanted her all to himself too. He paid, quieting her protests to split the bill, and within minutes they were waiting outside for their taxi.

She leaned into him, resting her head against his shoulder. He lowered his head and when he pressed a soft kiss to hers, she slipped under his arm, into him, and he wrapped her close. "Are you okay?" he murmured.

"Yes, I just need you so much, it scares me."

His heartbeat leapt at her words because he knew what she meant. He was on fire too, for her, and her alone.

"Hey," he whispered as he cupped her cheek. "We'll take it slow, okay?" Her lips were so sweet and close, and he brushed his mouth against hers, a soft, reassuring kiss. She hugged him tight, and he realized she might just need to be held like this more than anything else.

Twenty minutes later, their taxi pulled up to their apartment block. He held the door open for her and took her hand as she stepped out onto the curb. Soon they were alone in the elevator going up to their floor, her hand tense in his.

He glanced down at her. "If you're not ready, Marlène, if you don't want this, you just say the word."

"I need you like I once needed drugs, Ruben. Don't you dare walk out on me now."

Holy fuck. He was a lost cause. Even if he got a blazing hellfire of red lights in two minutes' time, screaming at him that she was that girl in the photos, he wouldn't be able to hold back. Not with her being so desperately honest with him, and him so desperately wanting to be with her too.

They exited the elevator and walked the corridor to their apartments, and he clutched her hand, possessively. Outside his door he wanted to pause but she carried on walking, taking him to her door. "I have condoms," she murmured as she let go of him to take out her key.

Her fingers were trembling, and he forced himself to pull back. "Marlène." She glanced at him. "Sweetheart."

"What?"

"You're shaking. I won't do this—I can't do this—if you're scared or anxious."

She bit her lip and looked away. "You won't understand."

"Try me."

When she didn't answer him, he took over from her to unlock the door and held it open for her. She dropped her clutch purse on the small foyer table, and he waited in the doorway, tense, dragging the courage to walk away from her out of the depths. Every light was shining orange now, and all he wanted was that final, overwhelming green. Would she open up to him, make him see her, without them dancing around each other like this?

When she looked at him again, tears brimmed in her eyes and shredded him. He closed the door and pulled her into his arms. "You're killing me here. Who hurt you like this?" he murmured, pressing soft kisses to her temple and ear. *Please open up to me. So that I don't have to cut into you to extricate your secrets.*

"It isn't that." She buried her face in his neck, wet and hot. "I'm trying to find myself, as you know. Getting clean for me has been about scraping away all the layers and remembering who I am without drugs, and without the numbing distraction of random sex. What if I don't like who I am?"

He sighed and hugged her closer. He understood this, better than she thought he did. "I'm here for you, for us. You know that. Regardless of who you are or where you've been." He didn't care, all he wanted was to love her as she needed and wanted him to love her. To love her as she deserved to be loved.

She quivered in his arms in the effort to suppress a sob. "I have so much to lose with you."

He had so much to lose too. His heart was made of glass, and she was holding it over a precipice. Shattering his moral code was the least of it. "Like what?"

"It's been two years for me, Ruben. Before that, I've had a lot of sex in my life. Love was hardly ever part of the equation." She met his gaze, uncertain. "With you, making love is all it can be. And to be honest, I don't—" She drew in a shaky breath. "I don't want to have just sex with you. Even if sex is what we both need, if it's going to be sex for sex's sake for you, I can't."

Ruben cupped her face. Now was the time to tell her, to ask her, and be open with her, as she'd been with him. But his heart was in it now, deeper than he'd ever realized, wrapping around hers and wanting to keep her safe. When had this momentous shift developed between them? How had they gotten this close? She searched his face, her tears waiting for him to break her. If he took the next step, he'd never be able to tell her what he knew, what he'd suspected from the start.

"Then allow me to make love to you." He lowered his mouth to hers, lifting her face tenderly to his, knowing he'd just admitted he was in love with her, and about to show it with every action to follow.

She gently collapsed into him with a sigh, her body relaxing against his chest, soft and willing like her lips, and he brushed his fingers from her cheeks to her neck, to her coat's collar to ease it off her shoulders. She shivered under his touch, but in a beautiful, sensual way. When her coat finally puddled at her feet, he circled her wrists to guide her hands around his neck.

He couldn't stop kissing her, but her hands were roaming, pulling his shirt from his pants, fingers warm on his skin. He still had his coat on and let go of her for a moment to shrug it off.

"Come here," he whispered against her lips as he gripped her butt in his hands and lifted her up so she could wrap her legs around his hips. Her high-heeled shoes dropped to the floor in soft thuds, and she clenched her thighs, rising up to rub her sex against his erection. He moaned at this move, and she smiled into their kiss.

"The things I want to do to you," she murmured as she kissed her way from his temple to his ear where she nibbled at his earlobe.

"The things I'm going to do to you." Ruben took wide strides to her bedroom where the floral scent of her perfume still lingered. He lowered her to the bed's edge and glanced at the feminine space. The golden glow from the nightstand's lamp provided just enough light for his somewhat hesitant investigation.

For a moment she only stared up at him as he stood, towering over her, taking in her beautiful, flushed face, eyes wide and trusting. She reached for his belt buckle, but he paused her by placing a firm hand on hers. "I get to play hide and seek first."

Ruben suppressed a groan. Why did he have to bring that up when all he wanted was to strip her slowly and bring her to orgasm before she'd even touched him? He'd wanted to slow them down, take his time with her, but of all the ways to do it, that one shouldn't have been his first pick.

She lowered her hand with a languid brush along the ridge of his cock. "Take your time then. And good luck." The last words were spoken with such a soft tease, he would swear she had no tattoos. That was a good thing, right? That was what he'd been praying for.

Ruben dropped to his knees in front of her and she bit her lip as she looked down at him. He stroked her feet, rounding his fingers to the back of her ankles, and up, in a slow brush of his fingertips, deeper, to the folds of her knees and the bit of thigh that wasn't resting on the bed. Stretchy lace kept her stockings up and he ran his fingertips over it. "Hmm, should have known you'd be wearing something like this."

"You like it?"

"I love it." He rolled each of them down, grazing her soft inner thighs, just shy of her sex, with his knuckles in the process, hardening more with her sharp inhales and strained exhales every time he did. Her hand was in his hair, anchoring her to him, but once he had the stockings tossed to the corner, he rose to his feet.

For a moment he breathed, willing himself back into control. He stroked his thumb over her wet bottom lip and then kissed her, rougher than intended, but fuck, her scent was an aphrodisiac driving him wild. He softly pushed her shoulder, urging her deeper onto the bed.

She complied, legs bare, dress hitched up to reveal a lacy black triangle between her legs. "My dress?"

"In due course." He pressed one knee into the bed, forcing himself to keep some distance as he lifted her left leg. With slow kisses and a close inspection as he went along, he covered the smooth, creamy skin to her knee. Then he took up the other leg and repeated the same micro-inspection, rubbing her foot in the process.

"No ankle tats here." He sighed his pleasure. "Well then. Onwards and upwards."

She smiled at him, her legs already falling open as he kneeled into her upper thighs and soon found his way to her epicenter, where she was glistening wet and begging through the lace.

"Ruben..."

"I'm thorough, so be patient," he murmured as he inched her dress up over her hips, to expose that scrap of inconsequential lace. Part of him wanted to rip it off so there was no delay in burrowing his tongue into her, but she was so beautiful, so perfect, he had to take all of her in first. Her breath was strained with anticipation of his next move and when he hooked his fingers under the bands of her thong, she lifted her hips for him to peel it off.

Her sex was trimmed, but not bare as he'd thought it would be, given that she would follow trends within the fashion industry she worked in. Her legs, where they had been relaxed to the side, stiffened under his touch.

"I hope you don't mind." Her voice sounded a bit lost.

"I love it. You're a woman, Marlène. It comes with the territory."

He stroked his palms over her thighs and felt her relax. "You good with this?" he murmured as he unbuttoned his shirt and stripped it off.

"Yes." She stared at his chest, hungry-eyed, making as if to sit up.

"I'm not done." He pressed down on her stomach and a frustrated groan escaped her lips.

"This is torture."

"Not for long." He inched his hand down to her mound and quietly massaged her with his palm. Her clit was peeking at him, teasing him, but all he wanted was to have her in this love-drugged state of anticipation for a few moments longer. With his other hand he lifted her thigh, kissing it, inspecting, lowering himself to her secret parts. When both thighs delivered no ink markings, he caved in and ran his tongue along the edge of her groin, up to her protruding hip bone, only to find his way back to her sex with a line of deep, teasing kisses.

"Ruben." Her voice was strained and when her hand

pushed his head down, he knew it wouldn't take much to drop her over the edge.

He ran a finger along the side of her slit, circling her wet entrance, dipping in and making her hips buckle. Marlène had seemed to give up, her upper body pushing back as she opened wider for him, offering herself to him. He fingered her then, slow and careful, seeing how much she could take. Her muscles clutched and he groaned. "You are so freaking tight."

It went with her delicate frame, the way she was built, and as he extracted his finger, she arched her back, begging for more. He pressed two fingers into her, rubbing deeper, harder, watching as her chest heaved. She was close, but he wanted to taste her, so he lowered his lips to her sweet clit and sucked and licked in the same rhythm as his fingers.

Her hand was in his hair and her moans tore through the room as she came against his mouth, wetting his fingers and seeping through to the comforter.

He drew every ripple of her orgasm from her, then gave her a moment before he slipped his fingers from her body. He traced a wet trail over her thigh with a soft kiss and a sigh. "No tattoos there."

She opened her eyes, seeming out of breath. "Best game ever."

He chuckled. "Yeah?"

"Oh yeah."

He reached for her hand to make her sit and found the zip of her dress at the back. "Good thing we're not done," he said as he unzipped her dress. She raised her arms and he peeled it off her, exposing her breasts with a soft bounce. "Holy fuck." Seeing her like this, naked, was almost too much for his poor cock, which he'd kept locked up in his trousers, the pressure just enough not to wish for more.

It only took one quick sweep of his eyes over her breasts

and stomach to know there was no ink tattooed on her pure, untarnished skin.

He cupped her cheek and kissed her as she buried her fingers in his hair. "Turn around for me, sweetheart. This is torture for me too."

She smirked and with a last soft kiss to his lips turned around to kneel with her back to him.

He closed his eyes for a second, unwilling now to face the moment of truth. He reached out for her then, blindly tracing the beautiful curves of her cello-shaped back, from the tips of her shoulders to the deep dip of her middle and out to her curvy hips. She inhaled at his touch, and he took a fortifying breath and opened his eyes.

Nothing. He scanned her back, following the breadcrumb trail of those first three deceptive little moles that took him on a fool's errand, down and lower to where her skin had more little specks of brown, but out of sync with what he'd expected. In the dim yellow ring of light, no black ink tarnished the purity of her creamy skin. There was no Andromeda constellation, no Chained Maiden.

Ruben dropped his head to her shoulder, his whole body shaking with the effort to suppress a sob.

34

MARLÈNE

Ruben's hands were clammy on her hips, his fingers pressing into the soft flesh.

"Hey." She reached for his cheek and lured his mouth closer to hers as she turned her head toward him. She kissed his jaw up to his cheekbone, her hand drifting into his hair, wet salt melting in her mouth. Her hand stilled. "Ruben? What's wrong?"

Her words brought him back to her, for his hands relaxed and ghosted up her sides to her breasts, which he cupped gently, his fingers circling her nipples with the lightest touch. He'd mastered her body one inch at a time, and she moaned as he traced his nose to her ear with a sigh, the heat of his breath fogging her skin, making goosebumps ripple to her breasts, where her already puckered nipples tightened more.

"You are so freaking beautiful," he murmured against her temple, and she leaned back into him, her love doubling up at his sweet words, whispered with a quiver of reverence, which echoed in his touch. "No tattoos. But are you going to tell me about these?" He squeezed lightly and pulled at her nipples, and she gasped at the sensation.

"Maybe. Later." The last thing she wanted to do now was to go over that bit of history. She needed him, all of him. And he needed her. Her hand stroked up his thigh that hugged her side, his erection pressing against her. "I have better things to do right now."

He smiled in her neck and nibbled kisses as he massaged her breasts, upping her need for him. "Bend over. Let me see that sweet pussy from this angle."

Marlène listened as he rose behind her and tugged the few pins and the hairband from her hair. She dropped onto all fours. His belt buckle clinked, and his trousers rustled as he stripped them off. She looked over her shoulder and let her hair cascade to one side, knowing the movement would perch her butt up even more, cheeky and inviting.

Ruben's erection was daunting in the soft light, and her whole body went liquid at the thought of having him buried deep inside her.

He stroked and splayed his hands over her butt and squeezed, opening her up. For all that Ruben had been cautious at first, it was as if something in him had shifted. His need and desire, which he'd held back before, seemed to roar to the forefront and she wanted to answer it, echo his every need until they were both limp, sated and breathless in each other's arms. He smoothed his thumb up and down her folds again, then wetting his fingers, he dipped them inside before trailing them out and up to her butt where he circled a divine tease before heading south again.

"If you'll let me," he grunted, "I'm going to claim every part of you as my own by tomorrow morning."

"God, yes." It was more a plea than anything else, but she didn't expect him to answer by dropping to his knees again and dragging her closer to the edge of the bed.

His hot tongue against her clit and the slow lick that followed up her perineum and tight hole made her shiver and gasp. She breathed through it. Oh, he was going to claim her. But this wasn't fair. She had plans too. "Ruben," she murmured on a moan as he licked her again. At this rate she was going to come again before she'd even touched him. She started to pull away, but his hand snaked around her waist to keep her where he wanted her.

"You're not playing fair." She laughed as she crawled away, and his hands slid from her body. She turned to lean back against the pillows, and he rose to his full magnificence, staring at her from the end of the bed with a smirk. "Not fair, hmm?"

"No. I want that." She pointed to his twitching cock. "I want you, and you're making me wait."

"Patience is part of the game, sweetheart." He rounded the bed to the nightstand where he opened her now-empty pill drawer. "Where are they? I'm not playing hide and seek with condoms."

"Other side," she said, hoping he'd circle the bed again so she could shamelessly ogle his body which her fingers itched to touch.

Instead, he sank down on the bed next to her and gathered her close for a deep, lingering kiss. "Hey," he said. "You good?"

She wanted to laugh and cry in his arms. He was always so sincere, checking in with her, making sure she was in a good space. She reached between them to stroke his cock, loving how he rocked into her gently, quietly asking—promising things only if she was on board too. "Yes. You?"

"Never better." He let go and reached over her to the nightstand drawer for the box of condoms.

She rolled to her side and watched as he got busy, as open with his body as he was that first night when she saw him in the mirror. The lamp light threw shadows over the ridges of his abdomen, into the deep cut of the v-line by his hip, and the dark gloss of curls that disappeared between his thighs. The scar from a knife wound near his pec looked faded, but the bullet and stab-wound scars shone in the low light. She ran her fingers up his muscled thigh and stroked his side, letting a fingertip cross over the old wounds within reach. She'd ask him about each of them, soon.

He caught her hand and as if he'd read her mind, kissed the wandering fingertip, and merely whispered, "Later."

"Okay."

He leaned over and brushed her hair from her shoulder, the soft gaze with which he took her in almost her undoing. With every touch, he worshipped her. Every gesture showed how he treasured her. Now he gathered her hands above her head, easing her onto her back, then coasted his knuckles down the inside of her arm. She sighed at the intoxicating rush that rippled through her body. When he circled her breast with his knuckles, she arched into him, and he rose to perch over her. She spread her legs for him to nestle in between, and he lowered his head to lick her nipples, tenderly sucking them into his mouth, one by one.

Of their own volition, her hips rose to brush her sex against his erection, for sweet tension was building in her again. He kissed a path up her chest and throat to her lips.

"Ready for me?" he asked against her lips.

"Yes." She closed her eyes as he guided himself to her entrance, focusing on every sensation as he pushed into her.

"Fuck, you're so tight," he said, but didn't stop his slow rhythm, giving her body the time to accommodate him.

He filled her and she trapped him with her legs, wanting to keep him close like this, connected and safe in his arms. Ruben brushed her cheek. "Look at me, sweetheart."

She opened her eyes and met his gaze as he steadily changed the rhythm of his thrusts, faster, deeper, fuller.

Harder.

Oh God. It felt so good and right and the tide swelled and swelled in her. "Ruben, I'm going to—"

"Come for me, sweetheart; I'm there too." His breathing came fast as his body strained, his hips pushing deep into her and as her orgasm vibrated through her, he pulsed and erupted into her depths. He still held her gaze, glazed over with passion, lips breaking into a deep chuckle as her body trembled. He thrust into her twice again, dragging their mutual release out.

"Fuck." Ruben dropped his forehead to hers and she clung to him, emotions welling inside of her. "I never knew how beautiful this could be."

"No?" She bit her lip, trying to contain her emotions. She never cried, but this, this came from elsewhere outside of her inner being.

Ruben's fingers combed into her hair and his lips pressed against hers in the most tender, reverent kiss. "Let's stay like this forever," he murmured.

Those words broke her, and tears slipped and sailed south, down her temple where they streamed over his fingers.

"Marlène?" He kissed her, even softer than before. "Are those good or bad?"

She couldn't answer. Where would she even begin?

"Sweetheart? Answer me or those tears will break me." He attempted to shift off her, but she clung tighter, not wanting him to move away from her.

"This was so normal," she choked on a sob, no longer trying to hide her feelings.

He slipped from her body and rolled onto his side, gathering her to him in the process, allowing her to cling to him. "Normal is good, right?" he said, searching her face.

"Normal is perfect."

"You're perfect."

She was broken beyond repair, but maybe here at last was a man who could live with all her shattered pieces.

35

RUBEN

Ruben leaned against the kitchen doorjamb as he watched Marlène speaking to her sisters on their usual Saturday morning video call. She hadn't bothered with make-up. This time, her cheeks were rosy from their intense night together, her eyes full of sparkle, and a naughty smile played on her lips.

She was a tease, and so freaking playful he seemed to have grown younger overnight by at least a decade. In that moment when he finally saw her back, the relief had almost suffocated him as emotion had gripped his throat. He'd had to force every haunting thought of his work and related anguish away to not break down and tell her everything he'd been holding back.

The growing pressure inside him, the heavy guilt, had drained away. Mostly. Maybe it would never dissipate completely. Maybe now was the time to tell her what work he did in Paris. Maybe she could help him think everything through and make sense of why he'd lost his shit on that night weeks ago. He'd keep it vague, like he had with Bryce. But honestly, all thought of work had drifted off into the vast wide ocean and he hoped it would drop off the face of the earth, never to be seen or heard from again for as long as he lived.

At least his mind and body—his heart—had been occupied with more pleasurable thoughts and pursuits. Making love with Marlène was something else. Nothing seemed to be off-limits with her, and yet he'd wanted to take his time, treasure each moment and explore at leisure. When it came to sex, she had years on him that he never intended to catch up on. Not that it mattered because she seemed to like his pace.

With them together, as they'd been last night and this morning before she lured him into the shower, only to go down on him again, his time left here seemed too short.

Screw Paris. The burning need to hunt down pedophiles had been doused by her passion. He needed a life—with her. More than anything else.

The coffee machine gave its last gurgle, and he took the cream out of the fridge. Marlène had her indulgences, that was for sure. She sat, legs crossed, with her laptop perched on the coffee table. As he carried her coffee over, she glanced at him, turning her head away from the screen. The tones and pitch of the other women's voices changed. He didn't need to understand the language to get the gist of their conversation now: they wanted to know who she'd spent the night with.

Marlène shot him a sly smile. "Come meet my sisters?"

He smiled as he placed her mug on the table, still out of view. "They speak English?"

"Of course. I had an English granny. Didn't I tell you?" She held out her hand for him.

"Nope."

He didn't allow her to pull him down to sit next to her but leaned in to smile at the two women on the screen.

"This is Vianne and that's Anaïs," she pointed, "and then there's Emily in Vianne's arms. Manon is playing somewhere in the background."

A chorus of *hello*s followed the awkward moment where he waved to them. "Nice meeting you." He didn't want to sit in on her call or take time away from her family. It was hard enough for her to be this far away from home. "I'm going to get some groceries."

"Okay. I'll still be a while. Wedding and so on."

"All good. Enjoy catching up." He kissed her softly for all to see and turned away and walked off, rolling his eyes as her sisters voiced their approval in teenage-like hoots.

That was it. Five more years younger. A full fifteen overnight. If he didn't watch it, he was going to slip back into his teens, and that was an age he didn't want to revisit for anybody.

When he knocked on her apartment door an hour later, she opened it for him with the quick excuse that she was still on the call. He walked in, closed the door with a gentle shove of his foot, toed his shoes off, and continued to the kitchen with his bags of groceries.

She was winding up the call now and seconds later came into the kitchen.

"That was a long catch-up," he said as he reached for her, and she slipped into his arms as if they'd been at this for years, not weeks.

"Sometimes I need to talk sense into their heads. As soon as Manon has a sniffle, Vianne rushes her off to our uncle. I know it's so easy, what with having a pediatrician in our family, but I just wish she wouldn't." Marlène bit her lip and shook her head.

Ruben pressed a kiss to her temple. She really had a dislike for doctors.

"And then there is Anaïs and her wedding," she said as she rolled her eyes. "She's over the top, sometimes."

Ruben grinned. "Sounds like she's nervous."

"No, a perfectionist. It would drive me nuts to live with her." Marlène laughed. "What did you buy that smells so delicious?"

"Cinnamon rolls." He pulled the box from the bag, and she

made space so he could open the lid. "From the bakery two blocks down."

"The same as last time?"

When Bryce had been here, and she'd been so sick. "Yep. Comfort food." He tore a piece off and held it out for her. She took a bite, and he popped the other half in his mouth as he placed the box on the counter.

"So yummy," she whispered, and licked her lips.

"Mm-hmm." He buried a hand in her hair and she didn't pull back when he kissed her, the buttery cinnamon taste of her still laced with coffee. "Yummy indeed," he murmured as his lips traced their way to her neck.

Her hands roamed too, urging him to peel off his coat as she led him out of the kitchen and into the lounge. She made him sit on the sofa and straddled his lap.

Ruben loved her like this, easy and light and filled with so much life. And love. He didn't want to think about her drug habit, which she seemed to have ditched years ago and not just the other day, or why she'd even picked up drugs in the first place. There was only this, her warm smooth skin under his fingertips as he slipped his hands under her sweater to find the back strap of her lacy bra. She'd be ready for him in seconds once he kissed her breasts.

As if she followed his thinking, she lifted her hands and he stripped off her sage green sweater. He groaned when her nipples peeked at him through a lacy pattern of florals, so frivolous, feminine, and summery.

She tugged at his T-shirt, and he chuckled as she helped him strip it off. Her lips were on him then, on his temple, racing lower to nibble at his ear. He gripped her hips and rolled her onto his already hardened cock, the perfume on her skin and the scent of her hair grounding him to her. She was all this—beautiful, giving, a joyful woman underneath whatever it was that bogged her down.

"This is so pretty, but it's got to go." His hands sidled up her waist to play his fingertips over the colorful embroidered surface of her bra, delicate, intricate, like her.

She pressed closer into him, the late morning light falling on her cheeks, lighting her up.

An angel. He'd call her that, but he barely got away with sweetheart. It still bothered him that she got worked up over those two words, *baby girl*.

"This one clasps in the front," she murmured, watching his hands on her body, waiting.

Marlène liked to instigate but didn't like to lead. She breathed heavily now, his fingertips on her nipples, the heat between her legs radiating to his cock.

She was so fucking hot. There was no way this was happening on the sofa. The condoms were in her bedroom, anyway.

He shifted to the edge of the seat and hugged her close, her arms circling his neck as she realized his intention. He stood and strode with her to her bedroom, where he eased her to the bed and stripped her leggings off her body in one smooth sweep. Her matching panties had a slit in the crotch and the visual took his breath away. Her sex, needy and wanting, peeked at him through negligible strappy bits.

It was on the tip of his tongue to whisper *naughty, naughty girl* but he bit back with a groan. *Fuck.* This *woman* was something else.

He'd been in the bathroom busy shaving when she'd dressed and thank God for that, for this set would never have made it this far. Ruben inhaled deeply and dragged his hands through his hair, happy now that he hadn't torn her underwear off, but had time to appreciate her in this state of undress. "Don't move," he breathed as he first stripped and then reached for a condom. Once he was ready, he lay next to her, cupping her cheek for a warm kiss. "You're not too sore?"

"No. I rather like it." She blushed as her hand smoothed over his chest. "I mean, I know it's messed up, but you're so big and it feels heavenly, being this thoroughly loved."

"Yeah?" Loved indeed. He trailed a hand down the flat plane of her stomach, to the gap in her panties that allowed him such easy access. He dipped a finger into her, and she arched her back into his hand with a soft moan.

"Ruben," Marlène whispered, an urgent plea. She was ready, so easy, so quick.

He rose above her and entered her, watching her intently, driving deeper, as the pleasure bloomed on her cheeks. Her chest rose as he felt her body gather, tightening, upping his need for release. She clutched his butt, forcing him closer, deeper, slower, and as her orgasm swelled and exploded, he released, feeling at last at peace with this world.

When he dropped to his side, he gathered her to him, and she snuggled close for a moment as they came down. He dealt with the condom, and pulled a blanket over their bodies, but she stopped him from drawing it to cover his chest and her shoulders.

Her hands stroked over his pecs, trailing down to where he got stabbed that first time. "I know you said later, but can you tell me now?"

Ruben caught her hand and singled out her forefinger. "Let's start from the top. This one," he said as he let her fingertip circle a bullet scar, "I got during a drug heist gone wrong. This one here, during a street shootout. These two stab wounds I got from a back-alley fight with a bunch of other teenage gangsters. It started with this one here."

She rose on her elbow and frowned. "How did they treat you for pain?"

Marlène caught on quickly, but then she knew his birth secret. "I only took non-scheduled pain medication."

"Was it enough?"

"I didn't ask for more."

"You're strong," she murmured, her gaze soft. "I could never be that strong."

"But you are." Couldn't she see what she'd achieved?

"I—" Marlène broke off and dropped back on her pillow, breaking their connection.

"Hey." He turned on his side and watched her profile as she cupped her face in her hands, collecting herself for a moment. "What's on your mind, sweetheart?"

She rolled back so they were face to face. "How did you end up in foster care?"

Of course she would have wondered and there was no reason why he couldn't tell her everything. "My mom was a victim of domestic violence, but I still had my granny. I stayed with her until she fell and broke her hip. I was ten when she ended up in the hospital, and that's when I got my first taste. She died eight months later, and I became part of the system. It took some time to find me a permanent home, I was shipped around a fair bit beforehand."

"Oh God. I'm so sorry. About your mom. About all of it. Were you there when it happened?"

"Yes and no. I was locked up in the bathroom. I can't really remember all that much."

She stroked his cheek. "I—"

"It's okay. I'm okay."

"But are you? There're all these horror stories about foster homes and abuse."

"Yeah. Shit happens." *Bryce.* Bryce knew all about that.

"Were you ever abused? Physically?"

"No. I got a few slaps but nothing that would alert the social worker, if you know what I mean."

"That sounds like more than enough to me." She sucked her lip, seeming to suppress her tears, her breathing strained.

It broke him to see her like this, so emotional as she assimilated his childhood trauma. After a long moment of quiet, she said, "Sorry, but I have to ask you this."

"What?" Their eyes locked, and in that moment, the world started to tilt.

"Were you ever abused…sexually?" She swallowed and blinked. "I know it's not something people talk about, but were you?"

He stared at her, at the lone tear that hovered in the corner of her eye, clinging until she blinked to set it free. How did she manage to just ask him this question, the one he'd wanted to ask her from that first night, almost impulsively and without flinching?

In him, the pressure that had seeped out on seeing her back, naked of any tattoos, pure and ink-less, catapulted right back.

No. He was never abused like that. His mind spoke out loud, but in his body, a soft whisper rippled through his groin. That feeling he'd had in Graham's office surfaced, even if it was only a faint echo of the sensation he'd experienced during the visualization. A fist clutched his balls and twisted.

"Ruben?"

"No." The blood drained, from his body, it would seem, into the mattress. "No." He couldn't. His head. His body. "No."

She scanned his face, and he reached out for her, gathering her hair behind her ear, anything to touch her and let this new thing in him fuck the hell off. His fingers quivered.

"You never found my tattoos," she said as she caught his hand against her cheek. "I need to tell you about them. I *want* to tell you about them."

No. Don't. "I thought you didn't have any."

"They were so small, insignificant really. Hardly visible unless you knew they were there." She swallowed, tears now flowing. "I had them lasered away years ago, but if you look closely, you can see where they were."

He wanted to stop her and go back to minutes ago where they were making love and not having this conversation. Some things don't need ink to be branded on you.

"Marlène—"

She sat up. "I need to show you. Please." She turned to kneel with her back to him, and his stomach turned. "Look, here." Her hand traced her back, her fingertips going directly to the spot where her skin seemed to have been bleached, almost invisible against her natural untanned skin. "And here...and here."

He closed his eyes against the visual of her fingertips reading the spots blind as if they were Braille.

"I need to tell you about these. Only you. And only once." Her body had stilled, only rising with her strained breathing. "Please."

No.

He got up off the bed and didn't look at her as he picked up his jeans and shirt. He walked out of the room. Out of her apartment and into his, the door still unlocked from his sex-induced negligence. He was, after all, only at his neighbor's.

He slowly slid down against the door to the ground, breaking.

36

MARLÈNE

For a long moment Marlène sat frozen, staring at the door through which Ruben had disappeared. Her apartment's front door had clicked closed maybe ten minutes ago, and she still couldn't move.

This was the first time she'd taken that step, the first time she'd built up enough courage and trust to open up to someone, and he'd gotten up and walked away without a single word. She always thought things couldn't get worse, that something couldn't hurt more, but this was a new level of rejection. As if Ruben had known what she was going to tell him, he had spurned her, turning his back on her, and walked out on her in that crucial moment.

The shame she wore like a second skin shrank and clung even tighter, suffocating her. For decades she'd been able to keep her tears at bay, but with Ruben, the level of intimacy and knowing he'd seen her at her worst and only seemed to love her more for it, despite it, had gained her trust, unexpectedly. Making love to him was more emotional than anything she'd ever experienced, and she couldn't stop herself. Her tears might have triggered him. Some men lived for tears; other men didn't know what to do with them.

No.

She sensed it in her gut. It had been something else. She inhaled a sharp breath, dread pushing up her throat. That last night in Paris and its memories that had never stopped haunting her. Her last horrible attempt to beg James for help had backfired, what with Damien always hovering, always meddling, always needing. Damien had lured James's sister Stacey to the swingers club he owned, and something had triggered her there. Stacey had crumbled at the foot of the bed in the open playroom and had coiled into herself as trauma she'd kept locked away for so long, had come roaring up from the depths of her unconscious. Damien had seen straight into Stacey's soul and sensed her trauma, so similar to theirs, and had whispered: *She is one of us.* Marlène had only wanted to hold her, to pull her close and be the barrier between Stacey and the rest of the world. But here had been someone she couldn't protect. She had been too late.

Ruben had said no three times, each of them in a different tone. She'd picked up on it, but now she knew she'd triggered him.

He is one of us.

Marlène wiped at her cheeks as she got off the bed and reached for her clothes, following the scattered trail through her apartment. By the time she'd dressed, her body quivered, the knowledge too weighty for her to carry. She went out to the corridor and knocked on his door.

No answer.

She went back to her apartment for the key Ruben had cut for her. Being alone was the worst. All she wanted to do was to hold him. Tight.

The apartment door unlocked but didn't open. It gave a little, but then pushed back.

"Ruben?"

He moved, a dull shuffle coming through the wood, and when she pushed again it opened a few inches.

"Marlène. Don't. Please."

He sounded so tired, and her heart squeezed.

"Don't what?" She needed to be there for him like he'd been for her. "What did I say that upset you?"

He didn't respond but through the small gap she could hear him breathing. "I need time."

"Don't do this, please. Let me be with you."

"Being with me is the last thing you should be."

Marlène dropped her hand from the door handle. It made zero sense. "Ruben, please."

She stepped closer to the door and leaned her forehead against it, biting her lip to stop emotion slipping into her voice. He was one of them, but she didn't know in what way. Abuse came in many shapes and forms, and until he opened up to her, she'd never see the complete picture. "Let me in?"

"You need to leave. There're too many things I have to get my head around right now."

"Okay." She hated the tremor in her voice, the way his rejection stung.

When he moved behind the door and the resistance gave, she stumbled into the room, but he caught her. He would always catch her. As soon as she'd found her balance, he dropped his hands from her arms and the cold gesture was so unlike him, the distance sudden and severe. This was the same man she was intimate with, to the point of telling him everything, an hour ago.

No. It wasn't. His face had the grey tinge of shock, and the brackets cupping his mouth cut deep. His hair was crushed and peaked into disarray as if he'd wanted to pull it from his skull. The worst was, his eyes were bloodshot with tears, tears which seemed to have watered the grey on his cheeks into a carpet of silver stubble.

"Ruben?" she said softly. "Let me help."

He shook his head. "Promise me you're going to be okay? You won't—" His voice broke. "You won't give in?"

Drugs had been the last thing on her mind. Since he'd taken her into his arms last night, every thought of a hit had been suppressed by him, his gentle care, his love. Now this.

"Of course." She would have to be strong, for Ruben. She'd promised Bryce. She'd promised herself.

He was leaving for Paris, soon.

Was he breaking up with her? This was one messed up way of doing so. But they weren't even together. For all she knew she'd been a stopgap for him. The mere thought was too much to swallow. "Will I see you again?"

"I need to speak to my therapist. Afterwards…I don't know." He dragged his hands over his face, a bone-weary sigh escaping from deep within him. "If we do see each other again, I can't be like this with you."

"Why not?"

He didn't answer her, and she stepped closer, but he rose his hand to stop her. "No."

"Is this about Paris? Because you're leaving? And we're getting in too deep?" That old feeling of being used came flooding back with a vengeance, creeping out from the shadows of the very cave she'd almost let him into.

"It's all about Paris." He closed his eyes as he pressed his hands in prayer to his lips. "Give me time. I have to—" He broke off and shook his head, checking himself. "I'm taking Caleb for lunch in an hour. I need to make a few calls, so I need you to leave."

"Okay." That was a polite *fuck off* if ever there was one. She wasn't someone to outstay her welcome. "If you need me, I'm next door."

She clung to her pride, turned, and walked back to her apartment. How bizarre that he spoke those words to her just the other day and now she didn't seem welcome at all. Did he use her, like all those other people had?

It might be that Ruben Scott needed to go fuck himself, but she knew men. She had, after all, been with a lot of them. Ruben didn't use her; he wasn't the type. It had been something else and for the life of her, she couldn't put her finger on it.

37

RUBEN

All the warmth drained from his body as Marlène walked away.

Ruben had no choice. He couldn't stay with her, not with what had just dawned on him for the first time in his entire life, or his stupidity shining like headlights into his eyes. The first thing anybody subjected to a forced tattoo would do was to remove it. She couldn't see them on her back, but the knowledge of them burned. Her fingertips had jotted the spots down as if they were a constellation she'd memorized and could blindly point out in the night sky.

Andromeda. The Chained Maiden. But to whom?

He reached for his phone, hesitating. He could cancel his lunch date with Caleb but leaving him in the lurch wasn't an option. Not when his sixth sense told him something was up with that boy.

He sank onto his sofa as he pressed Graham's number.

"Ruben?" Graham answered.

"Graham." His voice sounded foreign.

"Are you okay?"

"I don't know."

"Give me a moment." Graham moved away from family

noises and a door clicked closed. "I'm in my home office now. Do you want to talk over the phone, or do you want to come see me? Or do I need to come to you?"

"I don't know. I don't know anything anymore."

"That's okay. We'll figure it out." Graham waited for him to respond, but the words bottlenecked in his throat. "What happened, Ruben?"

"I don't know. She asked me if I was ever abused. First physically and then...you know. Sexually." He swallowed hard, the angst clamping down on his chest. Right at the moment when she'd built up enough courage to open up to him, his own revelation had roared in like a tsunami, destroying everything in its path. "Nobody has ever asked me that. It never crossed my mind that something like that could have happened to me. But it did. *Fuck.*" The last word exploded from him as he shot up from his seat, the iron hold on his anger slipping from his grip. "Jesus Christ."

"Where are you?" Graham asked, his tone calm.

"At home." He stomped around the room, wanting to do anything to rid himself of the rising red pushing up from deep inside his gut.

"Are you alone?"

"Yes."

"Breathe, Ruben. Sit down and breathe. Concentrate on my voice. Do only what I ask you to do."

He slumped back onto the sofa, trembling. He tried to do as Graham asked, but air wouldn't fill his lungs. An anger attack was the last thing he needed, just like that night in Paris. He tried again, Graham's steady voice drilling into his head, for many minutes, until the pressure on his chest eased and the fist he breathed into relaxed.

"You're better now? You're breathing?"

"I'm better. I didn't see it coming." In that sweet moment with Marlène, in the afterglow of intimacy, he'd never expected his life to disintegrate in a split second. But then, the months on this investigation in Paris, the time with Marlène constantly questioning, and finally, the work he'd done with Graham had been the scalpel cutting into the multiple layers of scar tissue that hid this malignant truth. Silent, waiting to be discovered, poisoning his life. He'd never suspected this.

"With the visualization work we did, this can happen. I tried to explain to you, but often clients don't even know what they're looking for. We're all feeling our way in the dark." Graham let his words sink in. "I suspect you've also been ready for this to surface."

"I don't understand. How? When?"

"When this happens, the trauma usually occurred when you were deemed too young to remember."

He closed his eyes and breathed into his fist again, biting down on the rising anger. Too young? He didn't want to go there. He didn't want to believe it. He didn't want to be— "How can I be so certain? It's so messed up."

"This is the thing. The body remembers everything, and the mind does too, even if not consciously. When the mind buries something, sometimes so deep, the body helps it remember, even decades later."

That day in Paris, when he'd lost his shit at work, the pressure in him at rocket-launch levels, he'd dipped in and out of a new photo collection of the same girl they'd been studying for months. Someone had emailed him, asking him to look at a recorded live stream of a small boy, wanting his input on the adult torso that had been in the frame.

He'd opened the clip. A toddler. Hardly older than two. He couldn't watch it. He'd stepped out and walked away and only come back hours later, when he'd thought he'd had his emotions under control. Marc was the last one still in the office, working on God only knew what. When his computer screen lit up, the image that had made him seize up had still been there, frozen on the scene. That had been it. He'd taken off like a rocket, despite every effort to contain his anger.

And this had been the source of all of it. He just knew it. On the inner walls of his being, the truth was scratched out in blood.

"What do I do now?" Ruben's voice broke as he dropped his head into his hand.

"You're going to have to give it time, Ruben, and when you're ready, we can work through it, together."

Therapy. The answer to everything. "I don't know. Digging doesn't seem like a good idea." All he wanted was to bury it deeper, so deep that it could never resurface, and go back to this morning, hours earlier with Marlène. "Fuck," he said, but it was more of a sob.

"I hear you, Ruben." Graham spoke as if right next to him. "I hear you, but therapy will help."

Yeah. Right. Marc would love for him to be *helped* so he could go back to his fucked-up job and put criminals behind bars. His track record was stellar, always happy to work behind the scenes and let others take the credit.

"Are you going to be okay?" Graham asked. "If you want to, I can come over. I don't have plans for this afternoon and maybe it would be better if you weren't alone."

He hadn't planned to be alone. He'd planned to check in with Caleb and to spend the afternoon with Marlène. And then some more *Marlène*. "There's something else."

"Yes?"

"I slept with her." He didn't need to elaborate. Graham would know who he was referring to.

"Okay." Graham waited for him to fill in the blanks.

"She's my girl." Ruben broke down. "I checked her back and when I didn't see anything, I thought it was a clear go-ahead. And then she told me afterwards that she'd had the tattoos lasered away." Because Marlène obviously couldn't stand the marks on her skin. This was harder than anything else. For a moment in her bedroom, once she'd started telling him about her tattoos, the rising horror of his personal discovery had been muted. What had happened to her had been worse, so much worse he couldn't get his head around it. "What do I do? What the hell do I do?"

Time ticked on as Ruben breathed, Graham quiet on the other side. "I can't tell you what to do, Ruben."

"She doesn't know that I know. How the hell do I tell her? *Do* I even tell her? Or do I just walk away from her?" Walk away from everything between them. The thought was a twist of the blade right in his heart.

"You were hoping she'd help you crack your case?"

When he'd had his first suspicions, it had been the driving force behind staying with her that Friday night. But the balance had shifted, so slowly he'd hardly noticed. He cared for her, so much, the cruelty of asking her to do this, when she'd just worked her way through the hardest withdrawal... "How could I ask her to do that? You don't understand, Graham. The things —" He broke off. "I can't think straight anymore."

"It's normal to feel this way. You've had a massive shock. And a breakthrough. Give it some time. You have a lot to process."

"Yeah. I know." Ruben wiped a hand over his cheeks. One thing was certain: he couldn't do anything on impulse. Marlène was the victim and he needed to respect that.

"You okay? I really can come over if you need me to."

"I suppose so." He was a victim too. It was going to take time to get his head around that. "I'll be okay."

"Phone me if you need to talk more. Otherwise, I'll see you on Tuesday?"

"Fuck. Yeah. Okay," Ruben said on a sigh. "This helped. Thank you for taking my call."

"Any time. Only—don't do anything rash, Ruben."

"Yep. Nothing rash. I'll see you on Tuesday."

They hung up and Ruben molded into the sofa, eyes closed, letting the exhaustion of the past hour flow over him. Eventually he forced himself to take a shower, although nothing would cleanse him now. A filthy layer covered him, like plastic wrap, clingy and stifling.

He had to get out for some fresh air to clear his head, but the walk across Manhattan plus a bus trip didn't stop the hundreds of questions circling in his head. By the time he reached Caleb's foster home, he was exhausted with too many unanswered questions. The only thing he could do was to box it all in and shove it back from where it had come. He'd deal with it later.

"You look like crap," Caleb said as he stepped outside. "Rough night?"

"Rough life."

"Yeah. Tell me about it."

He'd rather not. They walked abreast towards a pizza place where they sometimes ended up on his weekend visits.

"How was your week?" Ruben asked, forcing himself to be in the moment.

"Yeah. Things are ticking along."

"Schoolwork?"

"Yeah."

Ruben bought them some slices and sodas, and they walked outside into the cold to an adjacent park. The weather was bearable. "Do you want to catch a movie?" he asked as they sat on a park bench.

"Nah, I've got stuff to do later."

"What stuff?" He took in Caleb's body language. His clothes looked new and somewhat pricey for a foster kid growing up on this side of town.

"Just stuff. Weekend stuff."

"Caleb—" This was harder than he thought. He shouldn't

press himself to do this today of all days. But he didn't have time to waste. "I know foster homes are tricky. If there's something going on that you know isn't right, you'll tell me? Or someone? Right?"

"Nothing's going on there, boss." The boy replied too fast and shifted in his seat. "Nothing like what you're implying."

"I get you don't want to talk to me, but I want you to know that I'm here."

"Yeah. For now. It doesn't matter. I'm getting out of this fucked-up system as soon as I can, and things are looking up."

Ruben hitched his eyebrows. "In what way?"

Caleb shoved the last bite of his pepperoni pizza in his mouth with a shrug. "It's all good. Thanks for the grub." He stood and tossed his paper plate into a nearby bin.

Ruben stared at his own wilted slice. He didn't have the stomach for it and hadn't even taken a bite. "You want some more? I'm not hungry."

"Nah. Thanks. I gotta get going." Caleb didn't look him in the eye. "I've got a study group this afternoon."

Study group? Yeah, right. And this boy declining more pizza was a sure sign something was very off.

"Study group like a girlfriend?"

Caleb grimaced and stalked off but allowed him to catch up. "Girlfriends just cost money."

"You got yourself a job then?"

"You could say so."

"Why don't you just tell me the truth? I'm not going to interfere—"

"Not off the bat, you won't."

"You're dealing? You know that shit is the one thing I won't tolerate, and I won't turn a blind eye. I can't."

"No, sir. It's all good, a cop like you don't need to worry."

They'd reached the corner where they'd go their separate ways, Caleb home and Ruben to the subway.

Caleb held out his hand. "Not sure if I'll see you again before you head off to Paris. I'm kinda busy."

Ruben stared at him. Kinda busy? But with what? "Okay." He shook hands with Caleb, knowing he'd have to alert someone about this red flag waving like mad. "I'll keep you posted." And if Paris turned out to be another long stint, Caleb needed another mentor and maybe more than a social worker check-in. He watched as the boy sauntered home, kicking a discarded coffee cup off the curb. Never too young to get into serious trouble.

Ruben descended the stairs to the subway, wanting only to go home.

Never too young to remember. He grappled with the thought as he took the subway home, the warm rocking of the train weirdly comforting in the shock of it all.

His body had it all archived.

He didn't need to dig too deep to come up with a list of perpetrators. These things mostly happened close to home, in secrecy, behind closed doors. His mom had died at the fist of a fellow junkie who'd supposedly loved her. She hadn't had a parade of losers he had to pick the fucker from. There had only been one abuser in her life.

With his granny long dead, there was nobody to ask, except the dickhead still in prison, locked up for life. He clenched the railing tighter as his stomach turned. The heated bodies of his fellow commuters cornered him into one dead-end thought.

His mom had died trying to protect him from this predator.

He wasn't speculating; he'd come full circle. Seemed one was never too old to be hit in the face by solid truth.

38

MARLÈNE

Marlène sent Olivia, the editor-in-chief at the magazine, a desperate message on Sunday night asking if she could be back at work on Monday morning. One more day in isolation, cornered in her apartment, would drive her mad and the siren's call Bryce had warned her about would become a deafening screech.

After Saturday's disaster with Ruben, the loneliness of being without him had pressed down on her, and the quiet became unbearable. The quickest way to a cure was to go back to work.

Her withdrawal symptoms had trickled down to an occasional tremor and hot flush, and although she was still tired, nothing was worse than her head's incessant churning. She had to stay busy and stay miles away from the street corner where dealers hung out at all hours of the day.

Now she was dressed in her work attire, feeling more in charge of her life than she had done in years. It would be hard to keep a firm grip on her recovery, but she'd had Ruben with her for the worst of it. She couldn't be that pathetic and slip back to old habits once he'd moved on. He was only saving her from heartache, but it was too late for that. Funny how in the past she'd medicate all heartache away, but this time, with Ruben, she wanted to carry it for a while, if only to remember how it had felt to be with him, how it felt to be alive.

She headed out into the corridor, the narrow space her only link to him. Over the rest of the weekend, no noises had infiltrated between their shared walls, and she'd thought Ruben might have gone back to Boston to see Bryce. She still had no clue what had transpired on Saturday morning but understood Ruben might not be ready to talk to her, or anybody for that matter, about what was going on in his head. Or heart. Or body. She was one person in the world who could understand that more than anyone else.

As she locked her apartment door, she froze. In her peripheral vision, she saw Ruben coming around the corner with quiet, hasty steps. He froze midstride when he saw her, and shoved his hand into his jeans pocket, furtive, but not fast enough for her not to notice what he held in his hand.

A pill container. That looked like one of hers. She swallowed as a sudden thirst burst into her mouth, the need for water and one of those pills—maybe more than one of those pills—invading her whole being.

No.

She dropped her gaze but his cramped hand's funny shape in his pocket was like a magnet.

"Hey." Ruben took two steps toward her.

Marlène met his gaze and in her, all craving died. He looked as if he'd been to war and back. "Hey."

"Good weekend?"

"No. You?"

"No."

The silence between them stretched with the honesty they'd both put on the table.

"Where're you off to?" Ruben asked.

The Neighbor

As if he had a right to know. "Back to work. Better to be busy there than sit here, wondering what the fuck, you know."

He swallowed. "Saturday was a mess. I'm sorry."

"Yes, it was. Life is a messy business." Marlène let the thought hang and then took two steps, needing to get away from him, his warm body, his overpowering presence that made everything better...everything except this. How did she fall in love with him so hard and fast?

"Marlène—" His voice was edged with a soft plea, but nothing in his stance made her stop, so she walked past him, her heels quiet taps on the floor.

"I need to go, otherwise I'll be late." She didn't wait to hear more, but rushed to the elevator, relief mixed with heartache as the metal doors closed without Ruben coming back into view.

He was letting her go, just like that.

By the time she reached her floor in the office high rise on Greenwich Street, she'd contained her emotions and organized her thoughts. She was in time for their regular Monday morning brief and during the meeting, she sat and soaked up everything that had happened during her time off, as well as things that had to happen this week.

Since she'd worked her butt off to make sure the magazine could manage without her for two weeks, she had time for some side projects, so it came as no surprise when the editor-in-chief asked her to stay behind after the meeting. Once the others had filed out of the boardroom, she stood and moved to sit closer to Olivia.

"And? How are you?" Olivia asked as she closed her laptop screen.

"I'm fine, thank you."

"You had a good break?"

"You could say so."

The older woman searched her face and gave a deep sigh. "Your contract is up for renewal and maybe this isn't the right time for the discussion, and ideally I should've scheduled a meeting with HR present, but I do worry about you outside of work."

Marlène wiped at her brow, herding the anxiety in her chest into a corner, where it could wait. If they didn't renew her contract, she'd make another plan. She wouldn't go back to Paris, not yet. A sabbatical could be on her horizon as a last resort. She needed to solidify her recovery first, give herself a few more months to learn how to cope. "I hope you don't have issues with my work."

"I don't, but we can't skirt around the contents of your suitcase anymore, Marlène. I understand we all have habits, I mean, who here doesn't? But to mule drugs on company flights is the one thing I can't turn a blind eye to."

Heat rose to Marlène's cheeks as she recalled how her boss had stumbled upon her little habit. That day in Paris after Fashion Week, when Olivia, at the eleventh hour, had knocked on her hotel room door. Did Marlène, by any chance, have space in her suitcase for two new pairs of designer heels Olivia couldn't possibly leave behind? Things had dominoed into the rushed opening of a suitcase, the shuffling of items to reveal a bag of pills, not even bottled up, on full display. To save space, Marlène had bagged them up with the plan to split them back into the pill containers she'd hoarded back home. She had to pace her habit, after all, and couldn't dip in and out of a filled bag like it was a bottomless pit.

"I quit drugs," Marlène said. "I'm in recovery now and I promise—" She broke off. She shouldn't make promises when words sounded so empty. "They were for my private use. I had a problem, but it's all behind me now."

"Good. I'm in recovery too and have been for years. I would hate to hook you up for a hit next year at Fashion Week when it all becomes too much, you know?"

Marlène's eyes widened. "I—"

"I understand what you're going through, so I wanted to make it clear that you have my support. If you need anything, give me a call." Olivia dropped her gaze, and when she looked up again, clear honesty shone in her eyes, which were usually so guarded. "Sometimes it's good not to have any secrets between two people." Olivia gave a small smile as she stood. "This is obviously confidential."

"Yes, yes. Of course." Marlène rose from her seat.

"Fiona from HR will be in contact about your renewal. That is, if you were planning to stay?"

"Yes. I love it here."

"Excellent." Olivia picked up her laptop and gathered some other folders she had by her side. Her hands paused as she met Marlène's gaze. "Second chances are sometimes way better than first ones. So, stay strong."

"Thank you."

Marlène watched her walk out of the boardroom, relief washing through her. She wouldn't be going home soon. If she could stay clean, she'd never be going home. She was going to miss out on so much, things she already missed out on and that hurt—Vianne's girls growing up, Anaïs's own little ones who would be on the way as soon as her wedding vows were said. She'd be so far away, watching from a distance.

She picked up her laptop and walked to her desk, her steps going from brisk with good news to hesitant, as Olivia's words sank in. *I would hate to hook you up for a hit when it all becomes too much.*

Ruben. With one of her pill containers. She'd thought he'd flushed the whole lot while she was in deepest withdrawal, but now she wasn't so sure. What if he'd hidden them somewhere in his car or mailbox? There were many nooks and crannies. For all she knew he had a storage space and had access to all of it for when *things became too much.*

Whatever had happened on Saturday, something had been

too much. She reached for her phone, but she didn't have his number. How did that happen?

Her stomach was knotted by lunchtime, and she couldn't pretend anymore. She sent a quick email to Olivia, asking if she could go home early as she wasn't feeling great. At least her boss, after their conversation earlier, didn't protest and let her go.

By the time Marlène reached her apartment building, worry had eaten chunks out of her. Bryce and his warnings rang in her ear all the way home as images of Ruben's face, how he looked that morning and on Saturday, flashed in her mind's eye.

She padded down the corridor, hesitant now that the moment was upon her. What would she do if he'd taken something? Overdosed? Who knew what a few of those pills could do to someone who'd never taken anything stronger than unscheduled pain medication? When she reached his door, her breathing stalled. A sliver of light shone into the corridor, the door standing ajar. She bit down on her lip and pushed it open with a fingertip. No noise came from the inside; it was eerily quiet.

Marlène stepped into the apartment, where everything looked as it had before. The earthy scent of Ruben's morning coffee still hung in the air. The living room, his dining table, the windows screened with blinds against the grey November light, all looked the same. On his desk, his monitors were lit up and his laptop stood open. His chair stood swiveled toward her as if he'd stood and left his desk only moments ago.

Her pill container waited next to the keyboard, so innocent. Her hand burned to reach for it, but...*Ruben*.

She should go look for him in the kitchen, or his bedroom, but her gaze jumped from the pill container to the monitors, hovering over the images as unease fanned out inside her. She stood closer, zooming in, then took two more steps as the images became clearer. Her gaze flitted over the screens as her arm, which clutched her purse and laptop bag, weakened its grip. Everything slipped in slow motion to the floor as she sank into his chair, unable to peel her gaze away from the images. Her breath caught as a sudden chill prickled through her. With trembling fingers, she gathered her coat's lapels, trying to cover up her body.

She was staring at herself. In photos she'd never seen before.

A toilet flushed. A faucet ran and stopped. A door opened.

She couldn't turn. She couldn't stand. She could hardly breathe.

"Marlène." Ruben's footsteps came short and quick. "What are you doing here?"

"Your door was open. I was worried—" She swallowed but her throat jammed with every emotion the images vomited up. It was all bile, green and sour, pushed up by fear. Tremors ran through her with the shockwaves that came down on her. She couldn't peel her gaze from the monitor. "What are *you* doing here? With this? These photos? Of *me*?"

39

RUBEN

He should've known she wouldn't be able to stay away. This morning, when she'd seen him with her pill container, he should've aborted this venture. He'd only wanted to get the doctor's name and address on the script sticker, to see if he could track down a possible family connection. He recalled the name but wasn't sure of the spelling and needed the container's label to double check. What had seemed like a good idea at the time, and a way forward, had backfired, the bullets hitting Marlène in places he couldn't even begin to imagine.

Maybe this had been his fucked-up way to bring things to a head, but this wasn't how he'd wanted it to happen. Marlène sat frozen at his desk, her body trembling. Ruben leaned over her and closed his laptop screen, but when he reached for the nearest monitor to switch it off, she swatted at his hand. "No."

She shrank away in horror as the slap sounded through the quiet of the apartment, and when she glanced up at him, her eyes flashed naked fear.

No...please, no. He couldn't let her be frightened of him. For someone who knew what she'd been through, he'd messed up badly. Seeing those photos in his apartment, a safe zone for her, could cause a domino effect towards an entire range of raw emotions.

"This isn't what you think—" he started.

"Where did you get these? Why?" Her voice broke and he rested a hand on her shoulder, warm and gentle, but she pushed against the desk and rolled away from him.

If she weren't so stunned, she would realize he had drilled down deep into the dark web, but she was no longer looking at the monitors or at him. She'd gone deathly pale.

"Where, Ruben? Tell me."

He'd been in many awkward, horrible, and often inhumane situations, but nothing had prepared him for this. At least before, where he'd straddled two roles, that of policeman and first responder at a site of trauma, he'd had his armor and his training that kicked in. Those two things helped him stay objective and keep his emotional distance, but with Marlène it was too late. He had no armor and his training seemed to have evaporated. He defaulted to being a mere human with nothing more than a mountain of feelings for her that he had no right to have in the first place.

"They're on the internet, Marlène. I—"

She shot up from the office chair and took a step toward him, a finger pointed at his chest. "You look at this stuff? You're one of them! You lowlife, perverted asshole!" She was going at him now, punching his chest, the rage bouncing off her, but he caught her wrists before she could get in one good hit. Marlène squirmed but he held her firmly, struggling to find the words that would calm her down. She was comparing him to those perverts who'd done this to her? His stomach roiled.

"Was this what you saw in your head when you were with me? You pictured me like that?" she bit out. "While you *fucked* me?"

"No," he groaned. "And we didn't *fuck*, as you well know." Or should know. The chasm between them widened but he could blame nobody but himself.

Marlène tried to kick him now, but her tight pencil skirt prevented her from getting in a good swing, and he had her in such a strong, firm grip, she floundered like a fish out of water. Her arms tensed against his chest where he'd gathered her wrists at his sternum, twisting her palms to her face so she could only scratch herself. "Don't, please," he said, trying to keep his voice level. "Let me explain. It's not what you think—"

"Liar!" Her voice was laced with unspent anger, and he couldn't loosen his grip. Not yet. She strained again, giving it her all as she rocked into him, immobile since he'd forced a leg between hers to lock her one ankle behind his.

"Stop. Marlène. You're only going to hurt yourself and I can't bear any more of that." He bit down on his distress at having her like this, so close and yet so far. "Please, sweetheart, you're only going to hurt yourself and I can't let you hurt yourself again and again."

She clenched her fingers into claws, but her eyes closed at his last words, and she pressed her lips tight as if she could stop the sob that ripped through her. "You're so strong. Men are always so freaking strong," she whispered on a swallow.

"And fighting doesn't help. It only hurts more," he murmured. "And some of them thrive on it and want to hurt you. It's messed up, I know. I'm not one of them, Marlène. Please."

Eventually her fists relaxed, and she dropped her face into her hands, hiding. As the fight drained out of her, her body drooped against his. For a long moment he let her catch her breath, burning to hug her close, burning to go back and fix everything right from that first night she'd stumbled over him, but it was no use. It was impossible to erase memories. His own uncovered truth only underlined how futile it was.

Ruben made sure she could stand if he let her go. "Here,

come sit down." He helped Marlène to the sofa, feeling like a piece of shit. "I'm sorry," he murmured. "You're in shock."

He went on his haunches in front of her and fingered her hair from her cheek to tuck it behind her ear. She flinched at the caress, and he suppressed a groan. She didn't want to be touched and he of all people should respect that.

He reached for the extra blanket he'd slept under while she was still under his watch and wrapped it over her. "I'll make some tea."

As he walked past his desk, he switched off all the monitors, but it was too late. What had been seen, couldn't be unseen.

While in the kitchen, he kept an eye on her. She didn't stir except to kick off her shoes and hug her legs to her chest, dropping her forehead to her knees. She'd made herself as small as she could and he sighed, still unsure of how to handle this situation. He took the tea and placed it on a side table. For a moment he hesitated, then he perched on the coffee table in front of her. Honesty was the best policy and the only way out of this mess. Maybe he should have gone down that route from the start.

"I work for Interpol, Marlène," he started. He couldn't care less about his NDA or anything else. She deserved to hear the whole truth. He'd be happy if Marc let him go, to be honest, on this technicality. How was he going to go back to France after this weekend in any case? "I've been working with the team in Paris for the past nine months. We're trying to crack a child exploitation ring in Europe." He bit back on his own emotions and the fact that this endeavor had become fiercely personal over the weekend.

"It's me in those photos," she whimpered into her knees, keeping her face hidden.

"I know."

She glanced up, her gaze awash with anguish. "How? Where? I've never seen those photos before."

He'd been an idiot. Never mind Marlène being barely done with withdrawal and seeing him with her pills—he should have known her first day back at the office might not work out. To do this at home, when he'd cut her a key and told her to walk in any time uninvited. His office in Paris was behind several layers of security. But he wasn't at work. He'd gone on the dark web to find these images like any other fucking pedophile on the prowl. It hadn't taken him long; he'd known, after all, where to look. "I never meant for you to see those photos. Not like this."

"*No one* is supposed to see those photos," she murmured, face still hidden.

"They're being traded on the dark web."

"What?" Her whisper was so soft, he hardly heard her.

"Someone dumped them on a site we've been surveilling, but they were too old to give us any relevant clues as to who the perpetrators were or where the location could have been, or anything for that matter." Except those tattoos, a dead giveaway if they could find the girl whose back got inked in the afternoon light, for in the photos, sunlight beamed on her pale skin, the dark dots punctuation marks of torture.

"There're more?" For a second, she glanced at the dead monitor to see if the images were still there.

He nodded. "Yes." *You know there are.*

Silent tears streamed down her cheeks. "How many more?"

In general, probably millions. "Of you?"

"Yes."

Enough to document everything that happened to her as a child. "There's no telling. This was on one particular site."

"Please be honest with me."

"There are collections, Marlène. Different ages, the last ones are where you're being tattooed—" He broke off, the moment on him now. "I'm not sure how much you recall." He didn't want to go there, but how else? He needed Graham, but it was too late. Graham was stumped too. How did he do this? Here he was, a guy who recalled nothing from his own childhood abuse, in front of a woman whose every assault was captured in black and white. She *must* recall.

Marlène didn't move. She'd gone deadly still, but she clenched the blanket tighter and her knuckles turned white with strain. He didn't know what to do, how to help her in this moment of cold realization. Just like him on Saturday morning, she might want to run and hide from the world. It was one thing to live with a past, but to have it shoved in your face as an adult, out of the blue, knowing it was out there for anyone to see? He couldn't imagine what was going on in her head.

Eventually she unfurled, opening like a butterfly from her tight blanket cocoon as it slipped from her shoulders. She lowered her legs and stood abruptly, and he leaned back in surprise. Her legs brushed against his, but she moved fast, stepping to the side and collecting her things on the floor. "I've got to go."

He reached for her, his fingers stopping short of touching her. This was a bad idea. Fuck. He should've had her...what? Tied down, locked up, handcuffed?

"Marlène."

She didn't look at him. She evaded his eyes at all costs. "I can't."

"Marlène." He begged now as he glanced at his desk. The pill container, with its scant information, led him to over two hundred doctors with the name Phillipe Toussaint. He couldn't decipher much from the French websites and had gone to the dark web to see if he could trace anything there, but he'd been drawing a blank all morning. And then she'd arrived.

He didn't help her through withdrawal just to dunk her back into it, only this time even deeper. "Don't do anything you'll regret."

"Regret is par for the course, don't you think?" she whispered. "At least I've earned all my regrets. You're just another one."

She walked out of the apartment without looking back. His door clicked closed with a finality that cut through him, slick and clean.

40

MARLÈNE

Marlène closed her apartment door and pressed against it for a moment. One half of her wanted Ruben to stay well away. The other half pleaded for him to come beat down her door and excavate everything in her and imagined being emptied out once and for all.

Nobody knocked and the silence stretched from the corridor.

All she wanted was to collapse, but she should at least make it to her bed. She closed her eyes only to have visuals of those photos flash in her mind, the rhythmic clicking of a camera shutter adding a sickening beat to the stream.

Ruben had asked how much she'd recalled.

She recalled every moment. Every summer at the family's vacation home on the French Riviera. Her parents coming and going. Her mom leaving for modeling shoots. Her dad going back to Paris for a medical emergency. The local babysitter too young and more interested in her own summer dalliances. Random people, visiting, staying a few days, a constant flow of other family members, their partners, and friends.

She recalled *every* moment. Every time the shutter sounded with its satisfying click-click-click. Every shift of the photographer's feet. Every soft instruction. Every single time it had happened, quietly stitching together the monster that lived in her. A Frankenstein of her own making.

Inside her, that shadow stole half the air she breathed, listened in on every conversation, voiced her opinion, climbed in bed with her at night, and touched her lovers with ghostly fingers, claiming her fair share. She lived here, inside of her, in a cave nobody knew about.

Nobody except *him*. And *her*. Their friends. *Them*.

And now Ruben.

It was one thing to have your secrets buried inside, where no one could see them. To have the privilege of time to consider sharing them with someone else. To wait, to build trust, to finally crack open a tiny bit of herself so that he, the one trusted person in the world, could take a glimpse into her deepest, darkest crevice.

It was a whole other matter having your secrets laid out on a platter, for the world to pick from, a buffet really, of which Ruben seemed to have sampled every dish. *Collections* of her, which he'd seen? All of them?

Ruben had trespassed into a part of her she allowed nobody to see. Absolutely nobody.

Her shame swelled so thick she could hardly breathe. Her plan had always been to sketch a stick figure of the truth, but he'd seen layers of photos of her, each fleshing out her past. He'd met the monster without her even knowing.

Ruben had rushed away from her on Saturday morning, and now she could never look him in the eye again. If she did, his gaze would mirror back this knowledge of her, remind her of everything she only wanted to forget.

A landslide couldn't cover up her shame. Those photos

showed her naked body, on open display for any pervert hunting on the internet. Nobody would recognize her. Nobody except Ruben, who knew everything. Her willingness. Her participation. Her eagerness to please towards the end. It would all be there.

This must be why he'd walked out on her on Saturday morning. He couldn't contain his disgust. No honorable man with a lick of self-respect would want to be with her. Not once he knew the full truth like Ruben did.

Marlène peeled from the door and stumbled to the bathroom, her heels thudding.

Click-click-click.

She made it to the toilet in time and fell to her knees in front of the bowl, but nothing came up. The nausea just sat in her throat, sour and mean. She couldn't cleanse herself with a little bout of vomit. *Nothing* could cleanse her.

For two decades she'd tried to outrun her past. It always caught up. She was so tired of running, but there was no chance of taking a breather in this game. The thought left her cold and shivering, with the well-oiled need to numb every feeling in her mounting. She'd do anything to dial down this shameful anxiety, to avoid reliving every regret in full color. She'd take anything to return to life in black and white.

Why had she hurried home from work?

Ruben. With her pills.

Her fear and worry over him.

He had her drugs but had obviously not taken any. She could wrestle him for it, but he would win. Ruben was so freaking strong. Plus, it would involve looking him in the eye.

The guy on the street corner would be there. She might have passed him on her way home.

Marlène sat straight. Her wallet burned with two hundred dollars of cold hard cash. She had no clue what that would buy her. A pity the dealer wouldn't take a credit card. Money wasn't the issue, but her mind and body couldn't wait now for her to go draw more bills.

It was high time she learned how the rest of the world functioned.

She got up, her legs still weak, but every cell in her was swept up in this riot, propelling her into motion. Purse in hand, she opened the door, somewhat heady with the prospect of something that would numb her. As she stepped out of her apartment, someone moved in her peripheral vision.

Ruben leaned against the wall by his door, waiting. "Don't even think about it."

She should have expected this. Ruben, after all, knew everything about her. He had her cornered, reigning over her with his illicit knowledge.

"The drugs you get on the street are so far removed from the pure opioids you're used to." Ruben took a tentative step in her direction. "It's poison and will kill you if the dose doesn't."

Her hand stilled on the doorknob, her fingers clutching her key.

"Look at me, Marlène."

She couldn't. He came closer and she had nowhere to go, except back into her apartment.

"Can you please just look at me." He kept his distance now, but in the small space of this corridor and their two apartment doors, it was as if they were boxed in a stuck elevator. "I only want to talk to you." Two steps and he was there, his hand on her face, lifting her chin up, forcing her to turn and look at him.

His touch was so gentle. So soft. So warm.

She hated him.

Marlène pressed her hand against his chest to push him away, but he covered it with his other hand, over the frantic beating of his heart. "You need to understand. If I'd known you were the girl in the photos, I would never have taken things with us as far as I had on Friday night."

Yes. She hated him. Love and hate were two sides of the same coin, but how had it flipped so quickly? She hated herself because he still smelled of comfort and safety, with his shirt so soft against her palm, and his careful hold radiating heat to her arms. His voice was the same one that spoke to her through every dehumanizing withdrawal symptom, always patient, always caring. Every little thing of Ruben she associated with a safe haven, not this nightmare from her past.

"When did you know it was me?" she whispered, unwilling to meet his gaze.

"I suspected from the first Friday night."

"How?"

"I've been studying those photos for months, on and off. Searching for clues and links. Trying to find a connection and drill down deeper to figure out who did this to you. You wore a tank top that Friday night and your back, with your moles, jumped out at me." He swallowed hard as he curled his fingers around hers, pressing their gathered hands to his sternum. "The eye sees what it wants to see. And coming off the flight from Paris, still in a haze from the fuck-up at work and our inability to crack this ring...I don't know." He swallowed desperately. "Please. Just look at me."

She lifted her eyes to his and was startled at the intensity in his stare.

"You do understand I want to find the bastards who did this to you and lock him up for life, right?"

This was going to hurt. So, so much.

"Because you're so freaking good, right?" She tugged her hand away from his and stepped to the side. "You have trespassed into every last part of me, and you had no right."

"Marlène—"

"No! You don't understand. You have trespassed into my life, into my body, and into my heart, and you had no right to do so without asking me first."

"And how do you think I should've asked you? When chances were one in a million?" Ruben raked his fingers through his hair with a groan. "I wasn't sure. How could I be? None of those photos show your face from the front. And you're not the dark-haired girl in those photos anymore, Marlène. You're a woman."

And a fake blonde.

"A beautiful, gorgeous woman."

How could he still see her like this? "I might be a woman, but half of me will always be that girl, who did those things."

"You were coerced, Marlène. Abused. Exploited."

A quiet moment passed as his words filled the space around them.

"Was I? That's what you think?" She managed a cackle, in wonder as it sprouted so naturally out of her belly. "Bryce was right to tell you to stay the fuck away from me. You might be a good little boy, Ruben Scott, but I was a very bad, very naughty little girl. We really shouldn't mix."

Her words were a slap to the face, and she took his moment of shock to stride past him.

She made it to the elevator, got in and harassed the button for the first floor. Ruben rushed up but paused a good yard from the elevator, choosing not to step in.

"Trespasser," she whispered.

He shook his head. "If you cave in now, you'll only stay trapped by what they've done to you. Don't cave in, Marlène, not now, not this minute. Cave in tomorrow."

If she could only hold out until the next minute, the next hour, until tomorrow, she might have the strength to resist her cravings and come out stronger on the other side, but right now she didn't want to. She just couldn't.

She turned away from the distress in his gaze, the desperation in his voice. The doors whooshed shut, but in the quiet mechanics of her descent, his voice still rang in her ears.

You're only going to hurt yourself and I can't bear any more of that.

Yes. She hated Ruben Scott, for his words rang true. She was only hurting herself. The thought hammered in her head all the way to the first floor.

41

MARLÈNE

Marlène had escaped her apartment and she'd escaped Ruben, but as her heels clattered along the ever-busier sidewalk, the weight inside her pressed heavier. Her footsteps shrank until she came to a standstill at a red light.

Once she'd crossed this intersection, she'd be within arm's reach of the one thing that numbed every emotion known to man.

As she waited for the light to turn green, her phone vibrated in her coat pocket. It couldn't be Ruben. She didn't want to speak to anybody and pulled the phone out to kill the call.

Damien.

Again.

She'd been ignoring his calls for months now, probably almost half a year. *Maybe you should block him,* Ruben's voice whispered in her head. As she stared at the screen, the people around her crossed the road. She'd frozen in space and time. Blocking this number wasn't going to wipe away her past. Crossing this road would lead in only one direction, one with no return. Answering this call would lead in the very same direction. Both would lead her back to the space where she'd lived in a fogged-up glass cube, unable to see into life beyond. She'd be granted only glimpses of what could be for a few moments, when she cleared the fog with a trembling hand, only to block the visuals with her own breath again.

The phone stopped ringing and she slowly pocketed it, still hesitant. The light turned red and cars sped by as fellow pedestrians crowded around her. When she could cross again, a steady stream of people flowed past, bumping her with elbows and muttering their apologies, but she could only breathe through the seconds where everything balanced on a pinpoint. All directions seemed to tumble back into a fogged-up abyss.

"Which way are you going?"

Ruben's soft question seemed to come from afar. Damien and drugs were woven into her past where she could live out her life. Ruben asked her to look to the future. "I'm not sure," she said. She wasn't. Maybe she'd stand here forever, making no decisions at all.

"Whichever way you go, let me walk with you."

She closed her eyes for a moment, and when she opened them again, she glanced at his feet. He wasn't an apparition then, for his loafers stood firmly on the sidewalk next to her. "Why?"

"I want you to be safe...and make sure you don't overdose."

God. To overdose would be such a quick exit to all of this.

But Ruben... For all his knowledge of her, for all that she hated him, he still cared. He must be a guardian angel. Sent by the devil. That sounded about right. She swallowed, and as the light turned green, she stepped off the curb but changed direction to walk an extra block. "To Central Park." Away from the corner and the dealer and Damien and every morsel that fed the monster.

They walked abreast toward the nearest park entrance. Fall had immersed the park in yellows and oranges, spotted with brown and red. It was beautiful, and for a sweet second, she was so grateful to be here, to witness this beauty before nature bowed out from the stage until spring lured it back to the spotlight.

They took to the path that led around the pond, and for a long while they walked, almost companionably, in silence.

"Marlène—"

"Don't ask me who it was. Please. I can't tell you." This was what Ruben wanted. A name.

"Why?"

"Because it's a promise I can't break." Except with those photos out in the world, it could be that promises made to her were broken too. The thought made her stall. She hadn't had time to think about anything beyond the shock of this afternoon. Those photos were meant to be for him, and for her, for *them*, and *them* alone. How on earth did they end up on the internet? *Traded* on the internet? She collapsed onto an empty park bench, its cold surface reaching through her coat to spread deep into her core. Her world was collapsing, a house of cards meant to keep her sisters safe.

Ruben sat down next to her and clenched his hands on his thighs. "Can you tell me how it started?"

"No." She hesitated. She could give him this. "I don't know how it started." But she did. "The photos I recall. That started when she came into the picture. But the rest, no. I don't know. It was always there. This thing between him and me. I was taught that it was normal, until I was old enough to understand that it wasn't." She shook her head now, as if she could shake the memory. "I can't even recall ever being a virgin."

Ruben's fists trembled, but it could just be the cold. "Too young to remember," he murmured.

"Yes."

"Me too." He unfurled his fingers and rubbed his hands down his thighs.

"What?" She glanced at him, at the strain cupping his mouth, his gaze so far off. Surely she hadn't heard right.

"Me too," he whispered. "I was also abused when I was too young to remember. By my mom's boyfriend."

"Oh God." She wanted to reach for his hand, where his fingers dug into his thighs, but she stopped short. When she'd realized he'd been triggered, she'd known it was abuse, but not like this. Not like her. Too young to remember when it had started. "I'm so sorry."

"Yeah. Who knew? How many of us do you think there are?"

Millions. She didn't answer but clasped her hand over one of his and he stopped tearing at his jeans. He was so cold. "You're hurting yourself."

"Better than beating something up, don't you think?" He turned his hand in hers and their fingers slipped into a soft embrace. *You're only going to hurt yourself and I can't bear any more of that.*

They were one, an echo seeming to call back at each other.

"You think this is why you have those anger outbursts?"

"Maybe. Who knows? Maybe I can learn more with the support of a therapist. Not sure if I want to, though."

"Good luck with that." Talking was, after all, the reason why she avoided rehab. But this was something else. His hold was tender yet firm, as if he were clinging to her for support and not the other way around. Here was someone who needed her maybe as much as she needed him.

By the time he spoke again, it was growing dark. "How did it end?" he asked.

Ruben thought it had ended. Couldn't he see that, in her, it was a non-stop reel?

"I grew breasts and started menstruating." And she'd met Damien. Whether it was by pure fluke that Damien, after their initial acquaintance over that summer, had started at the same high school as her that fall, or whether he got shoved onto the stage by some director who manipulated them all, it had been as if he'd been picked for *her*. Ready. Eager. And with tattoos like her own. Instead of talking about what had happened to them, they'd chosen to feed off each other's needs for years, stumbling blindly into the underworld of desire and into addiction. No wonder she couldn't pick up the phone when Damien called.

"You said the photos started with *her*? What did they threaten you with to keep you quiet?"

"It isn't that simple."

"No?"

"The sexual aspect was one thing, but the photos were another. It started innocently enough, with me playing at being a model like my mom. My mom didn't want me near anything like that, none of us. She wanted all three of us to be as far away from modeling as humanly possible. But he—she—" She retracted her hand and pushed it into her coat pocket. "They always knew how to play me. It was our little secret, you see. The photos changed over time." Until there was no turning back. "My mom would've been furious with me for doing something she forbade, and I thought she would send me away. I was terrified I'd never see my family again."

"How old were you?"

"I don't know. Five? Six? Everything escalated later when I realized they were looking beyond me. To my sisters." A tear chilled as it ran its course down her cheek. "By then I understood how it would hurt them, and it was wrong, and it was sick. I also understood they would never touch my sisters, over my dead body. I went to him and his partner before they could go to my sisters. So you see, I'm as complicit as the woman who took the photos, as all the men I allowed to have me. We were in an agreement of sorts."

"Over what?"

"That I'd never tell anybody. And they could do as they

The Neighbor

pleased with me, as long as they and their kind stayed away from my sisters." And they *had* stayed away from her sisters, because she'd finally reached an age where she could look after them herself. No more distracted babysitters. No more afternoon naps when people had been left to their own devices. Only locked doors whenever he'd been there, with his fiancée and their fucked-up friends.

"Signed in ink."

"What do you mean?" Marlène shot him a side glance. "Signed in ink?"

"The tattoo on your back. It's Andromeda, the Chained Maiden."

Prickles spread over her skin, small fireworks bursting, burning. "The Chained Maiden?" Marlène repeated. "Andromeda?"

"It's a star constellation and in Greek mythology?"

"Really?" She shook her head in denial, because she'd never understood the tattoo or what it had meant. "No, it meant nothing. How could it mean anything?" She'd been too young and never asked questions. It had been safer that way.

"You didn't know that they were making a specific mark?" Ruben asked, his voice strained.

"No. How? I never knew what they did. I didn't see. I only felt what they did on the outside. I—" There was no way to explain to him how dead she'd been inside at that time in her life. "How do you know?"

"This is one of the things we do at work. We decipher things and look for clues. Make connections to all those dots."

"God." The old dread swelled in her again, unwelcome, unstoppable. "I never thought there was a meaning to any of it. They told me nothing." She bit her bottom lip as she clenched her fists, her nails cutting into her palms where she hid them from Ruben in her coat's pockets. *Chained to them...to her. In ink.* Sometimes, she still felt the piercing of her skin, the ink burning like a match just after it was blown out, the flame gone, but the scorching heat still there.

With brutal mental force, she pushed back the emotions wrecking her inside. "There's no more ink on my skin." And all deals are off. "But please, Ruben. Don't push. I won't talk."

"And yet, those photos of you are all over the internet."

She dug her nails deeper into her palms. She'd unpack her feelings about that tomorrow. For the rest of her life. The internet was forever and her only saving grace was that she no longer looked like that little girl. She was indeed a woman—a woman who took charge of her life, when she wasn't numbed by drugs or feigning being alive through a rampant sex addiction.

"Yes. It would seem so." She did after all see those photos on his monitor with her own eyes. Otherwise she wouldn't have believed him.

"What do you think happened that someone started posting those photos on the internet?" Ruben said. "The first collections appeared when I started working at Interpol at the beginning of the year."

To think those images of her were out for so long already, maybe even longer. What did it help to keep the monster inside, if other people allowed it to sneak out by the back door?

"I don't know," she said. "A relationship gone sour? More likely blackmail? You should know better than me."

"Are they breaking their promise to you?"

"Ruben."

"I only need a name. One name will do."

"Yes. You might only need one name. But think, Ruben, *you* might not need more from me, but it doesn't stop with a name. It *starts* with a name. A court case will follow and will demand so much more. It will demand everything." Marlène closed her eyes for a moment and breathed. "This will tear my family apart. I haven't given up everything to have my family shredded by this."

"It's a family relation then."

Weren't they always? Someone close? She didn't answer him. The territory was too tricky, the slide too slippery to deal with right now. She got up, cold to the bone. Ruben stood too, and in the dark, she glanced up at him. His eyes shone like marbles in the lamplight that didn't quite circle into their corner. She shook her head and turned away.

His footsteps fell in next to hers. "You think you're the only one? You might have protected your sisters, Marlène, but you understand there are more?"

This thought didn't catch her off guard but hearing it in his quiet voice made shudders rush down her spine. "No. I know I'm not the only one."

"And what if they're still doing this? To other girls?"

"And boys."

"Oh, for fuck's sake. Can't you see what I'm really asking is for you to stop this? To help prevent other young children from going through abuse like you did?"

"You don't know what you're asking."

"I'm asking for a name," he hissed.

"No. You're asking me to unearth everything I've been trying to forget for the past twenty years. You are asking me to let the monster out when all I know is how to keep it locked in."

"You should let it out and set yourself free in the process. Unchain yourself, at last."

She stopped midstride. "You don't understand. You don't recall the details of your own abuse, do you?" She finally stared back at him, sure she had him there.

"No. The details aren't surfacing."

"Well, go on your knees tonight and thank whoever it is you pray to."

"Marlène."

She walked off, not waiting for him to follow, but he caught up with her in two steps.

Her feet were killing her. She'd walked too far in her heels today. Stupid heels. Women were bound in so many ways. The pain was welcome though because it distracted her from the physical pain of sawing through the last inches binding them together. She needed to cut through the chains and let Ruben Scott go.

When she next stopped under a lamp's umbrella light, she met his gaze. "You must understand, Ruben, *he* isn't all bad. *He* has so much good in him too." As for *her*—

"Good that levels *this*? He must be a miracle worker for you to stand up for him like this."

"He is. In his own way. In his own fucked-up way." She pressed her hand on his chest, to put an arm's length between them.

"But beyond all that, it's more. It's more than a name. It's more than the court cases that would follow, whether the case is heard in a closed court or not. It's more than dragging my family's name and his through the mud." This was going to hurt, so, so much. "Can't you see? You're asking to use me. Like everybody else. Just on the good side of the coin. I've been a means to an end from day one. First for him. Then for them. And now, for you. I'm done being used."

She pushed at his chest, and he stumbled back with the little force, probably more from the horror of her words as they sank in than from the slight pressure or her hand. His expression told her more than a thousand words ever could.

"You allowed them to do whatever they wanted to protect your sisters. Marlène, you have nothing to be ashamed of."

He would never get it, would he? She limped on, one heel blistered, ignoring him. But Ruben was at her side again, reaching for her elbow.

"You haven't forgiven yourself, have you? You haven't

forgiven yourself for taking control of the situation and allowing it to happen to you. For taking part and acting and distracting and forever putting yourself forward to make sure they would be entertained and not look to those you were protecting the most."

"Leave me alone," she sobbed as she shrugged loose, hating the intensity of his words, the look in his eyes. He understood more than anybody ever would. "I don't want to see you ever again." The tears were streaming down her face, and she strode away blindly, only to collide with a police officer who rushed up the path, another following hot on his heels.

"Everything all right here, ma'am?" The officer already had his hand on his gun's grip.

"I'm good. Just tired," she said as she wiped at her cheek.

"No trouble with this man here?"

"No, no trouble, thank you. Don't know him at all. I just want to go home."

"Are you sure?" the officer asked.

Ruben didn't even appear in her line of vision.

"Yes. He just tripped."

The officer nodded and indicated with a hand that he would escort her to the entrance to the park.

Marlène didn't look back. She didn't dare see the look on Ruben's face because her last arrow would have hit the bulls-eye. She was done. She wasn't even going to go home. Chances of bumping into her neighbor there were one hundred percent.

She had dollars to burn, and for once she'd throw money at the problem. Credit card and all.

When she got to the intersection of Fifth Avenue and Fifty-ninth Street, she crossed the road and walked straight into the nearest hotel.

42

RUBEN

On Tuesday evening, Ruben arrived at Graham's practice, defeated. Marlène had not only walked out of Central Park, but out of his life. He couldn't follow her, not with a cop blocking him with a stance and a stare that meant business.

She hadn't come home. He'd waited in vain for her, in their corridor, like the night when they first met. No noises came from next door. No heels clicked on the floor. No beautiful Marlène tumbled into his arms, there where he wanted her the most.

By this morning, he was a wreck. What had she done to herself? He was on the brink of reporting a missing person, before he'd thought at nine to phone the magazine's office, feigning a business call to see if she'd made it to work. The receptionist had put his call through to Marlène's desk phone, indirectly confirming that she'd gone to work. Marlène hadn't picked up the call, and when the line had gone back to the receptionist, she'd confirmed that Marlène was in a quick meeting. He hadn't left a message, instead saying he'd send her an email, but when he'd hung up, he'd collapsed in relief. He couldn't stop his all-consuming worry about her, but she'd meant it when she said she didn't want to see him ever again. She'd moved out, on, and away.

So be it. He hadn't realized that, in the whole fucked-up situation, he'd fallen for her—completely and utterly and irreversibly.

"Ruben?"

He looked up to see Graham trying to get his attention. Two other clients were in the waiting area, and he hadn't noticed them come in. He needed to get a freaking grip on himself.

"This way," Graham said, indicating for him to walk down the short corridor as if this were their first consultation.

He didn't know how to do this. "What now?" Ruben said as he sat down. "I can't do any of this."

Graham got comfortable in his usual seat, and it struck Ruben that he hadn't even bothered to greet his old friend.

"You don't need to do anything you don't want to," Graham said as he picked up his notepad and pen.

For a long moment they sat in silence as Graham waited.

"Do you want to talk about what happened on Saturday?"

Saturday? That was years ago now. His own discovery had been muted by his concern for her.

"She did what she did to protect her sisters. She did whatever *they* wanted so *they* would never look their way. She took all the abuse, went to them to ward them off." Ruben rubbed at his eyes. He was still getting his head around the fact that Marlène's perpetrators were a man and a woman.

"You're talking about your neighbor?"

"Marlène, yes." Who else? "Who does that, at such a young age?"

"An old soul," Graham said. "Someone who loves deeply, unconditionally. Like a parent loves a child. People would go to extremes to protect those they love."

Like his mother. Ruben ran a hand down his face, in wonder at the layers of understanding that were revealing themselves one after the other. As a teenager, he'd thought his anger was fueled by his inner struggles. Once in the foster system, he couldn't come to terms with not being enough for his mom to quit her habit. Over the years and through his work, he'd learned that addiction was too complex, with no simple on-off switch. And yes, people did go to extremes to protect those they loved. In the end, his mom had protected him with her life.

"What are you going to do about the case?" Graham said. "You've spoken to her?"

He couldn't explain to Graham how thoroughly he'd fucked everything up. "It's a mess."

Graham waited for more, but Ruben shifted in his seat, unwilling to reveal how Marlène had come across the photos that made everything come crashing down.

"You're going to go back to Paris and continue with this type of work?" Graham said at last, as if only to break the strained silence.

"I have to go back to Paris. I have to finish this."

"I don't think that's a good idea."

"Nope, but it's cost me too much." He'd also gained too much, learning about himself.

He had to close the loop, for him, for every other child past, present, and future.

"What do you mean it's cost you too much?"

"I'm in love with her. I'm not sure how it happened. Even before the situation imploded. I've never met someone so strong, so unselfish, so brave. With all the sacrifices she's made, I owe this to her, to finish this job." To find the photos' source. "Without her help. I was an idiot to think she would talk."

"She's opened up to you. Understand it was a huge step for her too."

"More like a miracle." Ruben had digested all their conversations over the past weeks and concluded that Marlène had never told a soul.

"Give her time. This was a shock for her too."

"She doesn't want to see me *ever* again." Ruben groaned. "She didn't come home last night, and it freaked me out. I was done."

"But she's okay?"

"I checked her office. She was there." As if nothing had happened. As if his world hadn't fallen to pieces with her leaving. "I've got to let her go, but I've just found her." He couldn't stop his voice from breaking on those last words. His perfect fit. His magic match. His soulmate. He wanted to scream at the whole world, because he'd never been at such a loss.

"I know." Graham put his notepad to the side.

"I could kick myself. When I moved into that apartment, I saw her a couple of times, but never spoke to her. I'm not sure what stopped me. Something about her. If only I'd gotten to know her before all of this—" If he'd known her before Paris, he would've had a reason to stay in New York and wouldn't have taken on a job in Europe. But then, she would never have told him. He would always have had only half of her, the side she allowed herself to show.

"You've got to give her space."

He knew that. There were so many ways he could track her movements, but he wouldn't. Not knowing whether she was safe and staying off the drugs was going to eat him alive. But something in his gut told him Marlène was at work and not sky high. She was done with that shit. The thought was part prayer, part trust, based on the strength and determination she'd demonstrated last night. Yeah, Marlène had stepped two steps forward, and she'd never take one step back again.

"You've spoken to Bryce? About her? Or anything else?"

"No. I need time." He might never tell Bryce. There was no need to put this on Bryce's shoulders too. He had his own load and that was heavy enough.

"When you're ready, I'm here. It will help to talk through it.

Maybe develop some strategies for when you feel your emotions getting the better of you."

"Knowing is enough for now. I don't need details."

"Okay, but if in Paris something trig—"

"Yeah, I understand. You don't think going back is a good idea. I've got time and can still think things through before I need to decide. Either way, I owe Marc a face-to-face conversation." Marlène might not have given him a name, but at least he had *her* name, and the right search would narrow the possible perpetrators down, slowly but surely.

"I'll see you when you come back from Paris?"

"For a beer." He wasn't going to strip his memories naked for the promise of peace. Not yet. He first needed to deal with Paris.

"Sure. Anytime." Graham checked the clock. "We have more time left, if you need it?"

One thing had scratched at his subconscious this whole tumultuous weekend. "What shit do teenagers get up to nowadays?" Ruben sat forward in his seat. "In my day, it was drugs, sex, gangs, and street fights. But nowadays, with the internet and social media, there's too much of it and I can't read a situation."

"You're worried about someone?"

"My Little Brother, Caleb. Something's off and I don't know what."

"That's vague, Ruben, very vague." Graham chuckled. "It's the same things. Drugs, sex, gangs. We both know what goes on out there."

"Yeah." Regret washed through him. "I wish I could be here to rebuild the connection I had with him."

"You will be, and he might need you more in that moment than he does now."

"Stop being such a wise old man." Ruben stood and waited

for Graham to do the same. He was exhausted from yet another sleepless night.

"You do realize we've talked about everybody else, except you?" Graham's hand rested on his shoulder.

Ruben shrugged.

"It's a lot to unpack, but I'm a phone call away."

"Thanks, I know you mean it."

Graham nodded and saw him off at his office door. As Ruben strolled out into the street, he pulled up his coat collar. The air was nippy, and in his daze he'd underdressed. He picked up his pace as he headed towards the subway. It was the tail end of rush hour and people streamed down into the intestinal tract of Manhattan. Bland expressions, harassed steps, most slouching, all avoiding interaction, not even sparing their neighbors a glance.

He'd hate to know how many of them had those secret experiences, suppressed in the mist of time. For all he knew, it was more than half this carriage of sardined humans. Here again he was amongst a herd of people but had never felt more alone in his life.

43

MARLÈNE

Marlène counted the days and then added three more to make sure that Ruben would have left for France. Thanksgiving had come and gone, and the Macy's Thanksgiving Parade had passed right under her hotel window on the south side of Central Park. She'd had a proper bird's eye view of the floats and the childlike happy emotions they evoked had made her feel lighter. For the first time in a very long time, she had something to be eternally grateful for: she was clean.

Almost three weeks had passed since her last conversation with Ruben in Central Park. As she padded down the corridor to her apartment that Saturday morning, a small suitcase in tow with the new clothes she'd bought to avoid going to her apartment, she held her breath. What if she rounded the corner to their doors and he was there, coming out of his apartment?

She wouldn't be able to hold back and keep away from him. She'd missed him too much. Where some part of her had healed, other parts were raw with loss.

Three weeks was a lot of time to digest. Alone at night in her hotel room, there were no distractions. For once, words haunted her more than the need to numb her feelings. For the first time in her life, she slowed down, her mind clear, and for long hours she sat at the window, staring out into Central Park's light-dotted darkness, her gaze following the paths cut by the streetlamps. Her mind wandered through all the ways things had gone wrong and how they could have turned out differently. The past was the past, but she most often lost herself in his final words to her: she hadn't forgiven herself for the choices she'd made.

Ruben had been right. Forgiveness had never been on her radar. Maybe once she forgave herself, she could stop hating herself too. She couldn't change her history, but she could change her future. She'd already started doing so, by getting clean and taking back control.

Forgiveness was going to be her daily affirmation, until she could open the cage and at last drag the monster out. She knew what it would take, and although she wasn't ready now, she would be one day.

Marlène rounded the corner to their apartment doors, her heart in her throat, her pulse a riot. Her steps faltered in front of his door, and she stopped. As she let go of the suitcase, she listened, then turned back and lifted her fist to knock. She wanted to make sure he was gone, but what if he answered the door?

She'd been the queen of pretend, until Ruben turned up on her doorstep. It wasn't even about his work and her connection to that world. On their first Friday night, he'd seen through her withdrawal within an hour of meeting her. Even if they'd met via a blind date, as neighbors, and become acquaintances, friends, and lovers, he would have figured her out. He cared more for others than he did for himself. He cared for *her*. He would have loved her until she'd opened up. And then he would have loved her more.

The thought made a sob rip through her, and her knuckles

came down on the door in dull thuds. No one answered. How badly had she messed this up? She'd pushed him away, telling him she never wanted to see him again when all she wanted was to be with him forever.

With uncertain steps, Marlène continued to her apartment, and as she closed the door behind her, the old fist tightened in her stomach. The place was a bowl full of memories she didn't want to eat her way through. On the coffee table stood the roses Ruben had given her on their date night, now wilted with their petals dried and crisp. The sweetly sour stench of decay filled the room.

She had the weekend to make plans to move on. For all she cared, she'd rent a furnished apartment until she found a new permanent address. By the time Ruben returned from Paris, she'd be long gone.

The next morning, after her triple cream coffee, she went into the apartment block's basement where she had a locker, filled with appliance boxes and other crap that piled up. One night alone in her apartment had brought her lower than three weeks in a hotel room had. She needed to pack and stay busy with moving on or else her bad habits would creep up and consume her again.

As she walked past the line of wire mesh lockers, her eye caught the number next to hers.

Ruben's locker.

That day he'd arrived with a pill container in hand and she'd seen him in the corridor, flashed back at her. She peered through the mesh and there, shoved behind some boxes and a bike, was his suitcase from that first Friday night. Her fingers hooked around the wire as her mouth dried at the thought.

Marlène swallowed. This was so messed up, but that suitcase contained something she still wanted so badly. She rattled the cage door and tested the lock, but both held. Her breathing hitched as she suppressed the violence of her need. She couldn't do this again. She'd been clean for more than a month now and just because he'd left her, didn't mean she could cave in.

She hurried back to her apartment only to find herself en route to a hardware store twenty minutes later to buy a bolt cutter. She'd replace Ruben's lock and leave the new key in his mailbox as a final adieu.

During her years in New York, she'd been at this DIY store a few times and the maze always got to her. Maybe a Sunday morning would be better, but it was the Black Friday weekend and to go for some random shopping was utter madness. She weaved through other customers with carts full of discounted products, and by the time she found her way to the right aisle, her need had diluted. Inching along, eyes fixed, she scanned the shelves, so that by the time she stood next to him, it was too late. Her breathing stalled. He'd already turned in her direction and, as he tossed some pliers into his basket, he looked up and their gazes clashed.

"James." It had been more than two years. God, he looked so well. Tanned, as if he'd just spent weeks on a tropical island. Which he probably had. On honeymoon.

Her ex stared at her, eyes wide. "Marlène." His voice held surprise but not a slice of contempt as she'd always imagined it would.

Imagine seeing you here. Today, of all days. When I need someone like you the most. The words rattled through her head, but they didn't slip off her tongue. Instead, she swayed on her feet, feeling lightheaded for a second.

"You okay?" he asked as he reached for her shoulder.

She stilled under his touch. "I will be." She closed her eyes and bit down the swell of emotion in her. That he would touch her. Would he still if he knew?

"You didn't have breakfast, did you?" He squeezed her shoulder. "You look like you need to sit down. Come."

He knew her so well, except that he didn't.

James guided her out of the hardware store, discarding his basket along the way. "You should have more than a coffee before you head out shopping," he said as he held the door to a breakfast diner open for her.

"You don't need to do this. Really." James had always spent time in New York for work and had bought an apartment here after their break-up. That much she'd known. How bizarre that they'd lived in this city together for so long, and they'd never bumped into each other. The last time she'd seen him had been that night at the club in Paris with his sister, Stacey. Being in cahoots with Damien that night, and luring Stacey—someone she should have protected—to a swingers club, had been one of her last burning regrets that fueled her escape to New York.

James's lawyers had dealt with her and their Paris apartment and yet here he was, treating her with such compassion. In her current mental state, he would have her weeping in no time.

"Sit." James pulled out a chair for her and shrugged off his coat. "I know how much you hate DIY stores and tackling them on an empty stomach is a bad idea."

She clutched her hands together under the table, too cold to take off her coat, as the shock of seeing him settled into her bones.

"How is Stacey?" she asked, finally meeting his gaze again. "I lost contact with her after Paris." One of her many regrets.

For a moment, James dropped his gaze. He stared at the menu printed on a sheet that doubled as a tablecloth. His hands rested on the table, a titanium wedding band on his ring finger.

"Stacey is doing great." He looked up with an honest smile.

"She's living in Vancouver with her fiancé and working at some start-up."

"She's engaged?"

"To a doctor. He's doing research at UBC."

The waiter paused at their table, long enough for James to give a quick order for two egg and bacon breakfasts and some orange juice; long enough to let it sink in that she was sitting with him, her ex, in a diner, and that he was going to have breakfast too. James might not hate her after all.

And Stacey was engaged. "I should try reaching out to her. There were a lot of things left unsaid the last time we were together."

"You should. She'd appreciate it."

"James," she whispered and swallowed down her hesitation. This might be her only chance and she couldn't mess this up too. "I'm so sorry, for everything that went wrong with us, between us, with Damien."

His gaze pierced hers. "We were both at fault, Marlène. Please don't lay all the blame at your door."

That he could even think that tightened the knot in her throat. "I was never honest with you about a lot of things that mattered between two people." *Between two people who loved each other.*

"I know. But I didn't offer you the environment or show the courage you needed in me to open up, did I?" James said softly. "Even before you took up drugs, I knew there was something dark in your past that you struggled with. Something not of your doing. Something that broke you and that if it weren't for your own strength, you wouldn't be sitting here now."

It quieted between them as the waiter came with their orange juices. As she reached for her glass, James's hand cupped hers. "Bad things happen to good people, Marlène, and whatever happened to you, I know it wasn't your fault."

The warmth of his hand was an unexpected anchor in this

moment. A stick figure of the truth, that was all she'd promised she'd ever be able to give to anybody. This was what she needed to give James. It wouldn't right all wrongs, but it would help him understand.

"I still have contact with Damien," James said when she said nothing. "With my share in the club's sale and so on. He phoned me some time ago and let slip that he was—" He broke off and ran a hand through his hair. "It's hard, isn't it? I can't even say it out loud."

"Sexually abused," she whispered. "As a child."

"Yes."

She looked up and met his gaze. "We both were. By the same people."

Shock washed over James's face. It made her ache for him. Nobody wanted to learn this of anybody.

After a long moment, in which he clung to her hand, he said, "It wasn't your fault, you know that, right?"

"Yes," she whispered. It had taken forever to realize that it hadn't been her fault. It hadn't been only her body that had been messed with. It had been her mind too.

"Damien is sick with worry over you." His voice broke a little, and he cleared his throat. "When he phoned me, he said he's trying to reach you and that you're avoiding his calls. He hoped I could get hold of you, but with the wedding and everything—we've only been back since Monday and work has been hectic. I'm relieved to have bumped into you like this, to be honest." James squeezed her hand again. "Damien is worried. We both are."

James had been willing to hunt her down. Damien was desperate. They both still cared, even after everything that had passed between them. She pulled away from his touch, so foreign now, and took a tentative sip of her juice. "I've never been ready. Nothing, nobody has ever persuaded me to talk about this." It was so much easier to keep the monster quiet by feeding it.

"You might need to talk about it," James said, "if only to a therapist, or a person you trust and love. Someone you can open up to."

She couldn't stop the tear that cruised down her cheek. "I let him go."

When she met James's gaze, it was clear he'd realized she wasn't talking about him.

"The thing I've learned about us, Marlène, *through us* if I'm to be honest, was that I didn't understand what I needed. Not until she walked into my life, did I understand that I needed, and wanted, someone like Mila."

And not until Ruben had walked out of her life, had she realized she needed and wanted someone like *him* in her life. Someone who didn't need to dig into her history to understand and be there for her, but someone who came with that layered knowledge of her past and had a deeper understanding.

"What do I do?" she whispered. "I let him go and don't know what to do."

"You fight for him."

She wasn't sure how. She'd been too busy fighting to stay afloat, keeping her outward persona one step ahead of the inner demon and warding off her memories, that fighting for someone's love was an otherworldly concept, totally foreign to her.

The waiter placed laden plates of steaming breakfast in front of them, the smoky scent of the bacon making her stomach growl on cue.

"None of this gets attempted on an empty stomach." James passed her a knife and fork with a wink.

"Okay," she said and gave him a smile.

"And there it is," James said, his tone teasing, his gaze

honest and open, but with nothing but care in them. "The smile that makes men lose their heads."

"Oh, stop." She looked down to her food as a blush inched its way up her cheeks. That she could still blush was a miracle, but the way he said it reminded her why she'd found him so irresistible when they first met. Now, as they ate in silence, all she could think of was Ruben, in Paris, and too far away to fight for.

"What were you looking for at the DIY store?" James asked when the waiter came to take their empty plates.

"Bolt cutters."

"Come, I'll help you find them."

James paid, as she knew he would, and together they returned to the hardware store to retrieve his abandoned basket, which still stood where he'd left it.

After James had helped her find a bolt cutter, he hugged her goodbye.

She clung to him for a last long moment. "I quit too," she said. "The drugs. I'm done."

"I'm so relieved to hear it," he said and hugged her tighter.

"That's why I stopped talking to Damien. I had to."

"I get it." James's voice strained with emotion. "You still have my number?"

"Yes."

"Phone me if you need to, okay?"

She pulled away with a nod. He was so generous, as always.

"And don't doubt yourself. You're battle fit, if you'd just give yourself the chance to fight. By the sound of him, he's worth it."

"Yes." She needed to fight for Ruben, and she would. "Thank you, for breakfast. And everything else."

She'd never hoped to be forgiven by anybody, least of all the men in her life who preferred a woman to come with a somewhat clean slate, or at least the ability to pretend they could have a clean slate when prompted. Maybe if James could forgive her all her trespasses, Ruben would be able to forgive her the choices she'd made too.

When Marlène got home, she went straight to the storage locker, cut through the bolt, dragged Ruben's suitcase upstairs and in a final, decisive move, broke the lock and flushed all her pills down the toilet.

44

RUBEN

Ruben had scheduled a meeting with Marc but hadn't told him that he would be there in person. When he knocked on Marc's office door that Monday morning, two minutes before their scheduled meeting, Marc looked up and snorted.

"For fuck's sake, Ruben," Marc groaned as he stood. "You still have more than a week of leave left. What the hell are you doing here?"

Ruben walked into the office with a wry smile, closed the door, and reached over the desk to shake Marc's hand. "I sorted my shit out and didn't see the point in wasting more time."

"Yeah?" Marc indicated that he should sit down. "Wanna tell me about it?"

Ruben sat in the offered chair and placed his laptop bag on the floor. "Yes and no."

"Okay. Fair enough." Marc laced his fingers together and rested his hands on his desk. "I'm all ears for the yes part. Do we need coffee? Liquor?"

"I'm good. I'd like to get back to work."

"Right." Marc leaned back and his chair creaked. "So, about

the shit being 'sorted out,' you're not going to break something under my watch again, are you?"

The moment was on him, and his heart jammed in his chest, but he owed Marc at a minimum an apology, at max, an explanation. "I'm sorry about that night." He swallowed, but the truth of the moment pounded in his chest. Even if this never went beyond this office, which it wouldn't, the words didn't come easily. "I had some sessions with Graham, as you know, and it turns out that, as a child, I was...you know. Messed with."

"Okay." Marc blinked, frozen in his seat, for a few long seconds as the penny dropped. "Okay. I—" He closed his eyes as he dragged a hand through his hair, probably fleshing out the picture in his head. "Fuck. I don't know what to say."

"There's nothing to say." Ruben wanted to groan in relief but managed to exhale softly. In his chest, his heart was beating so hard, he could hear it. If this was how he felt physically on opening up to Marc, someone who he considered a close friend and who he'd known for years, how the hell did Marlène feel with all those memories she had and hadn't been too young to forget? No wonder she'd never told anybody. "This stays between us."

"Of course." At last Marc met his gaze again, but it seemed he had to force himself to do so.

"It explains a lot. The more I think about it, the more I see the pattern. The anger is there. It builds up until something triggers me." Ruben shook his head. "Let's just say, I'm surprised with what I know now that I hadn't had an outburst way earlier." In the early stages of this project, his urge to nail these fuckers had overpowered every other emotion. Until he'd cracked. Marc's nudge had been the right move. "I still have work to do and will go see Graham when I'm back in New York."

"Back in New York?" Marc shook his head. "You said you wanted to get back to work? Don't tell me you're resigning."

Ruben huffed out a breath, despondent.

"You're resigning, aren't you?"

"As I walked into the building this morning—" Ruben broke off and dragged a hand over his face "Fuck, Marc. I would've tried. I came back with the intension of trying."

"I know you. You would've given it everything. But I understand. It's just a complete mess. The team struggles without you. *I* struggle without you here."

It was nice to be missed. "To be honest, it's more than the work. I met someone in New York. I'm also quitting because of her."

Mark harrumphed. "That sounds intense. Bowled you right over, did she?"

"Yeah. Pretty much." He wouldn't tell Marc any more than that. The rest fell into the 'no' side of things. "It's complicated."

Marc sighed. "It's never easy. Not in our line of work."

That was just it. The line of work. Her being their shining star. Their Andromeda. A constellation of connections he was giving himself a week to tease out.

"Before I go, I have a fresh lead for us. I want to dig a bit and see where it goes."

"A fresh lead? You were supposed to be taking a break."

"Well, this one sort of stumbled into my hands." My life. My heart.

"We are freaking desperate for a lead. The worst thing is, we do all this work, we fight our way through all this shit to find and prosecute these criminals and then, you know what?"

"What?" Ruben asked. When Marc got going like this, he had to get something off his chest.

"These kids are now signing up for it themselves. We have a new team, looking into underaged sex streaming."

"What?"

"Yep. Teens. They sign up on these porn sites with some fake ID. The next thing they're live-streaming themselves teasing viewers to pay for visuals of them masturbating and other shit. It's so messed up. I don't know what to do anymore. On the one hand, we have children exploited around the world, and on the other, we have these older kids doing this type of thing—*willingly*. For the freaking money. For a quick buck. It's a tsunami."

Ruben bit down on his jaw, his stomach twisting tight. Yeah, this was happening and there was no way to put out all these fires. Teenagers with their whole lives ahead of them, and the first job they choose is in the sex trade, the oldest job in the world. What had happened to babysitting and mowing a neighbor's lawn?

"In any case, a new team is set up in the small boardroom for now, so that room is unavailable for a meeting. Have you checked in with the rest of your team or did you come here first?"

"I came here first."

"What's your new lead? Do you want to dig alone, or do you want the others to get involved too?"

"I need some French translators to help work on this. It's a name." Or two. The last one he wouldn't give away for the world. It was the least he could do for her. Marlène had been running for decades; he wasn't going to bring the party to her.

"A name? And you tell me this so casually?"

"I don't know if there's anything to it."

"How did you mine a name?"

"I'll tell you, maybe. One day."

Marc gave him a long, hard stare. "Why? You didn't do something extreme, did you? Something that would put us on the back foot should anything come of it?"

"No, of course not." He understood Marc's concern. As it

was, doing this work often toed the legal line. There was zero space for error.

Marc blinked and shook his head. "Something illegal?"

"No," Ruben said. "I did nothing extreme. I promise." Illegal, yep. Digging to find those images of Marlène was just that, but he only did so because he didn't have access to the database while in New York. That the situation wasn't entirely ethical wasn't something he wanted to discuss with Marc, now, later, or ever.

Marc cursed under his breath. "I'll call in Céline and Sébastien?"

"They'll be perfect, thanks."

Marc stood and walked out of his office, telling Ruben to wait. When he came back in moments later, Céline and Sébastien followed. Ruben stood and closed the door, then greeted his French colleagues. He offered his seat to Céline and with Sébastien leaning against the wall, Marc back behind his desk, the small office was getting cramped.

"We need to investigate a Phillipe Toussaint. He's a doctor, but when I search the name, hundreds of doctors with that name pop up in France. I suspect he must be in Paris or surrounds. For the rest, I have no clue and I can't decipher anything with the medical jargon that's thrown in."

"Anything else?" Marc prompted.

"Nope. That's it. My very long lead."

"It's more than what we have now," Sébastien said with a sigh. "We've not made much progress since you left. As soon as we break through a layer, the ring comes up with two more."

"We'll jump on it right away." Céline stood. "I would love to have something to show for it by the end of the day." She turned to Ruben. "Nice to have you back. Your empty desk has been harder to look at with each passing day."

Ruben smiled but his stomach churned. If he could save himself from seeing any visuals, he might make it through the day, but given the work environment, it was unlikely. Still, he trailed after the other two, calling back to Marc that he'd keep him posted, should they find anything.

As he walked with his colleagues to the secured office his team worked in, they went past the glass-walled boardroom which they kept for meetings. Now at least seven people were cramped in the small space, each with multiple monitors, some facing the glass wall to the corridor.

Nice. The least they could do was to stick paper up to prevent passers-by from seeing what they were investigating.

"I know," Sébastien said as Ruben shook his head. "It's a crisis. Everybody's complaining, but they're working on a deadline for new legislation that's going in front of the EU parliament next week. They want to amend some details on livestreaming and underaged users before they submit their proposal."

"The floor administrator will tape up paper to block out the windows," Céline added. "This team only moved in on Friday and worked through the weekend. They think because of *our* work, everything goes. *Merde.*"

Ruben forced his gaze away, but the images on a monitor caught his eye. A zoomed-in picture of a teenager, his eyes closed, a dreamlike pull to his mouth. He leaned in towards the glass wall as his stomach clenched.

This was so easy. So nonchalant. So disconnected. Just like Caleb had been, with him.

Was this what his Little Brother had gotten into over the past year while he hadn't been at home to support him? Ruben swallowed a curse and forced his gaze away to meet Sébastien's.

"Are you okay?" Sébastien searched Ruben's eyes as he hovered next to him.

"It makes me sick," Ruben said, his voice hollow as the urge to get back to New York washed through him again. Caleb needed him.

"*Oui.* It is a shitshow out there and once they're in it, it's hard to get out." Sébastien scrubbed his stubble and sighed. "Do you think the company who owns the porn site gives a fuck? They 'verify' these kids' ages but don't care to look properly for fakes IDs because they're making money. The kids are making money. They're all making money. And what's so wrong with that?"

45

RUBEN

Ruben sank into his desk chair and cupped his hands to his mouth. He understood how desperate a kid like Caleb could be, and if this was what Caleb had gotten into, Ruben had to get him out of it. Caleb was just a kid and whatever he'd put on the internet now could spread like cancer and kill his future. Even if it was only livestreams, someone always recorded, copied, posted, and spread the content.

Graham had been right. He'd be home for Caleb, probably at a time when the boy needed him most.

Someone placed a black coffee on his desk, and he looked up at Céline. "Your lead, what do you need?" she asked.

Ruben forced Caleb to the back of his mind, knowing he'd be back in New York soon. This was Paris, and he needed to focus on Marlène and this ring they'd been working on for years.

"Right." He took a deep breath, and on the exhale, focused back on the moment. "We need to narrow it down to doctors in Paris, find family connections and then—" He couldn't tell them to look for a link between Toussaint and Desrosiers, and that Marlène's mom was a well-known model and her dad a renowned heart surgeon. "And then we'll use facial recognition against our databases to see what comes up."

"Okay. It narrows it down. Do you want to sit at my desk, and we can go through them?"

Ruben was jet-lagged, and with this Caleb revelation, the wind was knocked out of his sails. "Sure." He could do with a bit of dead-eyed staring at someone else's screen.

He dragged his chair closer to Céline's desk and Sébastien leaned back in his chair to join their conversation. "We are only looking at medical doctors, yes?"

"Yes. And in any specialty."

On Céline's desk, a stack of French magazines lay discarded in the corner, front covers down. They all had a help-me-take-a-break crutch and Céline's was magazines. The back page had an ad for an anti-aging beauty product, and as Ruben scanned the page, slow knowledge sank into him. He pulled the magazine closer and stared at the older model. Her face was in profile, accentuating the elegant column of her neck, down to full breasts cupped in an evening gown to create the perfect cleavage, shoulders bare. Her hair was gathered in a classic roll, but for the rest she was unadorned, with only simple make-up, since her skin was the focus of the ad. The image struck him as so French, so...Marlène.

"Ah, Inès Toussaint," Céline said as she glanced at him and the magazine he was holding. "She's a French icon."

Ruben bit down on his jaw. *Toussaint.* It was a family relation then.

"She's striking." Ruben traced the line of her jaw down her neck to her collarbone, so similar to Marlène's, for hadn't he had the pleasure of trailing kisses down her daughter's jawline, her neck, her collarbone? Her breasts. Lower. *God, he missed her.*

This could be so easy, but he couldn't do it to Marlène. He dropped the magazine back on the stack. "Toussaint is a very common French surname?"

"Yep," Sébastien said as he stared at Céline's screen. "Just look, over two hundred doctors with that surname in Paris alone."

Céline had pulled a spreadsheet with names. "Where do we start?"

"With the ones that have most access to kids?" Sébastien suggested.

"Pediatricians," Ruben said, recalling Marlène's dislike for doctors and that she had one in her family.

"Right. *Pédiatre*. Sort." In a split-second Céline had isolated a single line. "Oh, good. There's only one with that name in Paris."

Her quick search showed exactly in what state of mind he'd been in back in New York, if he couldn't get here on his own. "Right," Ruben said. "What info do we have on him? Official info."

Céline's fingers flew over the keyboard and took them to a hospital's website where Dr. Phillipe Toussaint was listed as a specialist. Her eyes jumped over the information on the page, and she translated as she went. "Pediatric surgeon, specializing in heart surgery. Most noted surgeries are those performed with Dr. Henri Desrosiers…operating on European royalty and other cases that had no hope but pulled through and survived, because of him."

Henri Desrosiers. Marlène's dad. Céline droned on about more of Phillipe Toussaint's accolades, but Ruben had zoned out. All he heard was Marlène's words to him: *He has so much good in him too.*

And yes, Dr. Phillipe Toussaint was a devil disguised as an angel, who had been many a parent's last hope. Working together with Dr. Henri Desrosiers, they had given life where there was little hope or chance of survival.

Marlène's stance made sense now. With her mother on the back cover of magazines, visible everywhere in France if he'd only opened his eyes and looked, and with her father a renowned heart surgeon, exposing her uncle's crimes would be damaging for everybody. This would tear her family apart. Marlène hadn't done what she'd done to see her family shredded while under intense public scrutiny.

"Surely this man can't be your lead?" Sébastien said with a frown.

How could someone do such good on the one hand, and commit such horrors on the other? Ruben didn't know, so he just shrugged. "Let's see what he gets up to in his spare time." He hid his quivering fingers by pushing his hands into his pants pockets.

"Okay." Sébastien disappeared behind the screen of his desk, and Ruben waited as Céline did an internet search for Phillipe Toussaint for more informal content.

After ten minutes of going through random social media posts, Céline sat straighter. "Ha! Imagine this. This Phillipe Toussaint is the brother of Inès Toussaint."

Ruben closed his fists tighter, forcing himself to stay calm.

Céline had opened an article from a French gossip site and now clicked through a series of wedding photos. "Here, look, a family photo. All of them so beautiful. So chic."

Ruben stared at the wedding photo, recognizing Marlène and her younger sisters, Vianne in a ballgown-style wedding gown, between parents and other older family members.

"This is Phillipe Toussaint," Céline said and pointed to a tall and handsome man, graying at his temples. "He is engaged to Béatrice Martin, this woman here."

Him and her. Them. Ruben's gaze flittered over the woman who seemed too young to be engaged to such an old guy. As he looked closer, it became clear she'd had work done to keep looking this young. He homed in on the tattoos Béatrice had on her arms and shoulders, which were bare with her black, strapless dress, showing off her figure. He leaned in closer, his throat constricting. Her tattoos weren't bold or bright. They were an intricate web of fine lines. Zodiac signs. Stars. Constellations.

He swallowed convulsively and reached for his coffee to push back the bile. At this rate, he was going to be sick.

"Engaged to Béatrice Martin?" Sébastien said. "Why does that name sound so familiar?"

Céline shot Ruben a glance. "Marc met with Béatrice Martin three weeks ago, with her business partner, Christophe Morneau."

"Yes." Ruben barely managed to keep his composure. "Remind me why?" The puzzle pieces he'd had access to all this time were coming together to make a bigger picture. He had only to open his eyes, and *look*. And really *see*.

"They own a cybersecurity company," Sébastien said. "And run half the firewall and encryption software products on this side of the world."

Marc had scheduled the meeting while Ruben was still in Paris. He'd been supposed to attend the meeting too, but he'd been on leave. Before the incident with the chair in the break room, these names and people had been so trivial, but now a chill clawed its way up his back, spreading dread over his skin.

Holy fuck, they had a mole.

How else had this team not made a breakthrough for years? The only arrests they'd made were of petty pedophiles, those who were negligent or too eager. Someone inside had been feeding information to those who ran the dark web sites and security, making sure they were always one step ahead and police could never trace them.

"And apparently the meeting didn't go as planned," Céline carried on. "Marc said it was tense and Béatrice and Christophe hardly acknowledged each other."

"What the fuck." Sébastien's voice came from his cubicle. "If you can believe this shit, Phillipe Toussaint, Béatrice Martin, and Christophe Morneau has been in a ménage à trois for decades. Until a year ago, when they had an epic fall-out."

A ménage à trois? *Two's company. Three's a crowd.* A dirty break-up could fuel enough bitterness for revenge, and this wasn't just a clean cut between two people, no, this was a crowd.

The photo dumps of Andromeda had started around ten months ago, a few weeks before he'd started to work here. A bad break-up. Black mail. A relationship gone sour? *You'd know better than me* Marlène had said.

These could all be motives.

"Where are you digging up this dirt?" Céline's eyes were wide as her gaze jumped between Sébastien and Ruben.

"Where I usually get my dirt." Sébastien leaned over with his laptop in hand, showing them a site that was half porn, half sensationalist gossip, most of it AI generated.

"Guys," Ruben said, his voice strained. "Stop. Just stop right there." He brought his hands together as if in prayer and pressed them to his lips. He took a few deep breaths, and as the others looked at him, he made as if to zip his lips. This was enough. They had enough to run with now. They didn't need him anymore. "We need to go see Marc."

"Okay," the two chimed in unison, if a bit uncertain.

"Are you okay?" Céline asked as she got up.

Ruben gave her a curt nod and led the way to Marc's office. He was on this rollercoaster ride that only went in one direction.

Marc looked up from his laptop as they marched into his office.

Ruben closed the door and took a deep breath, hoping he was doing the right thing. "You need to investigate these three people and every person we've ever hired to do work from Béatrice and Christophe's company. And you need to go back years. I'm not sure how much you've been relying on outside resources, but I think we have a mole."

"What?" Céline hissed. "No."

"Impossible," Sébastien echoed.

Marc stared at them, one after the other, as the color drained from his face. "What? You can't be serious?"

"You met with Béatrice Martin and Christophe Morneau just the other day."

"Yes, but—"

"They have the know-how. Money and power. And the perfect screen to infiltrate our investigations and block us. They've been pulling this off for years." Ruben rounded Marc's desk and nodded en route for Céline to join him. "What site did you use for those wedding photos. Can you find them again?"

"Sure." Céline squeezed in and Marc stood to made space for her. She sat down with a thanks and took them back to the site and those wedding photos.

"Look," said Ruben, pointing to the strapless dress Béatrice wore, her intricate tattoos on full display. "This reminds me of something."

"*Mon dieu,*" Céline whispered as she expanded the image. "That girl. Andromeda. She haunts me. She haunts us all."

Sébastien came to stand next to them too and took in the details Céline traced with a finger on the monitor. "Constellations. On her skin," Céline said.

"Look, there," Sebastian said as he pointed to a tattoo on Béatrice's shoulder. "Andromeda."

The realization hit Ruben, hard, a punch to more than the gut, for it reverberated right through his body.

Trophies. They were trophies and marked as such. Marlène had never been the only one. There had always been more, they just hadn't found them yet.

Ruben closed his eyes for a moment. He'd just kicked the

hornets' nest. "You will need to keep this quiet until you have enough evidence. Trust no-one."

Céline cursed in French. "No wonder we've been having such a hard time getting anywhere. If we have a mole on this side, and Béatrice Martin and Christophe Morneau's company is dealing with the security of the sites, we'll always be on the back foot."

"Whatever you do, be careful," Ruben said. "*If* they are heading up this ring, or whatever it is—it could just be a couple of perverted sickos—don't let them to know you're on to them. And everything we do must be within legal boundaries. People with this kind of money could fight forever in a court of law. Or they could make things disappear, including themselves."

Ruben straightened from where he'd crowded Céline and Sébastien at Marc's monitor. This investigation was going to be a walk on a tightrope over a sea full of sharks, but for the first time since walking back into the building, he felt relief wash over him, because he wasn't going to be involved in any of it.

He looked for Marc and found him leaning against the nearest wall, pale, and clearly in shock.

For a long, tense minute, Marc just stared at him and said nothing. Ruben watched as the anger he could so easily relate to, expanded in Marc's body, pushing to his face, ready to explode.

"Fuck!" Marc pushed away from the wall and dragged his fingers through his hair as he circled the small space in the office, his chest heaving as he breathed into his hands. After minutes of pacing, he came back to the desk and leaned in again to look at the images on the monitor.

Ruben stepped away to make space for him, giving him a supportive squeeze on the shoulder.

Eventually Marc looked up and met his gaze. "I don't know what else happened in New York but I'm so fucking glad you went."

"Yeah," Ruben said with a nod. "The eye only sees what it wants to see and sometimes we need distance." A lot of distance. If it hadn't been for his time away, he would never have had this epiphany. "Everybody makes a mistake, sooner or later."

"And we'll be ready for them when they do," Marc said, his tone laced with the anger he barely had under control. "Ruben, I know we spoke earlier, but please, reconsider."

Ruben shook his head. "You can run with this, Marc. You have a solid lead, and once you've found the mole, the barriers will lift, and you'll find the evidence to bring these criminals to justice."

"I need you to be here—"

"No, you don't," Ruben said. Marlène needed him the most. "I'm done. I'll send you an official resignation via email."

Céline made a croaking sound and Sébastien's hands shot up in the air as if to stop him, but Ruben raised his hands to pause all arguments.

He had to get out. Out of this office, out of this building, and out into the open air. He'd come back to do exactly what he needed to do, even if he hadn't known what it was when he got on the airplane to Paris. He'd come to tip the first domino.

Marc took a step closer to him. "Ruben—"

"I'll catch you in New York, when all this is done." He slapped the doorjamb and then walked away, not looking back to see if any one of them would follow him and beg him to stay.

He wasn't going to be the guy who put a pediatric heart surgeon, saver of some lives, wrecker of others, behind bars. The police force had enough people to do the job and he'd rather have no connection to the case.

For him. For her. For them.

For Marlène's sake, he'd give up everything.

He was done.

46

MARLÈNE

Marlène zipped Ruben's suitcase closed and ran her fingers over the mutilated lock. There was no point in repairing her handiwork. She'd have to replace his suitcase.

It was lunchtime but she wasn't hungry, thanks to James's impromptu breakfast. If she put her mind to it, she could still manage to do a lot today. A weight had shifted in her. An anchor broken free from the boulder that had held her fast for years.

One thing was for sure, she could no longer stay in her apartment.

She breathed. If she'd come this far, it was only a matter of keeping the status quo. Keep busy, forget that she had a bruised and battered heart, and focus only on getting through the day.

But there was no forgetting a bruised and battered heart when, with every breath you took, your lungs swelled against it, pressing and squeezing the pain. There was no getting over—and no forgetting—Ruben Scott. Not in a lifetime.

With a sigh Marlène shoved her phone in her back pocket and wheeled his suitcase out of her bathroom. She paused to grab his apartment key and continued into the corridor, closed her apartment door, and unlocked his. With her hand on the doorknob, she listened. Maybe she should have knocked. But he wasn't at home. Since returning to her apartment, her ears had antennaed to each little creak, scratch or thump that could alert her to his return home. There had been nothing.

She opened the door and widened it, now a trespasser in that quiet act. In his space. Uninvited. This was her last message to him: an empty suitcase back in his apartment. She hoped he would interpret it in the way she wanted him to: *come find me, if I don't find you first.*

The windows were closed, the blinds down, his monitors switched off, not a light blinking. Ruben wasn't home. Her shoulders dropped in relief as she exhaled, her eyes closing in disappointment as tears welled behind them.

Soft footsteps fell behind her, those made by rubber-soled loafers. Her pulse skipped a beat in fright—she'd neglected to close the door. The footsteps stopped short, mid-stride, and so did the suitcase wheels, rolling along with them.

But nobody would come down their part of the corridor. Unless. She turned, only to meet Ruben's gaze where he stood, frozen.

Her stomach flipped as her hands rushed to cover her heart, its beats heavy and hard. "I thought you were in France."

His laptop bag slid off his shoulder to drop next to the suitcase. "I've been to Paris."

As he took a step forward, his gaze lowered to his ruined suitcase by her feet. When he looked up again, his eyes searched, and she held her breath.

"You're fine, aren't you?" he asked. "I knew you would be. That last night..."

God help her. She didn't want to remember the last night and how she spoke to him, as if she didn't know him at all. He must hate her.

"I—" She shrugged. "I only came to return your suitcase. I

flushed the whole lot down the toilet. I'm done. Well and truly done."

The light that shone in his eyes spread a slow warmth over her skin.

"Good." He dragged a hand over his jaw. "I went to Paris a week early and afterwards I went to Boston for Thanksgiving. And for Bryce's advice. I'm trying to figure out what to do next. Career-wise."

Marlène frowned and clenched her hands tighter. "What do you mean? Career-wise?"

He took two steps towards her. "I quit too. I'm done. Well and truly done."

"What?" She closed the gap between them as if he had a magnetic pull. "Why?"

"Because of you."

Because of me. "Ruben." She bit her lip and shook her head. "You can't quit. You know I'm not the only one, and I can't be the reason you stop the work you're doing." Her voice broke. "I won't allow it. You have criminals to put behind bars."

"Yeah. Turns out it isn't that easy. Not when all you can think about is this woman, this amazingly strong, resilient woman who fell into my life, only to lead me to one difficult choice after the other." His hand reached up and he ran his thumb from the corner of her mouth over her cheek, making her knees go weak. "In the end, I chose to come back here to see what would happen if, by chance, I walk into my apartment, and she was here, standing here as if she belonged."

"God," she whispered. "I missed you so much." She stepped into him, slid her hands up his chest and around his neck as Ruben, with a deep, relieved exhale, pulled her close to him.

"Best welcome home. Ever," he whispered into her hair.

Her emotions stampeded through her chest. He was here, he was holding her, he came back—for her. He quit—for her. "Please forgive me," she said on a whispered choke.

"What's there to forgive?" Ruben cupped her chin and made her look him in the eyes. "You were right that night in Central Park. To ask you to do—"

"No. Please, understand. You know everything, and I need to know that you forgive me for what I chose to do. Most days I can't live with myself and asking you to be with me, live with me, with what you know, is overwhelming. And it seems impossible to ask this of anybody." Least of all from this man who looked at her with such compassion as her words sank in and their true meaning seemed to break him.

For a long moment he searched her eyes, his jaw working as his whole face strained with his own emotions. Eventually his hands stroked up her back to her shoulders, and this time, he cupped her face with both hands and brushed at her tears with his thumbs.

"Look at me, Marlène." He waited until she was ready to meet his gaze. "I love you because of your choices, not despite your choices. I love you for who you are and understand that what you have become, whether by choice or force, has made you who you are. And I don't care how long this takes, it can take my entire lifetime, but I will prove this to you every day if you let me."

At his words, her love multiplied exponentially. "I'd love that."

He pressed his forehead to hers. "No more talking forgiveness, no more sorries, and no more regrets."

"Okay."

She closed her eyes as her fingers trailed around his waist and his coat covered her, warming her as she hugged his hips to hers.

Ruben tilted his head to the side to run the tip of his nose down her temple. "What were your plans for the rest of the day?"

"I've been thinking of—" Of moving out and away, too

scared to face him when he did come back from France. Too scared to see his investigations come to fruition. Too scared to be called in to be a witness. To be stripped naked for the world to see, again.

Now, all fear in her diluted and dissipated. He was here. And he'd quit. For her.

And yet in Paris, a team most likely was working on her case and at some point, something would give, and things would come to a head. But Ruben was here, with her, on her side when it came to that point and no longer on the side of law enforcement.

"Yes?" he encouraged her, his lips on her eyebrow, not quite kissing, more like questioning if this was all right.

"When you walked in," Marlène murmured, "I was contemplating coming to sleep in your bed. I don't want to be in my apartment, and it's as if, in my head, I could close my eyes and you'd be here if I didn't listen too closely to the silence."

He smiled as his lips teased their way to hers. "I would have loved to find you in my bed when I got home."

Ruben pressed his lips to hers, in the softest, sweetest kiss that forced her to cling to him as arousal flooded through her. She opened her lips and pressed him closer, his need evident where his jeans strained. Her hands tugged at his coat, and he let it slip from his arms to the floor. Ruben cupped her butt and lifted her up as they deepened the kiss, her hands in his hair, keeping him close.

He strode with her to the bedroom and lowered her to stand again, their bodies flush and pressing into each other. Her hands got busy with his shirt, and he loosened her jeans' button and unzipped them. Her cashmere sweater was suddenly too hot as his fingers splayed into the back of her panties to caress her butt. He nudged at her jeans and pushed them down until she could kick off the legs. They bundled to the ground with a soft thud as her phone hit the carpet.

At last, she'd worked her way down his shirt's row of buttons and her fingertips trailed over his chest, searching for and caressing each scar all the way to his shoulders. She peeled off his shirt and they broke their kiss, out of breath with their mutual arousal.

"We should slow down," he murmured.

"True. I've got nothing else planned for this weekend." He was here, he came back for her, and all her other plans had fallen away.

By the time twilight crawled into all the nooks and crannies, Marlène levitated with love and completion. She rested in Ruben's embrace, their skins sticky, her heart racing as they came down together again. His hand rested on her hip to nudge her closer. She turned on her side and looked into his eyes and his soft gaze locked with hers. She'd never felt this safe before. This treasured. This loved.

Ruben pressed his head close to hers, his lips on her ear, nibbling, kissing, whispering, "I love you."

Marlène turned her face to his, their noses caressing, their lips searching. They were so close that she could see the gold and amber flecks glimmering in his eyes in the afternoon light, like pathways through the darker brown that led straight to his soul. He brushed her hair from her face, the gesture so tender she burst inside with sparks of love for him. She cupped his cheek in her hand and stared at him as they stilled. "I love you too," she whispered back, knowing that for the first time in her life, this was true for not only half, but the whole of her body, mind, and soul.

Ruben closed his eyes and she watched as he drifted in and out of sleep. He needed more than a nap. She'd love the same, but every time she closed her eyes, images pressed against her eyelids, protesting at being locked inside.

A new urgency rose inside her. One she'd never anticipated.

She had to do something. She was going to do something. Or else peace would always elude her.

The new urgency made her restless and Marlène slipped from his embrace. Ruben's arm slid to his chest, and he stirred. She sat up and put her feet gently on the floor, her resolution snowballing.

"What're you doing?" Ruben muttered, sleep thick in his voice.

"I—" She swallowed as he shifted, waking up. His hand was warm on her back, there where she carried the miniature scars of dots made long ago on her skin, small insignificant chains. His fingertips caressed those same coordinates on her back, although he wouldn't be able to find them in this low light. It was as if Ruben had memorized where they were and with every touch, tried to erase them from her past. "I have to return a call."

Ruben sat up too and rested his hand on her shoulder. "Okay. A call? Your sisters?"

"We spoke yesterday morning." Not that she would mind speaking to them again, but with the time difference, it was too late for her sisters, especially for Vianne with her little ones.

The mere thought of Vianne's girls made her rile up. How easy it had been for her uncle to have access to her. He'd lived in their loft while he'd completed his medical residency at the same hospital as her dad. He'd been the ideal babysitter when her mom worked photoshoots and her dad worked his weird hours, always happy to take up the bedtime routine when her parents weren't at home. She'd been groomed so quietly, so on the side, normalizing it as part of growing up. By the time that woman had entered the scene, she'd been totally compliant.

Ruben gathered her hair from her face and brought her back to reality as she shuddered. She glanced over her shoulder into his eyes. "I need to call Damien." The boy with the tattoos, just like hers.

"Okay." His eyes filled with concern. "Now?"

"I have it in me now. I'm done with later too. It wants out." That monster in her with all its horrid memories was tearing at the trapdoor.

Marlène stood and reached for Ruben's discarded shirt, creased but soft and comforting with his scent. She closed a few of the top buttons as she padded to her panties where they were dropped to the floor.

Ruben watched her from the bed, concern etched in his gaze. "Marlène?"

She reached for her phone from the pocket of her discarded jeans and met his gaze. "I wasn't the only one, never had been, and this has been going on way too long with me doing nothing about it." She got dressed, feeling his worried gaze on her.

"Okay." He stood and reached for her. "I'm here."

She closed her eyes and leaned against him for a moment. "I know. If you weren't, I—" *I wouldn't be able to do this.*

He hugged her close. "I know. It's okay. I'm here."

She nodded and gave him a moment to pull on his jeans.

"He'll answer?" Ruben asked as he zipped up his fly. "It's late in France."

"Damien doesn't sleep," she said. "And he'll take my call, unless he's drugged out." She'd have to take her chances.

Ruben nodded, took her hand, and led her to the sofa. She was relieved that he understood—this call wasn't going to be made from the bedroom where they'd just spent hours cementing their love for each other.

They sat down and for a long moment she stared at her phone screen. Damien's handsome face stared back at her from his contact profile picture. She was at a loss, because his face held no trace of the inner trauma he too carried. Damien smiled in the photo, seemingly carefree. She knew better. "I don't know how to do this," she whispered now that the moment was upon her.

Ruben's hand, which rested on her lower back, swept up to her shoulder and he hugged her close. "I'll hold you every step of the way."

"I know." Ruben's body pressed tight against hers, grounding her in this moment.

"I love you," she whispered. "So much."

"I love you too," Ruben whispered back.

The soft assurance in his voice made her relax for a while in his embrace as she envisioned how this was all going to pan out.

"You'll be there for me, beyond this call? Through it all?" She still stared at Damien's number on her phone, her heart breaking for them both, quietly, inside, where they'd both been cracked so long ago. What she was about to set in motion was a destructive comet with a very long tail.

Ruben gently cupped her chin and turned her to face him. "Yes. Always. Whatever you need."

"This. This is what I need." She covered his hand with her own. Someone holding her tight, protective, strong, unflinching, not judging, just knowing, understanding and most important of all, accepting.

She pressed the dial button on Damien's contact, her heart beating so fast she heard the rush in her ears, unstoppable like a flooding river water.

Damien answered within two rings. "*Marlène? Finalement.*"

She swallowed on hearing his voice and those words, which spoke of every concern he'd had for her in the past months. "Damien, I'm sorry, I would have called earlier," she continued in English, her voice quivering. "I'm putting you on speakerphone." Seeing his face would be too much.

"*Mais pourquoi?*" Damien asked.

"I have Ruben Scott with me here. My—" She glanced at Ruben. *My forever.* "My boyfriend. His French, I think, isn't very good."

"Okay. Hi?" Damien replied. "Nice to meet you, Ruben."

Ruben glanced at Marlène. "Hi."

"Listen, Damien. I know we never spoke about Phillipe Toussaint. Or about Béatrice Martin. We always spoke around them. But I know, just like you know about me, that they abused you."

A stretch of quiet followed, and in her mind's eye she could imagine how Damien had paled and flinched at those names. He didn't respond, and when the quiet became too heavy, she took a resolute breath. "I don't know what hold they still have over you, but I'm done. I can't anymore."

"Marlène—"

"I'm doing it," she said, cutting him off before she could change her mind. "I'm actually doing it. I'm not going to be a terrified kid anymore, Damien. I won't let them intimidate me and I won't let Phillipe give me drugs to buy my silence. I won't—" Her voice broke. "Damien?"

"*Oui.*" Damien breathed haltingly into the phone, his agitation clear.

"Photos are out there. Of me. Of you too, no doubt. They broke their promise. But it's more than that. I need to do this. I'm ready to do this."

"You are?"

"Yes. And I want you to help. If both of us come forward, we can put them behind bars." She squeezed Ruben's hand and he hugged her back, his warmth reassuring, the rhythm of his breathing reminding her to breathe too.

"*Oui*," Damien whispered back. "I know he hurt you, so bad, Marlène. As for her—" Damien broke off as distress choked him. "Nothing I ever did or could be for you ever helped."

It hit her from out of nowhere that she was holding Damien back just as he had been holding her back. "Just like I wasn't your big escape either."

"We did the best we could," Damien said.

Ruben rubbed a hand over her back, and she leaned even more into him. "Are you willing to do this with me, Damien? It won't be easy." She closed her eyes and pressed her face into Ruben's neck to be as close to him as possible.

"*Oui. Oui,* at last." Damien's voice broke as he suppressed a sob.

"At last." Marlène exhaled, feeling queasy with the intensity of her emotions. "Ruben will help. He has experience of a different kind that will make this easier."

"Okay." Damien sniffed. "You're so resolute. And strong."

She broke into a teary chuckle. "I wouldn't be able to do it without him."

"Well, best I meet you, Ruben Scott. Sooner rather than later."

"Of course." Ruben smiled. "I suspect it's going to be fairly soon. We'll need to be in France to deal with this."

Exhaustion settled over her and it was time to end the call. "Can we speak later this week, Damien? To give you time to make sure that this is what you want? Think through the consequences first."

"Yes. Okay. Thank you." It was quiet for a moment as he breathed into the phone. He sighed. "This call isn't exactly what I expected, but that doesn't mean it's unwelcome."

"I know," she whispered, on the brink of breaking down.

Ruben kissed her hair, reassuring her that he'd be there every step of the way.

"We'll talk on Wednesday?" Ruben said. "Develop a plan, see which way to go forward. I have all the connections to make this happen quickly and we'll have people to guide us all the way."

"*Oui.* Wednesday." Damien's voice was choppy and for a long minute he just breathed. "Wow. I'll try get my head around this call, but maybe, just maybe, I'll sleep tonight."

"Yes," Marlène whispered back. "*Bonne nuit,* Damien."

"Sleep tight, you two."

She rang off and collapsed back into Ruben's embrace, exhausted by the amount of effort it took to make that call.

Ruben's lips caught the tear that crept out of the corner of her eye. "I've got you, sweetheart," he said. "I've got you all the way and back again. From beginning to end. All routes and detours and any other path this journey will take us on."

"All routes and detours and any other path." She no longer doubted. With Ruben by her side, she would never doubt again.

She would take control and she would dictate how this ended.

And no. This wasn't her ending.

This was her beginning.

Look out for Bryce's story, The Intern, to be published in late Fall 2022:

Izzy

Rules are there to simplify life and help people toe the line.

Rule number one: Don't let your boss catch you in a sex video you posted online, flaunting his company logo as if he were your biggest sponsor.

Rule number two: No tears in the boardroom. Ever.

Rule number three: If your boss wants to fuck you over, fuck him over right back but for heaven's sake…don't fall in love with the asshole in the process.

Bryce

All decisions in life fall into one of two categories: good or bad. I work every day to step away from my past and make good decisions, especially where my company and reputation are at stake. Rules make decisions easy.

Rule number one: My company's interns are off limits.

Rule number two: When an intern makes a hot AF video that lands in your inbox, company logo and all, don't keep it. Or watch it on repeat. Delete, delete, delete.

Rule number three: Don't break rule #1 or rule #2 and be the idiot that falls in love with her while you're at it.

As for Izzy…she might break more than my reputation, company, and bank balance. She might just break my heart.

Looking for something light, fluffy, and fun? I write those too!

One Sweet Summer releases 14 June 2022 and is the first book in my Ashleigh Lake series, set in small town Vermont. It's available for pre-order now.

One Sweet Summer

Life. Not my forte. Anybody who's heard of Raiden Logan will know that by now. But here I have my one chance to change the trajectory I set for my life when I ran away from home at sixteen. Building a tiny house for a televised competition and winning it might just put me on the map and get me that bank loan I need to start my own business. Losing isn't an option.

For this competition, I need an assistant. I'm not going to mess this up. I'm going to read all these resumes front to back and not choose the candidate by tossing the resumes in the air and going with the one that lands in my lap. My assistant isn't going to be a sexy Miami beach babe who wields power tools like she wields social media. And I'm not going to fall for Georgiana Wess either, because you know, business and pleasure shouldn't mix and can only lead to disaster. Nope. I'm going to nail this and get the kickstart I never had.

Not.

Life, remember? Not my forte.

ACKNOWLEDGMENTS

To all the lovely people who have stood by my side and supported me through this crazy endeavor.

My husband, Richard. A standard dialogue in our house goes something like this:

"I think I should go find a real job," I say, like every second day. I mean, there is a lot of underappreciated luxury in a 9-5 job that doesn't haunt you at all hours and to which you don't feel indebted all the bloody time.

"Don't go find a real job, just keep on doing what you're doing," Richard says with a sigh because he is tired of this conversation. "You've come this far already; you can't stop now."

More like, I can't give up now. I want to give up every second day. "But I'm not writing tropey stuff, none of my books are the same, and I think I'm confusing myself and readers." I should stop whining already. I mean, I'm only doing this to myself, aren't I? But this is how it happens.

"Well, you are who you are, and why would you want to change that?" Richard says, and my heart literally bursts out in tiny little hearts that batter my chest to get out and fly over to him. Because that's what he says, but what he means is, *I love you. I support you. I'm here for you. What you are doing is freaking hard and you put your heart out on a platter with every book and I get that. I'm freaking proud of you, and I think you are amazing.*

I just nod and quietly slink back to my desk and sob, because who gets to be loved like this in the world? ME!!

My book buddy and beta reader extraordinaire Caitlin

Bronaugh, who has read all my books as a beta reader and who says, "I can't stop now." I always love your feedback, honest, straightforward, and to the point!

My longtime friend and psychologist, Alison Dobson, who I almost 'killed' with this book. I think the first draft raised every red flag there could be in a psychologist's practice, and I had to rewrite the living crap out of it to make it pass. This version got a pass, but just barely. I think. Whatever. It's fiction, people. And my characters all want to cross the line.

My lovely sister Tilla, whom I subject to my raw work. Thank you for always reading, Dolla, and for letting me always count on you.

My writing buddy Meg Chronis, who I have teased with this book, rather relentlessly. Thank you for always challenging me and demanding more steam. This book is what it is because of you! I think if this one didn't deliver on the steam, Bryce's story definitely will. Look out for it, someone's coming soon.

My characters. Thank you for pitching up and never really shutting up. And I'm barely done with one pair when the next starts hammering on the door in my head. Sometimes two pairs are in a full-on fist fight to decide who gets to go next. Let's behave and keep on working together, shall we?

My readers: for those who have read all my books—thank you! I intend to do this for a long time to come (unless I actually go find a 'real job') and appreciate your support. For many of you I am a new-to-you writer: thank you for taking a chance on me. I hope it was worth it and that you will stick around for the ride.

And lastly, the BookTok community. You guys ROCK!

A NOTE TO READERS

Thank you for reading *The Neighbor*. If you've enjoyed reading this book and want to be in touch, please find me on the social media platforms below.

Sign up for my newsletter and stay up to date with latest releases and other news!

www.sophiakarlson.com

ABOUT THE AUTHOR

I've always been drawn to the magical escape of books and the safe journeys they take us on without leaving the comfort of home. This book was inspired by those questions that always bug me: "What happened to those people? Where are all those children now? How did life turn out for them?"

This was by no means an easy book to write, and the research was so hard, that to be honest, I just scraped the edges, so please forgive me any missteps and errors. It's weird how writing about a topic like this affects your own personal life, and I think a dungeon is best for writing books like these, where at the end of the day you can go up the stairs and leave it all behind in the dark. It's not that easy. All that said, my books have happy, hopeful endings, and this is what I want the most to resonate with you, the reader.

When I'm not being harassed by my characters, I'm a mom of two wonderful, witty children, two beagle dogs who sometimes fart me out of my office, and a wonderful husband, without whom none of this would be happening. Since moving to Canada (and arriving here just in time for Covid – thank you,

About the Author

universe), I've been lucky to explore this beautiful country, and planning camping trips has become one of my favorite pastimes. Last year we went on our first canoe camping trip, and that will feature in one of my books...soonish.

ALSO BY SOPHIA KARLSON

The Paris Apartment

She's been in love with him all her life.

His little sister's best friend is all grown up and the wait has been forever.

Will a chance reunion lead them to true love?

As an artist, Paris has always been Mila's dream destination. Being free of her family and the restraints they put on her only adds to the pleasure of exploring Paris on her own. Except that James, her best friend's older brother, is in Paris too, in the same apartment, and claims his side of the only bed.

They can't deny their mutual attraction and soon a one-night stand only leads to more temptation, but James has a secret. A secret that can kill their budding relationship. Can James steer clear and deserve Mila's love without revealing it all?

The Shrink

Apparently she's a bit crazy.

Apparently he's the shrink who will cure her.

Apparently they aren't allowed to fall for each other at all.

Stacey Sinclair's mother died in a gruesome car accident six years ago, and now everybody thinks she is finally losing it. Surely a few crazy actions on her part don't justify her seeing a shrink for months on end?

For a psychologist, Dr Ivo Linder is too decent, too caring, and too handsome to get a glimpse of what really goes on in her head. Stacey's unforeseen feelings towards him make her retaliate — she taunts him, never expecting to fall with him into forbidden lust.

As their attraction intensifies, the old adage stands: it doesn't matter as long as nobody finds out. But someone always finds out and when they do, will Stacey and Ivo risk everything to give their love a chance?

The Shrink is a sensual, emotional standalone contemporary romance that touches on hard topics that might trigger some readers.

Printed in Great Britain
by Amazon